"One Kiss Was All It Took, Right, Casey?"

"I don't plan to relive old memories with you, not when I find them repugnant."

Jess began to talk softly. "Repugnant, hell! Who're you trying to kid? You loved every minute we spent together that week. You know what's strange in all of this, honey? You've been protesting too much. I'm beginning to wonder who you've been trying to convince. Me or you?"

"This is the last time I ever want to see you. Are you capable of understanding that? I was seventeen years old when you were in Blythe six years ago. I'm not seventeen now. I'm—"

"Beautiful," he murmured.

"Jess . . . you've got to leave me alone. I can't take much more of this."

"Much more of what? We've seen each other exactly twice since I've been back."

"What do you want from me?" she asked.

"I think you know."

Dear Reader:

Welcome to the world of Silhouette Desire. Join me as we travel to a land of incredible passion and tantalizing romance—a place where dreams can, and do, come true.

When I read a Silhouette Desire, I sometimes feel as if I'm going on a little vacation. I can relax, put my feet up, and become transported to a new world . . . a world that has, naturally, a perfect hero just waiting to whisk me away! These are stories to remember, containing moments to treasure.

Silhouette Desire novels are romantic love stories—sensuous yet emotional. As a reader, you not only see the hero and heroine fall in love, you also feel what they're feeling.

In upcoming months look for books by some of your favorite Silhouette Desire authors: Joan Hohl, Ann Major, Elizabeth Lowell and Linda Lael Miller.

So enjoy!

Lucia Macro
Senior Editor

JACKIE MERRITT

RAMBLIN' MAN

SILHOUETTE *Desire*

Published by Silhouette Books New York

America's Publisher of Contemporary Romance

SILHOUETTE BOOKS
300 East 42nd St., New York, N.Y. 10017

ISBN: 0-373-05605-2

First Silhouette Books printing November 1990

Printed in the U.S.A.

Books by Jackie Merritt

Silhouette Desire

Big Sky Country #466
Heartbreak Hotel #551
Babe in the Woods #566
Maggie's Man #587
Ramblin' Man #605

JACKIE MERRITT

and her husband live just outside of Las Vegas, Nevada. An accountant for many years, Jackie has happily traded numbers for words. Next to family, books are her greatest joy, both for reading and writing.

One

The grandstand, which was located on the west side of the rodeo arena, was packed, and crowds of people milled around at ground level. The hot sun hadn't kept anyone away, Casey Oliver Maddox noted. The entire Oliver clan was there. And so was practically everyone else she knew, braving the glare and the ninety-plus temperature with dark glasses and wide-brimmed cowboy hats.

Casey's hat was straw, as was her son, Bobby's. Like most everyone else in the throng, mother and son wore jeans, cotton shirts and boots, and sipped cool drinks while the rodeo events unfolded in the arena. Through the public address system, the announcer's voice relayed participants' names, data on their past performances, and anecdotes, forming a continuous background to the din of voices, applause and laughter from the audience.

The annual July rodeo was a big event in Blythe, Wyoming, and many of the locals took part, although equally as many outsiders descended on the small town to vie for the quite substantial cash prizes. Casey used to be very good in the women's barrel-racing event and had a trophy at home to prove it. But that was before she'd had Bobby. After he came along, she had dropped out of a lot of the activities she had once enjoyed.

Today she was cheering on her younger sister, Kelly, in the final round of the barrel-racing contest. Bobby was cheering for her, too. While Kelly rode her horse around the barrels in the arena without a falter and gave a very near-perfect performance, Bobby was standing and yelling, "Come on, Aunt Kelly! You can do it!"

Bobby, a wiry little boy with nearly black hair and vivid blue eyes, was going on six. Casey loved him to distraction, but she never failed to see his father in her son. Bobby was the picture of Jess Lonnigan, a tiny replica of the man who had fathered him.

Kelly had been the second finalist in the event, and after two more young women had done their best, she was announced as the winner. Bobby whooped and threw himself into his mother's arms. "She won, Mom! Now there'll be two barrel trophies on the shelf."

Laughing, Casey glanced at her mother, and Lucille Oliver smiled back. All of the Olivers were in the stands: Casey's father, Ben, her two brothers, Buck and Brady, and their families, and her older sister Dee-Dee and her family. Altogether, the Olivers numbered eighteen—a large group, especially when they congregated to eat together. Only Casey, Bobby and Kelly still lived on the family ranch with Ben and Lucille, but the others all lived within a twenty-mile radius. Holidays were loud, confusing . . . and wonderful.

"Can I have an ice-cream cone now, Mom?" Bobby asked.

"Sure, why not?" Casey stood up, took her son's hand and began the precarious journey to ground level. When friends called a hello as she passed, Casey responded with smiles and waves, and in a few minutes she and Bobby were away from the grandstand.

They wound through the crowd to the refreshment stand and Casey ordered a chocolate ice-cream cone. "Don't you want one, Mom?" Bobby questioned.

"No, honey."

"How come?" Bobby's blue eyes contained total amazement that someone wouldn't eat ice cream at every opportunity.

Casey laughed and bent over to give her son a hug. "Because I'm already full of hot dogs and soda, that's how come. I don't know where a sprout the size of you puts it all."

"I'm just a growing boy," Bobby announced solemnly, parroting his grandmother's almost daily observation.

The crowd roared and clapped with approval. "What's happening, Mom?"

"The bull riding, honey. Someone must have had a good ride." Casey paid for the cone and passed it to her son. "Let's get back to our seats now."

"Yeah. I like the bull riding."

They hurriedly retraced their steps and settled down again. There were a dozen different bull riders to watch, and Bobby jumped around in glee over the colorful, agile clowns who were also in the arena. As comical as the gaily costumed clowns were, they weren't there simply to make people laugh. It was their job to draw the bulls' attention away from unseated riders.

Fifteen-year-old Kelly had joined the family and had been undergoing a lot of good-natured teasing. It was apparent every Oliver was proud of her performance and win, but it wasn't their way to gush over it. "When do you get your trophy, Aunt Kelly?" Bobby questioned.

"After the last event, Bobby."

"Will you get some money, too?"

Kelly grinned impishly. "Enough to buy some great new clothes, Bobbo!"

Lucille shook her head. "I hope you'll do a little more with your winnings than that, Kelly."

"Like what?" Kelly—with Casey and Bobby—was sitting a tier down from her parents, and she glanced over her shoulder with an almost belligerent expression.

"Like saving it for something important," Lucille retorted.

"Oh, Mom," Kelly said disgustedly, and faced the arena again.

Casey looked back and exchanged an understanding smile with her mother. Kelly couldn't stand having a dollar in her purse or pocket, but she was a good kid all the same.

The announcer's voice battled with the crowd's noise: "...a little surprise for you today, folks...award the trophies...we're proud to have such a rodeo star..."

"What's he saying?" Kelly demanded.

"Something about the man who's going to pass out the trophies, I think," Casey answered.

"...over six years ago...ranch in Clear Creek Valley...really great...Jess Lonnigan..."

Casey froze. But even worse than the immediate stiffness in her limbs and body, was the feeling that the blood had just drained from her head. Her thoughts were suddenly as disjointed as the announcer's words had seemed to be. *It can't be... No, I misunderstood... It can't be!*

Then she felt her mother's hand on her shoulder, and she knew she hadn't misunderstood at all. Lucille Oliver had heard Jess's name, too. Casey turned slowly and looked at her mother with pain-filled eyes. She couldn't speak about what they were both thinking, because no one else in the family knew about it. Casey's eyes darted to her father, and he gave her a warm smile. For the smallest fraction of time she wondered if he did know. There was something in his eyes....

But no, Lucille would have told her if she had related the old story to anyone. Ben didn't know. He didn't!

Casey's heart was suddenly pumping adrenaline through her body at a furious rate, and she turned away from her parents to wildly search the crowd. Somewhere in this crowd, *somewhere*, was Bobby's father. But *he* didn't know he was Bobby's father. Only two people knew that: Casey and her mother. Everyone else believed a lie about Casey and a completely fabricated husband.

But would Jess know if he *saw* his son? Would he see in Bobby what I do? Casey agonized.

Sick at heart, Casey got up. "Come on, Bobby. We're going home." She grabbed the little boy's hand.

"Home?" Bobby was clearly stunned.

Half of the Oliver clan called, "Why are you going before the rodeo is over?"

She was behaving too much out of character, Casey realized. Taking a deep breath she faced her family. "My stomach is really upset all of a sudden. I must have eaten too much junk food."

"Well, leave Bobby with us," Brady, Casey's oldest brother, suggested.

"No...no! I...he's better off with me."

Lucille said nothing, but there was a sad look in her eyes. Ben said nothing and just watched. Bobby looked ready to cry over leaving before the awards were distributed, and again Brady urged, "Leave him, Casey. I'll take personal responsibility for him. I promise not to let him out of my sight."

"Brady, that's not the problem. Thanks for the offer, but I want him with me," Casey replied firmly. "I'll see you all later," she added lamely, and tugged Bobby along. "Come on, Bobby. Don't drag your feet."

By the time they reached the ground, Bobby's big blue eyes were spilling tears. It was rare that his mother didn't smile and give him a hug every few minutes, and the little boy sensed there was something very different about her strange expression.

They passed the refreshment stand. Casey was walking fast, as if the very devil himself were on her heels, and Bobby was practically running to keep up. The parking lot was congested with cars, pickups and horse trailers, and the proof of Casey's state of mind was her reaching the Olivers' four vehicles before she realized she hadn't asked anyone for a key.

None of the vehicles was locked, though, and Casey opened the door of her father's car. "Get in, Bobby. I've got to go back and get the keys from Grandpa. I'll only be a few minutes." Guilt struck her as her son climbed into the car and huddled against the seat with silent tears running down his cheeks. "I'll bring you something from the refreshment stand, honey," she said with more gentleness. "What would you like?"

Bobby looked down. "Nothing, Mom."

"Come on, honey. Don't be like that. You know I wouldn't make you leave if it wasn't important, don't you?"

"I guess so. Are you really sick?"

Casey bit her lip and looked away from the shining innocence of her son's eyes. "I'm deathly sick," she answered dully, realizing how true the dire words were. But a five-year-old couldn't handle that kind of answer, and she quickly amended the admission. "I just need to lie down, honey. I'll be fine. Now, what can I bring you?"

A small smile shone through the tears. "Another ice-cream cone?"

"You've got it, honey. I'll hurry." Casey glanced around then. There were strangers present, people she didn't know, and her gaze returned to her precious son. She couldn't possibly leave him alone, and yet the prospect of taking him back into the crowd and risking an encounter with Jess Lonnigan chilled her.

Just then someone called "Hi, Casey."

Turning, Casey smiled. "Oh, Janice, hi. Listen, would you do me a tremendous favor? Bobby and I were leaving, but we got clear out to the car before I realized I didn't have Dad's keys. Would you stay with Bobby for ten minutes?"

"Well, of course. No problem." Janice Miller, an old school chum of Casey's, slid into the car with Bobby. "Hi, Bobby. How you doing, pal?"

"Thanks loads, Janice." Casey took off running, and dodged among the vehicles as she went. By the time she reached the grandstand again, she was out of breath. But she quickly climbed up to the level where the Olivers were sitting.

"I need somebody's keys," she announced, including the whole group in her plea.

Ben reached into his pocket. "I never even thought about keys, Casey. Where's Bobby?"

"In the car. Janice Miller's keeping an eye on him. I've got to hurry back. Bye, everyone. Catch you later."

She was back on the ground in seconds, dashing for the refreshment stand. There were three people ahead of her, and she got in line.

"Casey? Casey Oliver?"

The deep, masculine voice went right through her. Even after six years she recognized it. Jess Lonnigan. The situation didn't seem possible, it *wasn't* possible, and yet she was alternately hot and cold with indisputable shock.

Very slowly, Casey turned. "Hello, Jess," she replied coolly.

In a torrent of memories, the past came rushing back. For one week, six years ago, she'd made love with this man like there was no tomorrow. She'd been completely mesmerized by his rugged good looks and devil-may-care personality and drugged by the first adult passion of her life. It struck Casey that he looked the same—tall, dark and handsome—except for a few new lines at the corners of his outrageously blue eyes and maybe a few more well-distributed pounds.

He was studying her as boldly as the first time they'd met, and while she was as cold as ice inside, Casey felt heat in her face.

"I was *hoping* you were still around," Jess said softly.

Fury exploded within her, and she had to consciously remember where they were—in public, within hearing range of a dozen people. She kept her voice down, but it was no less venomous than what was in her heart. "Why? I'm not seventeen and stupid now."

"Seventeen!" Jess looked as if he'd just been slapped. "You weren't only seventeen."

Casey moved up a place in line, aware that Jess Lonnigan was watching her closely. She would have given her right arm to avoid this confrontation, but perversely, she was glad she looked good, glad that her jeans were tight and her bright red shirt was darted to fit just so. Her breasts were fuller than they'd been six years ago, but that was the only place she'd gained either inches or weight. Her hips and long legs were as lean and firm as always.

She was glad that her heavy dark hair was curled and fluffed below the straw hat, and that her boots were high-heeled and flattering. But most of all, she was glad that Bobby was in the car and out of sight.

"You weren't really only seventeen, were you?"

She gave Jess a disdainful look. "What are you doing back in Blythe? Besides passing out awards, that is."

Jess's frown added perplexity to his face. "You don't like me very much, do you?"

"Should I?"

"You seemed to like me just fine six years ago."

Casey took another step forward as one of the people ahead of her left with two handfuls of hot dogs. "Still a gentleman, I see," she hissed heatedly.

Jess's frown deepened. "I never pretended to be anything but what I was."

"A transient rodeo rider!" Casey sneered.

"That's not what I am now."

"Oh? Well, tell it to Superman. I'm not interested."

Jess kept staring. Casey Oliver was as pretty as he remembered—maybe prettier. She had big green eyes—which were presently well concealed behind dark glasses—a fabulous complexion and just about the sexiest mouth he'd ever witnessed on a woman. She'd knocked him for a loop six years ago, and as he'd told her, he'd been hoping she was still living in the area. He sure hadn't expected bitterness, though. Their week together during Blythe's big July rodeo six years ago had been one of the more memorable of his life. They'd danced, flirted, made love and had one helluva good time. At least *he*'d had a helluva good time. Was he that wrong about how she'd seen the whole thing?

And had she really been seventeen?

Impossible!

"If you were underage, why didn't you tell me?" he asked accusingly.

Casey looked disgusted. "Why didn't you ask?"

Jess's blue eyes darkened. "Because it never occurred to me that such a wise lady was really nothing but a kid," he answered in a lethally quiet voice.

Defensive anger sparked in Casey's eyes. "I was much wiser when you left, wasn't I?"

"Are you mad because I *left*? You knew the score. You knew damned well I was only in town for the rodeo."

"A one-night stand? Oh, pardon me. I meant a one-*week* stand."

"Stop being so nasty," Jess ground out tensely. "Obviously you'd prefer I disappear. Well, lady, you've got it. I've never had to beg crumbs from a woman, and I don't intend to start now!"

He spun on his heel and strode away, and Casey stared straight ahead, refusing to watch him go. *I hate you,* she thought passionately, mentally repeating it again and again. She did, too. There wasn't anything phony about the hot, burning hatred churning in her midsection.

"What'll you have, Casey?"

"What? Oh. One chocolate cone, Joe."

Casey drove home with exactly the upset stomach she'd invented only a short time ago. Bobby licked and ate his ice cream happily. Apparently he'd already forgotten being dragged away from the rodeo early. The blessed resiliency of childhood, Casey reflected, relieved that her beloved little son wasn't pouting.

Her hands clenched and unclenched on the steering wheel with every wave of new thought. *Why is Jess in Blythe? After six years, why is he back?*

And worse yet, *How long is he going to hang around?*

He knew how to find the Oliver ranch of course. It was only ten miles out of Blythe and easily located. But it wasn't likely Jess would drop in after the treatment she'd given him today. So, what she had to do was keep Bobby away from town for a few days. The rodeo was officially over this evening, and a few more days was the longest Jess would stick around.

Casey didn't have even a wisp of guilt at keeping Bobby from Jess Lonnigan. It wasn't Jess who'd been left behind, crushed by the desertion of a man she'd imagined herself in love with. Nor had it been Jess who'd nearly died of shame having to tell her mother that she was pregnant by a rodeo rider who'd been in the area one lousy week.

And when Jess had gone, that had been it—not a telephone call, not so much as a card. Two months later, when Casey had understood her condition, she had wept and pleaded with her mother to keep her shame from the rest of the family. *"Dad would never forgive me. Mom, never."*

"You underestimate your father, Casey."

"I could never look him in the eye again. Please…please…"

Lucille had given in, and together, mother and daughter had concocted an acceptable story. Casey went away to college that September, and within a month called home with news of an elopement that never really happened. She talked to her father. *"I'm Mrs. Don Maddox now, Dad."*

"Dammit, Casey! You've always been too impetuous. Why didn't you bring your young man home before you got married?"

"School, Dad. Don's in school, too. Neither of us wanted to cut classes."

At Christmastime she came home, obviously pregnant, and unhappy about a pretended divorce. *"I'm sorry, Dad. I made a terrible mistake. I know that now. Don doesn't want anything to do with the baby. Could I stay with a man who doesn't want his own child?"*

Lies, lies. During her pregnancy she'd lied so much it was a wonder Bobby hadn't been born a congenital liar. She'd lied not only to family, but to friends, as well. And oh, yes, she'd seen doubt in some people's eyes. After all, no one, not even the Olivers, had met Don Maddox. With her family behind her, though, other people eventually forgot, and it had been years since Casey had sensed an odd stare from anyone. Bobby was

Bobby Maddox, but he was one of the Oliver grandchildren, and in and around Blythe, the Oliver name merited respect.

But Jess's coming back could destroy everything she'd lied to protect. Casey knew her initial fear had been for herself, and in retrospect, from her present twenty-three-year-old viewpoint, she could see that she'd been scared silly at seventeen, willing to do almost anything to keep her predicament private. After Bobby came along, though, she'd stopped worrying about herself; her son was more important than anything or anyone else. But the lies were almost set in concrete now, and no one needed to learn at this late date that Bobby's real father was an itinerant cowboy who'd stopped in Blythe for a week, and that the little boy's mother had been the biggest fool of the century.

Gritting her teeth, Casey turned the car off the highway onto the half-mile driveway leading to the family home. The Oliver ranch was two thousand acres of prime Wyoming grassland, with a stately old two-story house that had sheltered three generations of Olivers, two massive barns, numerous other outbuildings and several thousand head of cattle grazing on its lush pastures. It was a productive, successful cattle operation and provided Buck, Brady and Dee-Dee's husband, Ray, with good jobs, even though the three families lived elsewhere.

It was home and, right at the moment, felt like a sanctuary to Casey. There were a dozen enormous elm and oak trees shading the house and yard, and after Casey and Bobby climbed out of the car, Casey collapsed on one of the front-porch chairs.

"Aren't you gonna go to bed, Mom?" Bobby questioned.

Casey smiled at her son. "I already feel a little better, honey. Maybe the sun was too hot at the rodeo grounds. I think I'll just sit here for a while."

"Are Julie and Mike coming over?"

Julie and Mike were Brady and Cindy's two children. Of Bobby's seven cousins, Julie and Mike were the closest to him in age and were his favorite playmates. "I'm not sure, Bobby," Casey replied.

"Well, gee, I hope they do," the little boy said, looking rather forlorn now that he was home and had remembered that all his cousins were still at the rodeo.

Casey leaned forward. "Why don't you run out and see how the puppies are doing?" One of the dogs, Pearlie, had just had puppies, and Bobby adored looking at them. "Don't pick them up, though," Casey cautioned as Bobby took off.

Sighing then, Casey sat back.

Jess Lonnigan. It still didn't seem possible that he was in Blythe again, even though she'd seen him with her own eyes. She'd come as close to fainting as she ever had when she heard his name. Her mother, too, probably. "Poor Mom," Casey murmured to herself. Lucille Oliver probably didn't know *what* she should be doing right now. Lies were even harder for Lucille than they were for her daughter, and Casey felt that her mother often wished she had insisted Casey tell her father the truth six years ago. It was probably the only secret between Ben and Lucille Oliver, and they'd been married for thirty-six years.

If for nothing else than that, Casey hated Jess. Some allowances for bad judgment might be made for a panicked seventeen-year-old; but Jess Lonnigan hadn't been only seventeen, and he'd given Casey every reason in the world to believe he'd meant everything he'd said.

"You're a special gal, honey."

"I love you, honey."

"You're the prettiest little thing these eyes have ever seen, honey."

Honey! Casey winced at the memories. How stupidly gullible she'd been. For one delirious week she'd worshiped Jess Lonnigan and followed wherever he'd led. She'd been putty in his hands—soft, pliable putty. She had thought him the handsomest, most wonderful man in the world. She had opened her lips, her heart and her legs for him, simply because she'd been so head-over-heels smitten, she hadn't even thought of saying no.

Then, his last night in town, he'd talked about leaving. Casey laughed bitterly now, when she thought of Jess's nonchalance. *"We've sure had a good time honey. It'll be a long while before I forget Blythe, Wyoming."*

"But I don't understand. You mean you're just going away? Why?"

Jess laughed. *"Why? What kind of question is that? You know I follow the rodeo circuit."*

"But I thought . . ."

"What would I do around here? Ask your old man for a job? No way, honey. I'm doing too good in rodeo to tie myself to a broomtail and ride fences for a few hundred bucks a month."

"Dad would pay you better wages than that. But you wouldn't have to work for him. There are dozens of other ranches where you could get a job."

"Sorry, honey. No can do. Come here and show me how much you'll miss me."

It disgusted Casey now to remember that she had done exactly as he'd asked: shown him how much she would miss him. In defense of her idiocy, she also remembered she'd actually thought that if she loved Jess passionately enough, he would change his mind and stay.

It hadn't worked, of course. The next day he was gone. And less than two months later, she'd realized she was pregnant.

It hurt so much to think of that terrible time that Casey couldn't stop the tears that filled her eyes, although it had been a long while since she'd cried over it. There had been months of tears that fall when she was supposed to be in school and wasn't, and sporadic bouts of crying sessions even after she was back home and safe again. After Bobby's birth, though, she'd cried very little. The wonder of her beautiful, perfect son had very effectively made her understand the old adage, "Every cloud has a silver lining."

Bobby had made her want to rejoin the human race and live again. It was caring for him and loving him that had matured her and turned the self-centered girl she'd been into a woman. She was no longer awed by masculine good looks and catchy, cocky phrases. Now, the rare times she dated were casual evenings with men who understood that she wasn't interested in anything beyond a movie or dinner.

She'd never been tempted, even once, to lose herself in a man the way she'd done with Jess. And that silly smugness over looking good to Jess today had only been a momentary regression, a never-to-be-repeated instance of femaleness that had unexpectedly struck her at the shock of seeing him. If she'd had a moment to think and compose herself, she'd have done much better at letting him know how much she despised him.

Well, he'd probably gotten the message, anyway—even if he had taken her by surprise. And it wouldn't hurt her a bit to stay on the ranch and out of Blythe for a few days. She did her work at home anyway, and any deliveries to be made could be handled by someone else.

Four years ago Casey had realized she couldn't keep living off her parents, even though they had both told her otherwise.

She wanted to continue living on the ranch because she honestly felt it was the best place to raise Bobby. But she needed a little independence, and after thinking about what she might do to earn her own money, short of leaving Bobby in someone else's care and taking a full-time job, she hit on the idea of a secretarial service. Casey had been a whiz on the typewriter ever since completing her high-school typing course, and there hadn't been anything even remotely resembling such a service around Blythe.

She had placed an ad in the local twice-weekly newspaper, then called on the businesses in town. Casey knew all the shop owners, of course, and everyone was willing to display a small poster in their storefront windows. Word soon got round. Her first customer was an elderly man who wrote freelance hunting and fishing magazine articles. Casey began typing Lloyd Abbott's manuscripts from hand-scrawled yellow pads, and went on from there.

If she'd had to completely support herself and Bobby from her earnings, things would be rather tight. But she made enough money to buy their clothes and pay for extras. What's more, she'd been told many times that if she opened an office in town she would get a lot more business, even though she did pick up and deliver. Casey had been giving it a lot of thought. Bobby would start first grade in September, and she could coordinate her hours with his. Lucille and Ben—even Kelly, on occasion—were willing to baby-sit, but Bobby was a responsibility Casey didn't take lightly and she seldom imposed on her family to care for him.

Thinking of the past six years gave Casey's pretty face a melancholy expression. She never let herself think too much about happiness or fulfillment or what it might be like to really be married. She loved her parents and was grateful that they were the kind of generous, supportive people they were. They were wonderful to Bobby, as they were to all their grandchildren, and growing up on a ranch among people who loved him was a definite plus for any little boy. But Casey still couldn't help wondering, at odd moments, what it would be like to have a home of her own.

She still slept in the bedroom that had been hers as an infant, she ate at her parents' table, and she listened to and took part in conversations that were as familiar as the seasons. She

had to admit, if only to herself, that if she didn't have a child,
she would try her wings in some far-off place.

But she did have a child. And she wouldn't trade Bobby for
anything in the world. More than that, she would *protect* him
from anything in the world, and that included his own father!

Casey didn't get a chance to talk to her mother privately
when Lucille and Ben returned from the rodeo. The entire
family accompanied them home for a barbecued-rib dinner,
and the large kitchen was chaotic with preparations for enough
food for eighteen people. As usual, all the women helped, but
it was Lucille's kitchen and she orchestrated the cooking and
salad making with a symphony conductor's sense of timing.

They were a noisy bunch. The kitchen buzzed with six fe-
males talking at once, four men coming in and out to get beer
from the refrigerator, and eight children vying for some kind
of attention. Everyone appeared to accept Casey's story of
feeling better once she got home, and she busied herself with a
macaroni salad, the dish Lucille had asked her to prepare. No
one seemed to notice that Casey's voice was the one least heard
or that she gave the salad an inordinate amount of concentration.

But then Casey nearly choked when Kelly made a remark
about the "handsome hunk" who'd awarded the trophies.
"His name is Jess Lonnigan," she announced while chomping
on a stalk of celery. "I wish I was five years older," the fifteen-year-old added with a sprightly grin.

"Stop talking so foolishly," Casey snapped.

"Well, what's wrong with you?" Kelly demanded testily.
"You never even saw him. Honestly, I can't say anything
around here without someone biting my head off."

"That's not true, Kelly," Lucille put in, with a warning
glance at Casey.

She was overreacting again, Casey realized unhappily. If
Kelly had made that kind of remark about a man Casey didn't
know, she would probably have teased her baby sister rather
than snap at her. "I'm sorry," Casey mumbled, and gave the
macaroni salad a stir it didn't need.

The apology brightened Kelly's countenance. "Anyway, Lisa
Mackey told me that he bought a ranch in Clear Creek Valley."

"*Who* bought a ranch in Clear Creek Valley?" Casey asked sharply.

"Jess Lonnigan," Kelly answered triumphantly. She was obviously pleased to be the bearer of such good tidings. "He has three national rodeo championship belts. Three! It's really thrilling to have a genuine rodeo star living only a few miles away, don't you think?"

Two

___

Casey didn't know if she was going to laugh hysterically, burst into tears or faint dead away. The kitchen actually swam before her startled eyes for a few seconds, and within the confused clamor of her own stunned brain, she was positive everyone was staring at her.

They weren't, of course—not even her mother. Lucille was at the sink with her back to Casey, and probably no one else in the room even noticed the odd set of Lucille Oliver's shoulders. The conversation was ebbing no more or less than it had, Casey finally realized, and with trembling hands she ripped a length of plastic wrap from its box, molded it over the salad bowl and placed the bowl in the refrigerator. Then she quietly left the kitchen.

Once away from the room she began to run, and taking the stairs two at a time, she raced to her bedroom. She closed the door behind herself and started pacing. *It can't be true, it can't!* she kept thinking wildly.

Why Blythe? Why, of all the millions of places in the world, why Blythe? A few miles away! My God, how can I keep Bobby away from him if he only lives a few miles away?

Why?

A soft rap at the door stopped Casey's frantic pacing. The door opened and Lucille came in. The two women looked at each other, then Lucille went to her daughter and put her arms around her. Casey clung to her mother and burst into tears. "Try to calm down, honey," Lucille soothed, though she sounded close to tears herself.

Taking a step backward Casey wiped her eyes. "He'll never get Bobby, Mom, not as long as there's breath in my body."

"Of course, he won't. No one's ever going to take that little fellow away from you, Casey. Even the boy's father couldn't do that, not when you've been such a good mother."

"He might try," Casey said sharply.

Lucille sat on the edge of the bed and regarded her distraught daughter. The older woman had a few lines in her face, but she was still very attractive. All of the Olivers were slender, handsome people, with pronounced similarities in facial features.

Years ago, Lucille had recognized that of her three daughters, Casey was the closest to being a real beauty.

Although Dee-Dee and Kelly are very pretty, too, she never failed to add when her biased opinion came to mind. With a mother's loving eye, Lucille couldn't really find too many flaws in any of her children's physical appearance. But there had always been something very special about Casey's looks.

Which, Lucille now acknowledged with a sad sigh, were probably what had drawn Jess Lonnigan's notice in the first place.

"Sit down, honey, just for a few minutes. I've got to get back downstairs, but I noticed you leaving and figured you might need a kind word."

Casey had gone back to her pacing, but at her mother's bidding, she sank onto the dressing-table stool. "I had been planning to keep Bobby out of Blythe for a few days," she recited bitterly. "It never even occurred to me that Jess might be in the area permanently."

"Why would it?" Lucille agreed quietly.

"Maybe I'll just take Bobby and go away, Mom."

"And leave your family? Casey, this is your home. It's Bobby's home. Where would you go? Please don't consider running away as one of your options."

"Mom, if I keep Bobby here and do nothing, sooner or later Jess is bound to see him."

Lucille nodded. "I know. But what you're overlooking is the fact that Jess knows nothing about Bobby's parentage. More than likely he doesn't even know you have a son. When he does learn about Bobby, he'll hear the Maddox name. And people are funny, Casey. We seldom know how we really look to other people. Jess might never see the resemblance you say Bobby has to him."

Casey shook her head with agitation. "When you see Jess for yourself, you'll understand my fears better."

"Possibly. Frankly, I'm very anxious to get a look at Mr. Lonnigan. I wish I had met him six years ago." Lucille leaned forward a little. "Casey, maybe it's time to talk to your father about this. If Jess should decide to come around..."

"He won't," Casey interrupted dully. "I saw him today after I got the keys from Dad."

Lucille's eyes widened. "You saw him?"

"Yes. I stopped at the refreshment stand to get another cone for Bobby on the way back to the car. Jess came up."

"You spoke to him?"

Getting to her feet, Casey went to the window and looked down at the backyard. The kids were running and playing and the men were sitting on the patio while Ben watched the beef ribs on the barbecue. It was a peaceful scene, vastly different from the storm in her soul.

"I wasn't very kind," Casey intoned. "I'm sure he understands that I want no part of him."

Lucille frowned. "You mean he intimated otherwise? For Pete's sake, it's been six years. What did the man think you were doing all that time? You could be married. Did he think you'd been sitting around waiting for him to come back?"

Facing her mother, Casey raised a speculative eyebrow. "Now that I think about it, you're right. At first he acted like he thought I'd be glad to see him. Can you even believe such an ego?"

Sighing with perplexity, Lucille stood up. "Well, I'd better get back down to the kitchen. Are you coming?"

"Not yet. I'd like to be alone for a while."

Lucille walked over to her daughter and gently brushed a lock of her hair back from her forehead. "Don't let this get you down, Casey. You don't have to pay for one mistake the rest of your life, you know."

"I'm not worried about me, Mom," Casey whispered brokenly.

"I know, honey. But think about something for me, all right? Think about talking to your father. I'm not saying I told you so, but I've never yet seen a case where lies didn't somehow come back to haunt a person."

Casey's eyes were misty again. "I'll think about it," she agreed, and studied her mother. "He doesn't know, Mom? You never told him? Today, at the arena, I had the strangest sensation."

Lucille's expression remained noncommittal. "Someday you're going to have to talk to Dad about it."

"I'm afraid to," Casey murmured.

"He'll understand, Casey. He loves you as much as I do." Lucille kissed her daughter, then started for the door. "I'll tell the others that you're still not feeling very well."

"Thanks, Mom," Casey answered raggedly.

Jess was puzzled, damned puzzled. On the drive back to his ranch in Clear Creek Valley at the close of the rodeo, he mulled over the strange meeting with Casey Oliver and what he'd learned about her later. She'd been married and divorced and had a little boy. Well, there wasn't anything so unusual about that information—certainly no reason for Casey to treat *him* like dirt. He sure hadn't done anything to hurt her. Hell, he'd shown her a great time six years ago.

Of course, he hadn't known she was only seventeen years old at the time. Who would have guessed?

Jess's brow creased with a frown. Had she been a virgin?

Damn, he couldn't even remember. There'd been so many women before and since Casey, it was hard to sort them out.

But he'd thought of her when he found himself seriously considering Wyoming as the place to raise the quarter horses he loved. And he'd also thought of Blythe, the pretty little town surrounded by the must beautiful rolling hills of grass he'd ever seen.

After twelve years of rodeo he was ready to settle down. He'd saved his earnings, which had amounted to a substantial sum once he'd started winning the bigger purses. Then, after taking the first national championship, there'd been endorsements and paid personal appearances. He'd done all right, and now he owned twelve hundred acres, with a nice house to boot. There were stables and a barn to build before winter, but he looked forward to getting into their construction. He'd already ordered the lumber and tools he would need.

That part of his life was planned and gratifying. But seeing Casey again—a prospect he'd been anticipating—had really given him a jolt. He'd considered the chance that she might be married now, although he'd sure been hoping she wasn't. But all his speculations about Casey Oliver hadn't even touched on the possibility of her just not wanting anything to do with him.

It made no sense, either—not when they'd had such a great time before.

Why, she'd acted as if she actually hated him. Whereas he thought of Casey with only the fondest of memories . . . and a few that were downright arousing, even six years later. She had made him very happy during that long-ago week, and he'd been under the impression that he'd made her happy, too.

Now he had to revise his thinking: and ever since he'd stalked off, leaving Casey in line at the refreshment stand, Jess had been trying to figure out the icy reception he'd gotten from her.

It made no sense at all. None. Not from any angle.

Well, he'd leave her alone for a few days, then either drop in at the Olivers' ranch or give her a call. Maybe she'd just been upset over something that had nothing to do with him. That made more sense than anything else. Casey had probably only been in a bad mood. She'd come around.

On Monday, as there was no longer any point to hiding on the ranch, Casey went about her business as usual. Ordinarily, when she made pickups or deliveries, she took Bobby with her. That was the only deviation from her regular routine this Monday; she left Bobby in her mother's care. Tuesday, she stayed on the ranch and typed Lloyd Abbott's latest article, plus six letters for a new customer—an attorney who'd just opened an office in Blythe and seemed to be procrastinating about hiring a secretary.

Wednesday morning, Casey got ready and drove into Blythe—alone again—to deliver the work she'd put out the day before. First she stopped at Lloyd Abbott's house, then she drove to the hardware store and parked on the street. Wesley Upton had rented three rooms above the store for his law offices, and when Casey had picked up the cassette for transcription, the attorney had been painting the drab walls.

He was still painting, Casey realized as she caught fumes of fresh paint while climbing the stairs. "Mr. Upton?" she called.

"In here." Wiping his hands on a paint-spattered towel, Wesley Upton came out of one of the rooms. "Hello, Casey."

He was a big man, stockily built, with thinning brown hair and glasses, probably around thirty-five. "Hi. Still hard at it, I see," Casey commented.

"Almost done. Come on in."

Casey followed the attorney into a room that had been efficiently transformed into an office. She looked around at the shelves of law books, the massive desk and the comfortable-looking chairs. "Very nice."

"Thanks. Got time for a cup of coffee?"

Casey laid the manila envelope she'd been carrying on the desk. She'd seen a glint of admiration in Wesley Upton's eyes at their first meeting, and if she wasn't tied in such knots today she might have accepted a cup of coffee. But not one minute had passed without worry since the last day of the rodeo, and she was too tense to participate in small talk or an attempt to further a brand-new relationship into something more than it was. Like everyone else around Blythe, she had heard that the new attorney in town was a divorced man. And while he wasn't really handsome, Wesley Upton was pleasant looking. If Jess Lonnigan wasn't hovering over her head like a threatening black cloud, Casey knew she would probably have welcomed the chance to get to know Wesley better.

"I'll take a rain check on that, if you don't mind. I've got to run today."

Wesley Upton nodded. "Anytime. I have another cassette ready."

"Great. I appreciate the business." Casey accepted the new cassette. "Thank you. I'll deliver the day after tomorrow, as usual."

She hurried away, already forgetting Wesley Upton. Casey felt that she was living on the brink of disaster.

She was driving one of the ranch's pickups today, and with her mind so overloaded, she didn't even notice someone sitting in the truck until she was only two steps away. Casey reeled with shock; Jess was smiling at her through the open window of her own vehicle!

She took one more step. "Get out of my truck," she demanded hotly.

Jess's smile disappeared. "Not until we talk. Get in."

A woman walking by slowed down. "Morning, Casey."

Casey's head jerked around. "Good morning, Stella."

Stella Patterson stopped, making Casey cringe inwardly. Stella was one of the biggest gossips in Blythe, and it was more than apparent that she was interested in the little scene unfolding in front of the hardware store. Her avid gaze was on Jess. "Aren't you Jess Lonnigan? I saw you at the rodeo on Saturday."

"Yes, ma'am," Jess replied with a look of amusement.

Stella stuck her hand in the window, inviting a handshake. "I'm Stella Patterson. I heard you bought a little ranch in Clear Creek Valley."

"Yes, ma'am."

Stella beamed. "Well, isn't that nice. You'll have to come to dinner some evening. Do you have a telephone?"

"Yes, ma'am."

"Wonderful. I'll give you a call. Casey, tell your mother hello for me."

"I will," Casey agreed stiffly. But when Stella was out of earshot, she muttered something unintelligible.

Jess had caught the gist of the comment, if not the words. "Afraid to be seen with me?" he asked quietly.

Casey's green eyes narrowed. "Get out of my truck," she repeated tersely.

"I want to talk to you."

"We have nothing to talk about."

"That's what's bothering me, honey. How come you and I don't have anything to talk about?"

Casey's jaw clenched. "Don't you dare call me honey."

Jess's dark blue eyes bored into hers. "Get in, Casey. You're going to tell me why you hate my guts."

"I'm telling you nothing!"

"Then I'm sitting right here. It sure doesn't bother me if every citizen in Blythe sees us fighting in front of the hardware store."

Casey was trembling with frustrated anger. "You arrogant jerk," she whispered.

"Make a scene, honey. Go ahead. Scenes don't bother me one little bit."

The bell on the hardware store door jangled, and behind her Casey heard two men talking. A quick glance backward lowered her spirits another notch; she knew both of them. "Hello, Casey." "Hi, Casey."

Responding with a weak "Hello," Casey marched around the front of the pickup, opened the door and climbed behind the steering wheel. She didn't say a word or glance at Jess as she started the motor and pulled away from the curb.

Jess was watching her closely. "Where you heading?"

Casey ignored him. Covering the main street of town took only a few minutes. At the edge of Blythe she turned the truck onto a dirt road, drove a silent half mile and stopped in a secluded wooded spot. Switching off the key, she stared straight ahead. "Say your piece and get it over with," she said coldly.

Jess was studying her with a frowning, questioning expression. "All I want to know is why you so obviously hate me."

"Why?"

"Why, what?"

"Why do you want to know? If my feelings are so obvious, why not let it go at that? Isn't a big rodeo star capable of accepting that every woman he meets isn't falling at his feet?"

"Why are you being so damned sarcastic? Can't you talk about this in a normal way?"

"No."

"Look at me."

"No."

Tension was in the air, heavy and thick. Jess felt anger in his gut. She might have a reason to despise him, but he had a right to know what it was. He slid across the seat. "Dammit, you *will* look at me," he muttered, and grabbed her.

They struggled, and there were several minutes of curses and grappling before Jess had Casey in a grip she couldn't escape from. "Big man," she taunted. "Does it make you feel good to subdue a woman?"

Jess was breathing hard. He stared down at livid green eyes and a beautiful face that contained nothing but hatred. "Just tell me why," he ground out angrily.

Her breasts were pushed into his chest, her arms held to her sides by his and their faces were no more than an inch apart. Irrationally, she registered the blue of his shirt as being the same color as his eyes, and his scent as something spicy and masculine.

"You don't just hate me, Casey. You'd like to see me squirm. I wouldn't be questioning your feelings if all I picked up from you was dislike. But there's a helluva lot more to your sarcasm and insults than dislike. Between the last time we saw each other and now, something happened. I can't even begin to imagine what it was, but—"

"Don't bother to try," Casey snapped. "I just grew up. Apparently you didn't. You still think you're the greatest thing since sliced bread."

"See? That's what I mean. You've handed out insults as though they were gifts both times we've seen each other. *That*'s what I can't understand, Casey. Dislike is one thing. But you act like you've got some kind of personal vendetta against me. Have you felt this way for six years?"

"Don't flatter yourself," she sneered. "I never even thought of you once!"

Their eyes met and held. Casey's face was flushed, her lips grim. Jess felt her the same way he had six years ago—somewhere deep inside himself. How had he forgotten Casey Oliver so easily? Holding her, even with anger between them, was bringing everything back. How many times had they made love during that week? Six times, eight, a dozen? "Are you really only twenty-three now?" he asked hoarsely, approaching the issue of her age six years ago from a safer direction.

"How long are you going to keep me in this disgusting position?" she returned tautly.

"At least you're looking at me now."

"I can hardly do anything else, can I?" she jeered.

"And you find being in my arms disgusting?"

"I'm not in your arms! I'm being held against my will!" To prove her point, Casey began to struggle again. "Take your hands off me," she yelled angrily. Her left arm eluded his hold, and she went for his face with her fingernails.

"Whoa, there," Jess growled, catching her wrist just in time. "You little hellion, what're you trying to do, scratch my eyes out?"

"It's a thought," Casey retorted, gulping a mouthful of air. Escape was impossible. He could hold her there all day if he chose. She was getting hot and sweaty, although the open windows allowed the passage of a warm, gentle breeze. Casey stiffened with a new fear and an immediate denial: she wasn't getting warmer because of Jess, she absolutely was not!

But why, after all the misery he'd caused her, was she so aware of the width of his shoulders and the hard bulk of his chest? And why did she keep looking at his mouth? She'd caught herself doing it several times. Oh, traitorous soul, she lamented in a bout of anguished self-castigation. How could she even notice that he'd only grown better-looking in six years? That the few silver hairs she could see mingled with all that black were dazzling, and that the crinkled corners of his eyes looked like perfect spots to plant tender kisses?

"I hate you," she whispered raggedly.

Jess stared directly into the centers of her tormented eyes. "I know you do. The big question is why? You loved me the week I was here before."

"I did not! I never loved you. No more than you loved me!"

"Well, honey, if that's the problem, rest assured. I loved you like crazy that week."

Casey's heart had already been beating hard, but now it raged in her breast. "You don't know the meaning of the word! Love isn't something you turn on for a week, then turn off again like you would a spigot!"

Jess was watching her with acute circumspection. He was beginning to understand Casey's scorn, or he thought he was. "Is that what happened to you? You couldn't turn it off?"

The implication of the conversation blasted Casey. "I *never* loved you!" she shouted.

"You don't have to yell. I'm not deaf."

"You're not only deaf, you're blind! What's it going to take for you to see that I wish you had never come back to Blythe? Nothing would make me happier than to hear you had disappeared from the face of the earth."

Jess's face was suddenly dark with anger. "You sound like you need some lovin', Casey. How long has it been since you've had some real lovin'? How long have you been divorced?"

She was torn with two debilitating emotions: fury over his crude remarks and fearful astonishment that he'd already learned about her "marriage" and "divorce." Did he also know she had a son? "That's none of your business," she cried, struggling wildly again. "Let me go."

"I will," Jess stormed. "But first . . ." He grabbed the back of her head and brought his mouth down on hers, hard. Casey's gasp of surprise was muffled, nearly soundless. She twisted her head, trying to tear her mouth away, but Jess only kissed her harder and pressed his full weight against her. The door made ridges in her back, and the buttons on his shirt pressed tiny indentations in her breasts.

Her mind alternately raced and stood still. Jess's lips had quickly grown kinder, more sensual. She felt his tongue and her own stronger heartbeat, and vaguely realized one had caused the other. She might loathe and despise Jess Lonnigan, but he was still the sexiest man she'd ever known. Having had Jess as her first lover, was it any wonder she'd found little to respond to in other men?

She was kissing him back, she realized, opening her mouth for his tongue. His body weight relented a little, enough to allow room for his hand between them. It found a breast and closed around it, and she felt how agitated the contact was making him. His palm chafed her nipple through her blouse and bra, and the resulting sting of pleasure shooting through her system had the impact of a lightning bolt. Her responsive moan drifted on the July breeze filling the cab.

Jess's lips moved against hers, and he whispered, "You don't hate me, honey. You want me, just like I want you." Before she could agree to or deny the sensual accusation, Jess's mouth opened over hers again.

Breathing in short pants, Casey felt her fear growing in a direct ratio to her desire. She was getting lost again. Jess was commanding her senses again, just as he'd done six years ago. She had to stop this, she *had* to!

Working a hand upward, she slid it past the muscles of his chest and shoulder. Thinking she wanted to twine her arms around his neck, Jess adjusted, giving her more space. At last both her arms were free, and Casey grasped two handfuls of black hair and yanked his head up.

Jess looked down at her, surprise in his eyes. "What's wrong?"

Casey's irregular breathing made speaking normally difficult. "Do you intend to rape me?"

"Lord no!" Jess sat up and away from her. "Why would you think such a crazy thing?"

Flushed, Casey tried to smooth her disheveled hair. "I won't make love with you, Jess," she stated, her voice raspy and husky.

His eyes narrowed. "You want to. Or, you did. A man knows, Casey, and you wanted exactly what I did."

"Maybe for a minute or two. All that proves is what you accused me of—needing a man. If I do, he's not going to be you."

"Why not? Casey, you're the most dumbfounding woman I've ever been around. You kiss like no one else, and—"

"*You* kissed me." Wishing her hands were steadier, Casey reached for the ignition key. Before she could turn it, Jess covered her hand with his.

"Just a minute. I started out kissing you, but you kissed me back."

"It won't happen again, I can assure you." She felt his eyes on her, searching every angle and curve of her body. She was wearing a simple green knit sleeveless blouse and white cotton slacks, but she suddenly felt as if her clothing were evaporating. "Stop looking at me like that," she demanded heatedly.

"Like I'd like to undress you and make you whimper, sweetheart?"

She swallowed hard. "You're crude," she managed weakly.

"Not crude—truthful. We both know what happened a few minutes ago was no accident, honey. The same thing happened between us six years ago. One kiss was all it took, right?"

Casey shook his hand away and turned the ignition key. "I don't plan to relive old memories with you—not when I find them repugnant."

Jess snorted. "Repugnant? Hell! Who're you trying to kid? You loved every minute we spent together that week."

Shooting him a black look of resentment, Casey turned the pickup in a circle and started back to town.

He began to talk softly. "You know what's strange in all of this, honey? You've been protesting too much. I'm beginning to wonder who you've been trying to convince with all those bitter words. Me or you?"

"You're talking pure drivel."

"Am I?"

Casey was a seething mass of confusion. She had accomplished nothing beyond whetting Jess's curiosity even more than it had been. And pretending coolness over kissing him back when she despised herself for being so weak was making her furious, at herself as much as Jess. But she couldn't scream at herself.

She slammed on the brakes, slapped the gear lever into Park and turned on Jess. "This is the last time I ever want to see you. Are you capable of understanding that? If we meet on the street, I intend passing you by without so much as a blink. By way of an explanation, which you seem so bent on getting, I was seventeen years old when you were in Blythe six years ago. I'm not seventeen now. I'm—''

''Beautiful,'' Jess murmured.

She took a shaky breath, realizing deep inside herself that she was getting very close to hysteria. ''Jess . . . you've got to leave me alone. I can't take much more of this.''

His brow knit. ''Much more of what? We've seen each other exactly twice since I've been back.''

Casey dropped her gaze. ''What do you want from me?'' she asked in a ragged whisper.

Jess leaned closer and touched her hair. When she cringed back from his hand, he didn't press her. He withdrew his hand and said, ''I think you know what I want.''

Her eyes darted fitfully, evading the hot light she saw in his. ''Why'd you come back here?''

''I always liked Wyoming.''

''Wyoming's a big place. You could have bought a ranch hundreds of miles from Blythe.''

''Yeah, I could have. Something drew me back here. Was it you? Maybe I never really forgot that week, honey.''

Her expression grew colder. ''You're lying.''

Jess laughed easily. ''Not lying, honey. But maybe exaggerating a little, huh? Truthfully, I was so busy the last six years, I never looked back at much of anything.''

Sighing. Casey turned and slipped the lever back into Drive. In all honesty she respected Jess's ''truthfulness'' a lot more than she did his glibness. It didn't matter, anyway. She knew he hadn't thought about her all those years, so it wasn't news now. It didn't even hurt—not when she had another much more serious ache in her heart: Bobby. The little boy's big blue eyes were Jess's. Bobby's thick thatch of black hair was Jess's. Bobby's special half-smile, so endearing on his handsome little face, was Jess's.

Casey saw a dozen other similarities between the two—in expression, in movement. A child didn't have to grow up around a parent to imitate him: it was in the blood, a trick of genetics.

''Where do you want to get out?'' Casey asked quietly, strangely coiled into numbness after the onslaught of emotions she'd undergone the past half hour.

"My truck's close to the hardware store. I was inside making a purchase when you drove up." Jess cocked his head in Casey's direction. "I understand you have a little boy."

"Yes," she replied through numbed lips.

"How old is he?"

"Five."

Jess frowned. "Then you must have gotten married right after I left."

"I did."

"To a local guy?"

"No. I met him in college that September."

"How long were you married?"

Casey shot him an angry look. "That's enough, Jess. I don't plan to give you a day-by-day update of the past six years." With tremendous relief, she steered the pickup into a parking space in the same block as the hardware store.

Jess didn't immediately jump out, though. He sat for another minute, then looked at her. "Would you go out with me some night?"

Her eyes widened. "You never give up, do you?"

"Not when I see something I want."

Casey took an impatient breath. "All right, I'll say it again. No, I will not go out with you. My most ardent wish is that it will eventually sink in that I want nothing to do with you—not today, not tomorrow, not next year. Just forget we even knew each other, because that's how I look at us: as total strangers."

The pupils of his eyes seemed to grow darker. "You're lying through your pretty teeth." Jess reached for the door handle. "One of these days I'll figure out why. See you around, honey."

Casey drove home, alternately crying and cursing.

Three

A week passed—an unholy week with Casey peering at every pickup she met on the road and constantly looking over her own shoulder in town. She was positive Jess was lurking around every corner, just waiting for another chance to challenge her. But she never saw a sign of him, and after a while she began to breathe a bit easier.

Casey had told her mother about Jess confronting her that day. She didn't mention Jess's personal advances, though, simply because she could hardly bear even thinking about the episode, let alone talking about it. But she did relay the fact that Jess had already heard that she'd been married, divorced and had a little boy.

Lucille's response was a seriously posed: "Did he seem to doubt what he'd heard?"

"I don't think so," Casey replied honestly.

Lucille smiled with apparent relief. "There, you see? You were worried about nothing. By the time he sees Bobby, *if* he does, he'll be so used to the story he won't see anything but a very handsome little boy."

"I hope you're right, Mom." Casey still wasn't so sure of that, however. Whenever she looked at Bobby, she saw Jess—

even more strongly now than she had before she'd gotten another look at Jess. Just to play it safe for a while longer, she continued to leave her son at the ranch when she made her trips to Blythe.

Wesley Upton had quickly gained a few clients, and his work was taking up more and more of Casey's time. The attorney offered her a cup of coffee whenever she made a delivery, and one afternoon Casey accepted. They sat in Wesley's office, Casey in one of the big chairs in front of the desk, the attorney seated behind the desk.

"Your offices turned out nicely," she remarked.

"Thank you. By the way, please call me Wes."

"If you like."

Wes smiled rather warmly, then put his cup down and leaned forward. "I'd like to ask you something, Casey."

"Go right ahead."

"Well, I've been wondering. I like your work very much, but I can see a time coming when I'm going to need a full-time secretary. Would you ever consider giving up your business and going to work for just one client?"

Casey hesitated. "I've been thinking of moving my business to town, Wes. Quite a few people have indicated I'd get a lot more work if I were closer. However, I really don't want to make any kind of change until Bobby is in school."

"And next summer, when he's out of school again?"

"I don't mind admitting that's been bothering me. My mother is very generous about taking care of Bobby, but I couldn't impose on her time for three months every year."

"Other mothers work, Casey. I would imagine pretty well all of them are faced with the problem of their children's summer vacations."

Casey nodded. "That's true. But I've never left Bobby with anyone but family. Anyway, as you can see, I haven't made a decision on the matter yet."

"Will you give my offer some consideration?"

Rising, Casey smiled. "Of course I will. I appreciate it, as a matter of fact."

Wes walked to the door with her. "Perhaps we could have dinner together some evening," he suggested.

"Perhaps," Casey agreed pleasantly. "Bye, Wes, I'll see you in a few days."

After three more deliveries, Casey started back to the ranch. She was driving with her eyes on the road, but her mind was on Jess Lonnigan. Maybe, as her mother had suggested, she had gone a little overboard about Jess's return. It was only because she didn't want Bobby's life disrupted with some kind of parental clashing, but it really wasn't very likely that Jess, being the type of man he was, would lay claim to his child, anyway—even if he should become suspicious. Rationally thinking, it wasn't even very likely that Jess would do more than catch a peek at Bobby now and then, possibly spot him from a distance in Blythe.

She felt a little better about it, Casey admitted to herself. The shock of hearing Jess's name, seeing him, then learning he was living only a few miles away, had caused her to panic. If she were going to be totally honest with herself, wasn't her own reaction to Jess much more dangerous than the slim possibility of him figuring out Bobby was his son?

The morning Jess had cornered her, for example, she, herself had made Jess suspect there was more to her animosity than mere dislike. *Dislike.* Casey smirked grimly. To her, the word denoted mild feelings of ill will. For six years she had *hated* Jess Lonnigan. Small wonder she couldn't stop herself from using sarcasm and insults around him. But she could see now that her open hostility had only aroused his curiosity. If—or more likely, when—she ran into Jess again, it would be much wiser to behave with less bitterness—if she could.

On the other hand, if he tried something personal again, she'd ... She'd what? Frowning, Casey struggled with the obvious: Jess still had the power to turn her knees to jelly. She could despise him—and she did—and still, she couldn't halt a tide of desire when he kissed her. Why? Why was she able to handle every other relationship—granted, they'd been few—but have absolutely no control with Jess?

A horn behind her blasted her reverie, and Casey glanced into the rearview mirror. A black pickup was right on her bumper, and quickly Casey veered to the right to give the impatient driver more room to pass. The horn honked again.

"What's wrong with you?" she muttered. "How much room do you need?" The road had only two lanes, but there wasn't another car in sight. The honking continued.

Slowing way down, Casey frowned into the rearview mirror again. Only this time, she got a good look. Jess!

Automatically she speeded up, just wanting to escape. But the black pickup stayed right on her bumper, although the intolerable honking had stopped. Then Casey realized that Jess would follow her clear to the ranch, and her heart sank. She could convince herself all day that Jess wasn't the kind of man who would want his son, even if he knew about him, but she wasn't ready to take that chance. And the minute she drove up, Bobby would run out to greet her. He always did.

She let up on the gas pedal and pulled off the road.

In the rearview mirror, Casey watched Jess get out of his truck, toss his hat back in and start her way. She faced front and waited.

"Hi," she heard at the open window.

"What do you want?"

"Are you going to talk to me without looking at me again?"

Reluctantly Casey turned her head a fraction and gave him a cold stare. "Why are you following me?" *Do you have to be so damned good-looking?* In the bright sunlight, Jess's black hair, tanned face and vivid blue eyes were radiant.

Jess was seeing the same kind of thing in Casey: the purity of a flawless, creamy complexion, clear green eyes and a head full of thick, dark auburn curls. He cleared his throat. "I've been doing some thinking about us. We got off to a bad start."

Casey did nothing but raise one eyebrow slightly.

"I'm not the same guy I was six years ago, Casey."

"No? So far, I've seen nothing different," she said coolly.

"I know. But you riled me that day at the rodeo. I was glad to see you and I didn't expect what you dished out."

"So, what you're saying is that it's my fault you manhandled me last week in my own truck?"

Jess gave her a hard look. "Is that what I did, 'manhandle' you?"

"What would you call it?"

"Did I hurt you?"

Casey looked away. "I assume there's a point to this conversation?"

"Yeah, there is. I want to see you."

Her eyes flashed his way again. "No."

"Why not?"

Rolling her eyes in exasperation, Casey took a long breath. "Are we going to go through that again? How many times...?"

"As many as it takes."

"You think you're going to wear me down," Casey accused heatedly. "Well, you're not, Jess. Once was enough with you."

"What if I promise to keep my hands to myself? Would you see me, then?"

She laughed grimly. "I can't believe this. Why would you want to see a woman who so obviously doesn't want to see you?"

An approaching car drew Jess's attention, and he watched it speed toward them, then whiz on by. He turned troubled eyes and a frown back to Casey. "I honestly don't know," he confessed quietly, almost sadly. "There's some kind of pull...hell, I don't know what it is. I only know I keep thinking about you."

Something swirled within Casey. Resentment, maybe. She had thought of Jess a lot, too. At first. For months, after he left, she had cried herself to sleep every night thinking about him. If he suffered a hundred times more than she had, it wouldn't be enough. He'd been right about that personal vendetta. She would love hearing him say "I love you" with meaning instead of lust, so she could laugh in his face. And she'd push him into it, too, if it weren't for Bobby. With her son at stake, she couldn't risk revenge, as sweet as it would be.

But she had already decided to soft-pedal her hostility—for Bobby's sake—and remembering that decision, Casey kept her expression passive. "I'm sorry you don't understand me better. I rarely date, and I have no desire to renew a mistake I made at seventeen. That's all there is to my refusals. Don't try to read more into them than that."

A flush darkened his face. "I didn't know you were only seventeen, Casey. I never would have gotten so physically involved if I'd have known your age."

"I accept full responsibility," she answered sharply, then took a calming breath. "I should have told you. I knew you were older."

Shaking his head, Jess looked away for a moment. "I just grabbed at fun in those days. One town blurred into another. Women—"

"Blurred, too, I'm sure. Forget it. I have." *Grabbed at fun?* Casey's stomach was aching.

Jess gave her a direct look. "No, you haven't. You haven't forgotten at all. That's the problem. I know that now. You got emotionally involved, and when I left—"

"You're wrong!" Casey's mouth was suddenly dry and her heart pounding. "You're wrong, Jess. Look, I've got to go."

He put a hand on the window frame. "See me, Casey," he pleaded. "Go out with me. I promise I won't lay a hand on you. We'll take in a movie, or have a drink someplace. Dinner. Anything. You name it."

She shook her head sharply. "No. I can't. Please don't press me."

"Dammit, I *will* press you! You melted in my arms last week."

Casey met his eyes. "I'm the first to admit that I'm a fool sometimes. Please move back from the truck." She watched his eyes narrow.

"I'm not giving up, Casey."

She lifted her chin. "I guess that's your decision. Goodbye." Slipping the truck into gear, Casey eased it away. Looking in the rearview mirror again, she could see Jess, and he was standing in the same spot, just watching.

"Have you thought anymore about talking to your father about Jess?" Lucille asked.

They were sitting on the back patio. Casey had just told her mother about Jess stopping her on the road, and they had agreed that Jess's promise to "keep pushing" could present some problems.

Sighing over the question she hadn't really faced up to yet, Casey replied, "Yes. Whenever I think about it, I see Dad's face. It's cowardly, I know, but I'm just plain scared to tell him."

"Casey, there's no reason for you to be afraid to talk to your father about anything."

"I'll do it, Mom. Just give me a little more time."

Lucille nodded. "Just don't put it off too long."

Casey grimaced. "I've already done that, haven't I? I wish I had listened to you six years ago and told him then. Mom, what if Dad resents your part in it?"

Lucille looked away. "I don't think we should worry about that right now. Jess is back in your life, like it or not, and we have to think of Bobby."

"Yes, we do."

Lucille looked thoughtful. "Casey, I know what Jess did to you. I know you were devastated by what appeared to be desertion six years ago. What I'm getting at is, you've changed a great deal. Could Jess have changed too?"

"I don't understand."

"Well, every child needs a father and—"

"Mom! You're not suggesting I *tell* Jess!"

Lucille sighed. "I don't know what I'm suggesting. But it has occurred to me that Jess might have grown up, just as you did. He seems to have settled down, at any rate."

"He was grown-up six years ago," Casey argued. "He has to be ten years older than me."

"I meant emotionally, honey."

With her elbow on the arm of the chair and her chin in her hand, Casey stared morosely at her feet. "I won't share Bobby with a man who didn't have an ounce of concern over seducing a seventeen-year-old girl and then running off like it never happened."

"I thought you said he didn't know how old you were. Casey, you were pretty headstrong in those days. Try and remember yourself as you really were. No, Jess didn't do right. But neither did you, honey. Your father and I thought you were spending that entire week with a girlfriend in town."

Casey heaved a sigh. "I know. I gave you and Dad fits back then. When I see Kelly doing a lot of the same things I did, I feel like smacking her."

Lucille laughed. "It's just part of growing up, honey. After raising four other teenagers, I don't think Kelly's any better or any worse than the rest of you were."

"Dee-Dee never gave you any trouble."

"You're right. Dee-Dee was always pretty level headed. Buck and Brady were another story. Dad and I never knew what they were up to."

"None of them did what I did."

Lucille's blue-gray eyes softened. "It never made me love you any less, Casey. And there's a bright side to the whole thing— Bobby. Let's not forget that without Jess, we wouldn't have Bobby."

Casey smiled, though her eyes were misty. "He's my life, Mom."

"Yes, he is. But maybe it's time you expanded your life."

"With a man?"

"With a man," Lucille agreed solemnly, regarding her daughter with maternal concern and affection.

Stripped to the waist, Jess worked at unloading the first of the lumber he'd ordered for his new barn and stables from the back of his truck. The sun was hot, and his face and back glistened with perspiration. Hauling boards off a truck and stacking them near the proposed building site took little concentration, and as he did more often than he liked, Jess was thinking about Casey while he worked.

He knew she wasn't the same woman she'd been six years ago, even if that long-ago memory had a lot of fuzzy edges. Although he had easily recognized her at the rodeo that day, Jess realized. The changes in Casey just weren't apparent on the outside. She had the same beautiful face, glorious mane of hair and exciting body. Where she'd changed was inside. Instead of the soft, pliant girl he remembered, Casey was now guarded, caustic and hard. How come?

Had her marriage been bad enough to turn her into a manhater? Maybe that was it. Maybe she treated *all* men the way she'd been treating him.

Jess knew she still lived on the family ranch, having picked up that detail at the same time he'd heard about her marriage, divorce and little boy. Well, whatever had caused her bitterness, she sure had been something six years ago.

Wiping his forehead with the back of his arm, Jess leaned on a board and looked off into his own past. Blythe. It had been full of people that week, just as it had been during rodeo week this year. The sleepy little town came alive during rodeo week, and the restaurants and bars had been overflowing with customers six years ago. Jess had had a few beers at one of the bars, then went back to the rodeo grounds to tend his horse.

A group of young women came along. Yes, now he was remembering. That's how he and Casey had met. She'd been strolling around the evening-quiet rodeo grounds with some friends. They'd stopped to talk—the whole group laughing and flirting. Then they'd wandered off.

Attracted by her startling green eyes and husky laugh, he'd picked Casey out. He hadn't once thought of how old she might be, even though now, he remembered that her girlfriends had seemed pretty young.

He'd found her again. It hadn't been a problem. People had been all over the streets. Somehow the two of them had ended up at a dance in the high-school gymnasium, and they'd danced a few dances, then left together. He had asked her to go for a beer, and she had said she didn't go into bars. Damn, that had been another hint she'd been too young! Why hadn't he taken it?

He'd been bowled over, hadn't he? That was his only excuse. She was beautiful and dazzling, and he'd known she was dazzled. He'd bought a six-pack and asked her where they could go to be alone. She'd shown him a place by a river about five miles out of Blythe.

Jess's jaw clenched. Now he was remembering a lot.

He'd spread a blanket on the grassy bank of the river. The moon had been big and bright. They'd sat down on the blanket and she had taken sips from his can of beer. He'd teased and flirted with her, and she had laughed and flirted back. He'd kissed her, tentatively at first, then with more passion. She'd surprised him with a wild response.

Jess wiped his forehead again. Oddly, his hands weren't very steady and his mouth was dry. Dropping the board he'd been leaning on to the stack on the ground, he strode to the house. Popping the top on a can of icy beer, he came back outside and plopped down on one of the chairs on the porch.

She *had* been a virgin. He remembered that evening very well now. He'd been stunned; she'd been consoling. The week had progressed from there.

Damn! Double damn! She hadn't been the kind of girl to make love with a man for a week, then forget him. What kind of horse's patoot had he been back then? His damned brain had been so full of rodeo and the next town, the next contest, that he'd gone off without a thought for what Casey might be feeling.

Was it any wonder she hated him now? He might have put that week and Casey behind him with the first sign of open road, but apparently she hadn't forgotten quite so easily.

Putting the other bits and pieces of her life together, Jess remembered her saying she'd met her husband that September in college. She hadn't wasted any time. Had she married on the rebound?

Then she had a son.

When?

How long had she been married before the boy was born?

Jess became as still as a statue. *How long had she been married before the boy was born?* "My God," he mumbled as the thought took form and grew to something almost unbearable. Had she had *his* child? Was that what she was hiding?

"How old is he?"

"Five."

Five. Five and what? Five and a half? Dates stormed Jess's mind. He'd been in Blythe in July. That would make a baby due the following April. Jess gulped a big swallow of the cold beer. If it was true, if Casey had gotten pregnant that July, then he had a son.

A son.

He put the beer down and covered his face with his hands while something hot and anguished flowed through his body. A son. He'd never had a family. He'd been kicked around as a kid, shunted off on one reluctant relative after another. His mother had run off with some guy; he'd never even known his father. At sixteen, he'd split, gone off on his own. It had been tough. He'd taken odd jobs to eat, then met an old cowboy named Ace Goodfield. Ace had sort of adopted him, giving him a roof over his head, even making him go back to school.

Ace was dead now, but if it hadn't been for him, Jess never would have gotten a high-school diploma. He never would have gotten into rodeo, either. Ace had introduced him to horses and the exhilaration of rodeo. The rest, he'd done on his own.

Jess raised his eyes wearily and stared across his land. A son. Damn Casey Oliver's selfish soul. She could have told him. The past was irrevocable. He couldn't go back and change inconsideration and thoughtlessness into something good. He'd been a jerk and there was no way around that. But keeping a man's son from him was just about as low as anyone could get. If it was true, the punishment far exceeded the crime.

He'd better find out if it was true. He'd never have a peaceful moment again until he knew for sure, one way or the other.

Casey was helping with the dinner dishes. While Lucille put leftovers away, Casey rinsed the dishes in the sink and stacked them in the dishwasher. Kelly came bounding in, her long, blond hair flying, her blue eyes excited. "He's here! Out on the porch with Dad."

"Who's here?" Lucille asked with only mild curiosity.

"Jess Lonnigan! He's sitting on the front porch with Dad. He is only the most gorgeous hunk that's ever been on our front porch."

"Don't overdramatize, dear," Lucille admonished softly with a worried look at Casey.

"Oh, honestly," Kelly groaned, and dashed out.

"Casey? Are you all right?"

She was facing the sink. The water was running and she was holding a plate, but she wasn't moving. Her shoulders rose as she stopped holding her breath. "Why would he come here?" she whispered, and turned to her mother.

"He told you he intended to press you, Casey."

"Yes. But, here? That takes a special kind of gall, Mom." Casey's eyes darted wildly for a moment. "Where's Bobby?" Grabbing a dish towel, she dried her hands hastily. "I've got to find Bobby," she tossed over her shoulder as she ran from the kitchen.

Lucille sighed sadly. She'd seen Bobby only a few minutes ago, playing in the front yard with the dogs. There was no way Jess could have missed seeing him.

Feeling choked, Casey dashed through the house, praying that Bobby was in front of the TV. The living room was empty. She reached the front screen door and saw Jess, her father and Kelly on the porch. Just beyond, rolling around on the grass with the dogs, was Bobby.

He was giggling, and looked so adorable she wanted to run out and hug him, then hide him. Her hands were itching to touch her son, and her heart was aching to protect him. She heard her father's laughter, Jess's voice. They were getting along very well.

Weakly, Casey slumped back against the foyer wall. Her mind raced. Hadn't her father and Kelly immediately seen the strong resemblance between Jess and Bobby? Why weren't they already in the house, questioning her, accusing her?

Had Jess noticed it?

She heard her father's voice. "I'm glad you stopped by, Jess. A man should meet his neighbors."

Then came Kelly's voice: "Everyone is so-o-o excited about you moving here, Mr. Lonnigan."

"Call me Jess, Kelly."

"Oh, thank you."

Casey's stomach turned over. Why hadn't she gathered her pitiful supply of courage and confessed the awful truth to her dad? It was going to be even harder to do now. *Dad, that man who dropped in last night—Jess Lonnigan? Well, he's really Bobby's father.*

Oh, God, what a mess she still was making of her life!

"Is Casey around?" she heard Jess ask.

"Do you know Casey?" That came from Kelly, sounding totally amazed.

Casey stiffened, anticipating Jess's answer with bated breath.

"We've met," was Jess's noncommittal reply.

Then came Ben's voice again. "Well, she's around here somewhere. Kelly, go see if you can find her."

Casey ducked into the foyer closet while her sister ran past. Then she opened the door to eavesdrop again.

"You've got a beautiful place here, Ben."

"Yeah, it is. It's home, Jess. Three generations of Olivers have lived here."

"I'm just starting out, but someday, maybe Lonnigans will be able to say that."

"Gonna raise quarter horses, I hear."

The men were soon in a technical discussion on the qualities and characteristics of the quarter horse. The conversation was so impersonal, Casey was feeling a little better—but only a little. Jess's nerve at just driving up and apparently introducing himself astonished her, even while it angered and frightened her.

"I'm starting construction on a barn and a stable within the next few days," Casey heard.

"A barn? Do you have any help lined up?"

"I hired a couple of guys to give me a hand."

"A barn's a pretty big project."

Bobby let out a whoop and Casey slipped from the closet to peek out the screen door again. The little boy was running as hard as he could, with the dogs yapping and chasing after him. Both Jess and Ben were watching the chase with big smiles.

"Oh, there you are."

"Kelly..." Casey began, on the verge of warning her sister to keep quiet.

"Casey? Come on out, honey." Ben had heard.

Taking a deep breath, Casey pushed the screen door open. Jess slowly stood up. "Hello, Casey."

The second she looked into his eyes, Casey wanted to flee. Jess knew. No one else knew, but Jess did. Ben hadn't seen the resemblance, it had escaped Kelly, but Jess knew.

Her voice was dull, her spirit dead. "Hello, Jess."

His gaze flicked over her. She was beautiful in white shorts and a green T-shirt, her long, tanned legs dark in the waning light and in contrast to the white fabric of her shorts. "I've been having a nice talk with your dad."

"Have you?"

"And your sister Kelly." Jess gave Kelly a glance that the teenager responded to with a bedazzled smile.

"I also enjoyed watching your son playing."

Casey's eyes darted to Bobby. "He... he's a wonderful little boy," she said hoarsely.

"I can see that." Jess turned to Ben. "Would you mind if I asked Casey to take a ride with me?" Kelly's eyes had grown as big as saucers.

Ben looked from Jess to Casey. "That's entirely up to her, Jess. I wouldn't presume to tell that little filly what to do."

It was a joke, but Casey wasn't laughing. "No... no," she stammered, then looked at Jess and wilted inside. It wasn't exactly a threat she saw in his dark, cold, blue eyes, but it was something that sent a chill up her spine all the same. "All right," she amended quickly.

Lucille stepped through the door. "Oh, honey, meet Jess Lonnigan," Ben piped up. He dropped an arm around his wife's shoulders. "Jess, this lovely lady is my wife, Lucille."

Casey watched this nightmare unfold as if she were a great distance away and looking down on the front porch. Her skin felt clammy and cold, and though the evening was warm, she wanted to heave a mighty shiver.

Lucille extended her hand. "I'm glad to meet you, Jess," she replied in a clear, controlled voice. "I've heard a lot about you."

Jess cocked an eyebrow over the handshake. "I hope it wasn't all bad, Mrs. Oliver."

"Well, I suppose that depends on what one considers bad, Jess."

Kelly looked ready to burst. "Casey's going for a ride with Jess, Mom."

Lucille looked at Casey. "I'll put Bobby down at his regular bedtime," she said quietly.

"Thanks, Mom." Casey bit her lip for a troubled moment, then gave her mother a kiss on the cheek. "I won't be long," she whispered.

Smiling, with her husband's arm still around her, Lucille stood on the porch and watched Casey and Jess walk out to his pickup. "He's very good-looking, isn't he?" she murmured softly.

Kelly gave her a sharp look. "He's only a dream, that's all," she retorted dryly. "Lucky Casey. I sure wish I was older."

Ben laughed. "Your time will come soon enough, little girl."

"Little girl!" In a huff, Kelly dramatically swept into the house.

Sighing, Lucille sat down. "What did you think of him, Ben?"

Ben took a minute, then nodded solemnly. "He seems like a real nice fellow, honey. A real nice fellow."

Four

___

Neither spoke. Jess stared straight ahead while he drove. Casey stared out the side window. They were miles away from the ranch before she realized where he was going—the river. She clamped her teeth together to keep from telling him not to go there. It was where they had gone again and again six years ago. She hadn't been back, and she didn't want to go now.

But there was so much tension in the truck. What they were both feeling was in the air, thick, heavy, as dense as pea soup. She couldn't determine clearly what was in Jess's mind, but she sensed how tightly coiled his emotions were.

He jerked on the knob for the headlights, though it was still twilight. Lucille would be bathing Bobby about now, hearing his prayers soon. Casey chewed her bottom lip, then a thumbnail. What did Jess intend to do? She would fight with every drop of blood in her body: he would never get Bobby away from her. Never!

Jess turned onto the bumpy, rutted road leading to the river. The pickup bounced and rolled for a mile, then Jess braked it to an abrupt stop and switched off the motor. The silence of a Wyoming evening permeated the cab of the truck.

"He's mine, isn't he?"

The words slashed the quiet, increasing Casey's pulse, breaking her heart. She felt hot, burning tears threatening. "No, he's mine," she whispered.

Jess swiveled in the seat and leaned forward. His eyes were hard, his face tense. "Did you think I wouldn't figure it out? Did you think I wouldn't know when I saw him?"

"I knew you'd know. That's why—"

"Why you tried to turn me off with insults," Jess interrupted harshly. "I want him, Casey."

"*No!* You can't do this, Jess. Think of him."

Jess remained cold. "What poor sap did you marry to give Bobby a name? What *is* your married name, by the way? That's one piece of information that eluded me."

"Maddox," she replied numbly. "But—"

"Forget it. I don't give a damn who the guy was. The only thing that's important right now is my son. *My son!* Lord, I can't believe you hate me so much you'd want to keep Bobby away from me."

Casey turned on him, fury erupting. "I have every right to hate you. Don't you dare make me the heavy in this. You're not the one who had to lie and sneak around, to leave Blythe and pretend to be in college, damn you! What do you even know about what I went through? Nothing! Did I have even the slightest idea how to find you? Did I have any reason to hope you might come back?"

Stunned, Jess absorbed her rage. "All right, all right. Don't come unglued. Maybe we can figure something out."

"Like what? Let me tell you something, Jess. The day you make trouble for Bobby will be the sorriest day of your life! He's a happy little boy. He lives among people and family who love him. He's got cousins and pets to play with, and he's got—"

"He doesn't have a father!" Jess's voice lashed the air. "What do you tell him when he asks? Does he think that other guy is his father?"

Casey swallowed. "I ... told him ..."

"Then he has asked?"

Hesitating, Casey realized she hated admitting that Bobby had asked. Of course, he'd noticed that his cousins all had fathers: *"Where's my daddy, Mommy?"*

"You have Grandpa, honey."

"Yes, he's asked," Casey said in a low voice.

"And what did you tell him?"

Enraged again, Casey stormed, "Could I tell him his real father ran off before he was born? He's only five years old."

Breathing hard, Jess retorted scornfully, "I didn't run off, and I never would have left at all if I'd known you were pregnant."

"Oh, sure," she scoffed flippantly. "You thought so much of me, didn't you? That's why I never got as much as a postcard from you."

Jess looked away, stung for an answer. Casey's anger was justified as far as his lack of consideration went. When he brought his eyes back to her, he released a heavy breath. "Look, fighting like this is getting us nowhere. All I want is a chance to get to know my son."

"No," Casey whispered, battling tears again.

"You can't stop me, Casey."

"I *will* stop you. I'll take Bobby and leave. You'll never know where we went, even if I have to completely break all ties with my family."

"You wouldn't do that."

"Oh, yes, I would. I've already thought of leaving, but my mother talked me out of it."

Jess was silent a moment. "Your mother knows, doesn't she? I'm not sure about your dad, but your mother knows."

"She knows," Casey admitted with misery in her voice. "Don't underestimate my threat, Jess. If you cause Bobby one moment's pain, you'll never see him again. I swear it."

Miserable too, Jess sat back. A long pause ensued, and the night silence descended around them.

"All right, you seem to have all the answers," Jess finally responded. "What do you propose we do?"

Another silence stretched while Casey fought with herself over the sadly limited alternatives.

Jess spoke again. "We could get married."

"What?" Her eyes practically glowed with righteous indignation.

"We've got a good reason to get married, Casey—a lot better than some couples have."

"Where do you get your conceit? Do you actually think I would even consider marrying you? Haven't you gotten the message yet? I loathe the ground you walk on. Is that clear enough?"

Jess's voice was thick with sarcasm. "Is that why you kissed me back, because you loathe me so much?" He moved quickly and grabbed her arm, pushing his face very close to hers. "Who do you think you're kidding, sweetheart? I could make you want me right now. Should I prove it?"

Casey cringed back against the door. "Just stop it! I won't be manhandled again. Not by you, not by anyone!"

He glared at her in the near darkness for a minute, then backed off. "You're right. I'm sorry."

Sitting upright again, Casey rolled her window up against the cooler air coming in. Her shorts and T-shirt were great during the day, but it always cooled down after sunset.

"Are you cold?"

"I'm fine," she answered stiffly.

"Look, there must be a compromise we could make."

"If I let you see Bobby on occasion, what would you do?"

Jess's heart leaped. "See him how?"

Casey thought a moment. "At the ranch. You could come by once in a while."

"As what?"

"What do you mean, 'as what'? As a friend. As a neighbor."

"How's the boy going to get to know me if I can't tell him who I am?"

"Don't you dare tell him! Don't you dare tell anyone!" Groaning, Casey buried her face in her hands. "It will never work. Why don't you just disappear back to wherever you've been for six years?"

Jess looked at her, his heart in his throat, then opened the door of the truck and got out. He gave the door a slam and walked away, going closer to the river. Despair gripped him, and he stared at the dark water moving past, at the silvery touches of moonlight rippling across its surface. He was right, Casey was right, and the boy was in the middle. There was no solution to the dilemma.

For Bobby's sake he couldn't make trouble. Besides, he believed Casey's threat. She obviously loved their son and would do whatever she felt offered Bobby the best protection. And if that meant Jess was out of the picture, so what? So damned what? Who was Jess Lonnigan, anyway? Just a guy who had hurt her. A guy like that didn't have feelings, did he?

Cynically, Jess wished he didn't have them. It would be a lot easier to deal with this without emotion.

He'd almost died from feelings when he'd sat on the Olivers' porch and watched his son playing with the dogs. That handsome little fellow, that bright-eyed, sturdy little boy was his son. Jess Lonnigan's son. It didn't seem real.

Well, maybe it wasn't real. He'd had hope for a few hours... but what the hell? The boy was a lot more important than he was—any day.

Jess went back to the truck and climbed in. Casey was huddled against the seat and sniffing, obviously winding down from a good cry. "Stop worrying," he told her wearily. "I won't do anything."

"You won't? Oh, Jess..." Sobs shook her again, and she reached a hand out. "Do you have a handkerchief? I came away with nothing."

"Sure." Pulling out a white handkerchief, Jess pressed it into Casey's hand. She wiped her eyes and blew her nose. Her dry sobs sounded like hiccups, and she had to blow her nose again.

"I...don't know what to say," she said huskily. "But you have my thanks."

"I'll tell him when he's an adult, Casey."

Tears choked her again, and this time they were for Jess. She never thought she'd be crying for Jess Lonnigan, but she was. She felt his pain in her soul, the sorrow he had to be suffering over gaining and losing Bobby all in one evening. Casey tried to put herself in Jess's place and imagine how she would feel if she were him. "I can't bear this," she sobbed.

Sighing, Jess slid across the seat. "Com'ere," he muttered, and pulled her into his arms. He rested his chin on her hair and held her while she cried her heart out.

They were close, as much in spirit as body—both parents, both thinking of their child. It was a long time before Casey calmed down. She sat up and blew her nose again. "You can see him, Jess. Come by whenever you want. It might be good for him to—" She stopped and wiped her eyes. "I can't seem to stop crying."

"You've been a good mother, haven't you? I can tell, Casey."

"Yes," she whispered brokenly. "He's very easy to love."

Jess rubbed his eyes, as if he were worn out. "Lord, I wish I'd had more sense six years ago." He heaved a sad sigh. "Casey, for what it's worth, I'm damned sorry I treated you the way I did. How can I explain what kind of guy I was then? The only thing that meant anything was getting to the next rodeo. The fun and games along the way were only that: fun and games. I wish I could tell you that I intended coming back, that circumstances kept me away. But that's not the truth, and whatever else I am, I'm not a liar."

"I am," Casey said sadly. "I lied so much for a while it's a wonder my tongue didn't fall out. I even lied to my dad."

"But not to your mother."

"No. I had to tell her. I had to tell someone, and Mom's always been easy to talk to."

"And your brothers and sisters? None of them know?"

"Only Mom. After you came back, she asked me to tell Dad the truth."

"Are you going to?"

"I...don't know. If I do, it will be the hardest thing I've ever done. Dad is the kind of person who sees mostly good in others. Mom's more of a realist, although she does have a stubborn streak about her own children."

"You've got a nice family. You're lucky, Casey. Really lucky."

"I know I am." She looked at him. "What about you? Don't you have any family?"

"No."

"None?"

"No one."

"Oh, Jess, I'm sorry." She sighed forlornly, then added, "What a mess. I was such a fool at seventeen."

"Why were you?"

"A fool?"

"Yeah. Why were you so...?"

"Easy?"

"Cooperative. You were very nice to me, Casey."

Something began to tremble within her. "I had never met anyone like you before, I guess."

"You were a virgin."

She gulped hard. "I'm surprised you remember."

"I remember a lot about that week," Jess said quietly. "This is the place we came, isn't it?"

"Yes. Why did you pick it tonight?"

"I don't know. I just kept driving."

"Maybe it's appropriate." Casey sighed again.

"Yeah, maybe it is. Casey...?"

"Yes?"

Jess moved closer. "Casey, let's forget everything except you and me and Bobby. We could be a family, honey, a real family. My ranch is small, but it's going to be a winner. It's got a nice house, not as big as your folks', but it's nice. You'd like it."

"Jess, I can't," she groaned unhappily. "You don't understand. Too much has happened. I've been here for six years..."

"Hating me."

"Yes. I can't turn my feelings around that fast."

"I wouldn't expect you to. I wouldn't push you. I swear I wouldn't. We could even have separate bedrooms. Your family is great, Casey, but don't you wonder what it would be like to have you own home? Your own life? I've seen those posters in Blythe's store windows. I know you're trying to contribute to Bobby's care. Honey, let me take care of you both. I've got money in the bank. You wouldn't have to work—"

"I don't have to work now, Jess. Both Mom and Dad have told me that. I'm working because I want to. Please don't go on with this. We've made some headway tonight, but this kind of talk could ruin it."

He leaned closer, and his arm stretched along the seat behind her head. "Casey, listen to me. Please. Life's too short to dwell on the past. Bobby will shoot up. You'll only have him a few short years. Let me share those years. Give Bobby his father. What bigger or more precious gift could you give him?"

Casey's heart was pounding, and she wasn't sure it was from what Jess was saying or because he was so close. "Please, you're crowding me. Give me room to breathe, Jess."

He took her chin and held it, turning her face up to him. "Will you at least think about it?" His voice was ragged, hoarsely tense. "Casey, don't throw it out without some thought. You could lay down the rules. I'd sleep in another room. I wouldn't touch you."

Casey pulled his hand down from her chin. "Like you're not touching me now?"

"Aww, hell," he groaned, and fell back against the seat. "You're right. I'd touch you. How could I help it? You're a sexy, beautiful woman. Of course I'd touch you. I'd do it right now, if you'd let me."

Casey watched the river a moment, then faced Jess again. Her face and voice were sad. "You'd make love to any woman who came along, Jess. You might have changed some, but apparently not in that respect. Let me say something here. If and when I marry, it's going to be for love."

"Marry again, Casey. You forget the 'again.' And it's all well and good to hope for some kind of great love to come along, but don't you think that's kind of a foolish fantasy? What about the reality of what's happening right now? I'm offering something now, not five or ten years down the road. What would be so terrible about marrying me?"

"It's out of the question. I think we should go now."

"You're mad again."

"No, I'm not mad. But you're so insensitive I can't believe it. You've got some crazy picture in your mind of a happy little threesome—you, me and Bobby. Jess, you and I don't even know each other. We spent one week together six years ago and we've seen each other exactly four times since you've been back. Do you think I would uproot Bobby from the only home he's known and move him in with a complete stranger? That's what you are to him. In all honesty, that's what you are to me, too. A stranger."

Jess had listened and he was beginning to understand Casey's point of view. They *were* strangers. A week of flirting, dancing and making love six years ago sure wasn't a foundation for a relationship—any kind of relationship. He was willing to take the chance that they could work everything out after the ceremony, but Casey wasn't. She might have been impulsive six years ago, but it was all too obvious she was anything but that now—especially where Bobby was concerned.

"All right," Jess said quietly. "I think I see what we have to do."

"Oh?"

"Yeah. You and me have got to get to know each other better."

"Jess!" Dammit, that wasn't what she'd been trying to get across. She'd relented on Jess seeing Bobby because the alternative was taking her son and leaving Wyoming. She'd also been deeply moved by Jess's unselfish announcement that he wouldn't make trouble. But she had no intention or desire to further her and Jess's personal relationship. His marriage proposal was almost insulting. Live under the same roof with a man who had treated her so shabbily? It was unthinkable.

And "getting to know each other better" was almost as unthinkable.

Casey set her chin at a stubborn angle. "I don't want to know you better," she said, as emotionlessly as she could manage with the hope of maintaining the uneasy truce they'd somehow reached.

"You've got to give somewhere, too, Casey. So far, it looks to me like I'm doing all the giving."

"Are we adding up sides here? Does it matter who has the most points, you or me? Bobby's what's important—not that you might have given a bit more for his sake than I might have."

"You've had him for nearly five-and-a-half years," Jess accused softly.

Casey's pulse leaped with renewed fear. "You said you wouldn't do anything!"

"I won't. Neither Bobby nor anyone else will ever hear a word about this from me, not until he's an adult. You have my word on that. But it wouldn't hurt you to give a little, too."

Casey's voice wasn't quite steady. "I have given. Didn't I say you could see him?"

"Yes. And I appreciate it. But if there's a chance, the slimmest chance that the three of us could be a family, I think we should at least make the attempt."

He sounded so sincere, and as if his heart had been irreparably broken. Casey's innate kindness was responding. Only with Jess had she ever been so cold and waspish. It wasn't natural for her to play judge, jury and prosecutor. Yet, she couldn't even begin to forget the pain Jess had caused her. "You have no right to that argument," she whispered, frightened that her defenses were weakening. "You're using Bobby to make me feel guilty, and that's not fair. He's happy—"

"Are you?"

Her head jerked around so she could see him. "Would I be happier with you?" she snapped.

Jess raised a hand and gently touched her hair. "Maybe you would. I'd do my best, honey."

For a single moment a flash of the magic that Jess had dazed her with six years ago inundated Casey. Frightened by the strong, sensual feeling, Casey pulled away from his hand.

"Don't try physical persuasion," she warned sharply. "I'm not a kid anymore, Jess. I've learned to think before I leap into something."

"Maybe you've become a little too cautious. Maybe you're afraid to take a chance now. Is that it? Are you afraid of getting hurt again? Or have you blamed and hated me for so long, you're afraid of losing the biggest part of yourself if you gave up despising me?"

"Don't be silly," she scoffed, but she knew he'd given her something to think about. Had she clung to hatred because she had no other emotions to hang on to?

Jess was silent a moment. "All I'm suggesting is seeing each other for a while. If we get along okay, then bring Bobby into the picture. We could do it gradually, Casey—spend a few evenings a week together."

"And do what?" she questioned suspiciously.

Jess sighed. "Nothing you don't want to do. Maybe just go for a ride so we could talk."

Did he deserve that? Did he deserve even a dram of her consideration? There was something sad about Jess's position in all of this, but hadn't he brought it on himself? Was it her fault that he used to live for nothing but rodeo and "fun and games"? She'd paid her dues during the terrible year following rodeo week six years ago; wasn't it time Jess paid his?

She was confused, ambivalent, sorry for him, protective of herself. "I just don't know," she admitted wearily, tired of the battle.

"Will you at least think about it?"

"Yes, I'll think about it. Please take me home now."

"So what did you tell him?" Lucille inquired quietly.

Sighing, Casey got up from the kitchen table and went to the window. Bobby was playing in the backyard. Dressed in blue shorts and a red T-shirt, his black hair glistening in the sun, he was a lovely picture of health and boyish enthusiasm. "I told him I'd think about it," Casey replied dully. "I wish he'd never come back," she added after a moment.

"But he did, honey." Lucille stood up. "Well, you've got quite a decision to make."

Casey turned, and every inch of her body conveyed unhappiness. "Tell me what to do, Mom," she pleaded.

Lucille shook her head sadly. "I can't do that, Casey."

"What would you do?"

With a thoughtful expression, Lucille sat down again. "What would I do?" she repeated, as if asking herself the question. "It's impossible to put myself in your shoes, Casey. I'm older and see things differently than you do."

"You think I should do it, don't you? Deep down, you think Jess should have a chance."

"I'm only thinking of Bobby," Lucille cautioned. "What Jess asked isn't that terrible." She paused. "Your father said he thought Jess was a pretty nice guy."

Casey rolled her eyes. "Dad saw him for five minutes. Besides, when's the last time Dad met anyone who *wasn't* a nice guy? He likes everyone."

"Honey, if Jess was just passing through again I'd be dead set against him disrupting Bobby's life in any way. But he bought a ranch here, he's making his home here. And," Lucille added softly, "he *is* Bobby's father. Everybody makes mistakes, Casey. Would there be any real harm in spending a little time with him to see if the two of you couldn't come to some kind of understanding?"

"He doesn't want an understanding. He wants marriage."

"I know, and I'm certainly not suggesting marriage is the best conclusion for the two of you. I'm in complete agreement with you that a marriage based on anything other than strong emotional ties doesn't stand much of a chance. In short, love— a very deep, abiding love. I don't expect you and Jess could ever reach that point. But there are other levels of communication that might be very important to Bobby. Apparently Jess is going to be a part of his son's life, with or without your blessing."

"Not as a father," Casey reminded with strong conviction.

"Whatever the relationship evolves into, wouldn't it be easier for Bobby if you and Jess were on reasonably good terms?"

Casey looked crestfallen. "And how do I deal with my feelings for him? How do I forget what he did?"

Lucille smiled gently. "People don't forget, honey. They just learn to live with unhappy memories. Maybe once you get to know Jess, there'll be things about him that will make the past less meaningful."

Casey was about to respond with doubt when Kelly swept in. "What's for lunch, Mom? I'm starving." She looked from her mother to her sister. "Did I interrupt something?" Unconcerned despite the question, Kelly opened the refrigerator to check its contents. "How'd your date with the hunk go, Casey?"

"It wasn't a date," Casey retorted, and left the kitchen.

Wide-eyed, Kelly looked at her mother. "What's wrong with her?"

Lucille sighed and got up from the table. "Let's make some lunch, Kelly."

Jess looked up from the blueprint he'd been studying. The print was a plan for a barn, and he'd recently purchased it, along with another for a stable, because he'd had little experience in construction. Now, with the print stretched open across the hood of his pickup, he was beginning to realize the complexity of his undertaking. Joints, joists, beams, window frames, flooring—it was hard to relate the stacks of varioussized lumber beside the pickup to the terms he'd been studying.

The truck kicking up dust on his driveway was a welcome reprieve from the print, and Jess rerolled the several large sheets and secured them with the broad rubber band that had come with them. He went to meet his visitor.

Surprised to see Ben Oliver getting out of the pickup, Jess hurried over and offered his hand. "Nice of you to stop by, Ben."

Ben looked around. "Just wanted to see what you've got here, Jess. Looks like a good house."

"It is. You can see I'm short on outbuildings, though."

They walked toward the stack of lumber. "This is the barn site," Jess said. "I plan to get it built first, then the stable."

Ben grinned. He had a pleasant round face, hazel eyes and iron-gray hair. "How would you like a little help?"

"I've got a couple of men lined up—"

"I mean real help. The kind that will put that barn up in a weekend."

Jess flushed clear to the roots of his hair. No one, other than Ace, had ever offered to "help" Jess Lonnigan. "I'm not sure what to say, Ben."

"Say yes and tell me when you want us. That's what neighbors are for, Jess. A man doesn't build a barn alone around these parts."

"Tonight?" Casey echoed weakly. She clutched the phone with white knuckles, all of her strength seemingly having gone from her voice to her fingers.

"Around seven."

"Jess—I haven't made up my mind yet," she stammered.

"Do you have other plans for tonight?"

"No, but that's—"

"I'll see you at seven, Casey."

The line went dead. As she put the phone down, a spark of anger infiltrated Casey's numbness. She was being railroaded. Jess was completely ignoring her doubts, and even her mother was on his side!

When Jess arrived a few minutes before seven, Kelly was on the front porch, obviously determined to get another look at "that hunk." From her upstairs bedroom window Casey watched Jess get out of his pickup. He was wearing new-looking jeans, a fitted, Western-cut white shirt and highly-polished black boots. He looked fresh from the barber, with his normally unruly black hair smoothly in place. He was all "slicked up," and it made Casey madder than hell.

A sense of helplessness made her mad, too. Things were happening that she didn't want to happen. She didn't want to go out with Jess, not even for a ride. He was dangerous to her emotional health. She hated the silly, female reactions she felt whenever he touched her, and she didn't trust him not to take advantage of his sensual influence. Why couldn't he have been content to stop by now and again and spend an hour with Bobby? It was more than he deserved, if one were to get down to hard facts. She'd made one enormous concession in agreeing to him seeing Bobby at all; how many more was Jess going to demand?

Casey saw Bobby run around the corner of the house and heard Kelly call, "Bobby, come say hello to Mr. Lonnigan."

Through narrowed eyes, Casey watched her son cautiously approach Jess, who squatted to be on the same level with the little boy. They shook hands, with Bobby's small hand getting lost in Jess's.

Casey dropped the curtain as tears filled her eyes. She simply had to stop feeling sorry for Jess. He'd caused his own misery, and hers. He had no right to intrude on her life now. He especially had no right to try and push her into marriage.

Marriage. The mere thought was ludicrous. What would the reality of such an unlikely liaison be?

"Casey? Jess is here!" rang from the foot of the stairs. It was Kelly, yelling out what she thought was good news.

Casey called from the doorway, "I'll be down in a few minutes."

She went to the mirror, gave her hair a pat and checked her lipstick. She was wearing a faded denim skirt, a white eyelet sleeveless blouse and sandals—good enough attire for the totally wasted evening ahead. She would not be talked into anything, above all a marriage that repelled her.

With a sweater, in case she got chilly again later, and a small purse, Casey slowly descended the stairs. Everyone was on the front porch—her mother, her father, Kelly, Bobby and Jess. Their laughter and friendly voices annoyed Casey no end, but when she stepped outside and saw Bobby sitting on Jess's lap, her annoyance turned to bitterness.

"Hi, Mommy."

"Hi, sweetheart." She wanted to snatch her son away from Jess, and it was all she could do to stop herself.

Jess was looking at her with wary eyes. "Hello, Casey."

"Jess," she allowed stiffly.

"Sit down, honey," Ben invited. "I think our Bobby's made a new friend."

"I see that," Casey replied coolly.

Lucille spoke. "Casey, your father and Jess were discussing the barn raising."

"What barn raising?"

Jess answered. "Your father was kind enough to offer help on my barn."

"Not just me." Ben laughed. "There'll be a hundred men there, Jess. I like your place, and—"

"You've been there?" Casey interrupted, astounded.

"Today, honey. Jess's got a nice place."

"Oh, great," Casey muttered, and turned to Jess. "If we're going somewhere, let's go."

"Casey!" Ben exclaimed over her rudeness, and his wife laid a restraining hand on his arm.

Jess stood up, with Bobby still in his arms. "Well, pardner, I'll see you again in a few days, okay?"

"Okay," Bobby agreed as he was lowered to the porch. Jess turned to Casey.

"Let's go."

Casey quickly kissed Bobby, then her mother and her father. "I'm sorry, Dad," she whispered.

And when she and Jess left the porch to go to his pickup, everyone had to hear Kelly declare, "Well, I never! If somebody doesn't tell me what's wrong with Casey these days, I'm positively going to explode!"

Five

———

Exactly like the night before, they drove away from the ranch in stony, cold silence. But Casey didn't wait for a destination tonight. After a few minutes she stormed, "What are you trying to do? Get my whole family on your side?"

Her gaze fell on Jess's hands gripping the steering wheel. She saw frustration in their hold, anger. She heard the same intense qualities in his voice when he growled, "Aren't you the one who said, just last night, that we shouldn't be adding up sides? Who's doing it now, Casey?"

"You're forcing *me* to, that's what's happening. I'm on to you, Jess. You think if you put on a nice-guy image, my family might try to influence me in your favor. That's dirty pool," Casey fumed.

Jess threw her a dark look. "Did it ever once occur to you that I might really *be* a nice guy? You're judging me by what happened six years ago. Would you like me to judge you based on that week? You were very—"

"Cooperative?" she drawled sarcastically, beating him to the punch.

"Easy," Jess retorted.

Casey gasped. "That's a cheap shot."

"What do you expect me to do? Keep taking your crap without fighting back? My good nature only goes so far, honey."

"Your good nature? Now, there's a laugh. And don't call me honey. I'm not now, nor ever was your 'honey.' "

Jess laughed humorlessly. "The hell you weren't. For one memorable week, that's exactly what you were. A travelling cowboy's 'honey.' Baby you were—"

"Stop it!" Casey covered her ears with her hands. When he gave her a surprised look, she dropped her hands to her lap. "Last night I actually felt sorry for you," she said disdainfully.

"Don't feel sorry for me, Casey. I don't need or want your pity."

"No, you want my son," she snapped, bitterness tinging the accusation.

"He's my son, too."

"A biological accident."

"Well, that's how you got him, too, *honey*. By accident."

"I loathe and despise you."

"Except when I kiss you. You don't loathe and despise me in a clinch, lady."

She was so wounded she couldn't speak for a moment. Maybe it hurt so much because it was true, but Jess's saying it made her feel totally degraded. "Turn this truck around and take me home!"

"No way. You'll cool down in a few minutes. Then maybe we can talk like two reasonably intelligent people."

This is it! Casey thought. *This is the last time I spend so much as five minutes with you! I'm taking Bobby and leaving.*

Her mind spun with the enormity of the decision. Where would she go? She'd never been entirely on her own. She didn't have much money.

She fell silent, brooding over the situation. Jess drove, keeping his eyes on the road ahead. They reached the outskirts of Blythe, and the pickup slowed down to the speed limit. The evening streets were quiet, almost deserted. Jess drove to the opposite end of town, then turned around and started back.

"Want a beer, or a soda?"

"No, thank you," she replied coldly.

Jess shook his head grimly. Casey saw his disgust, and all at once felt totally drained. She put her head back against the seat and closed her eyes. All this fighting and dissension were taking a toll. She wasn't a fighter; she never had been. She'd been keyed up ever since Jess's name had come over the PA system at the rodeo, and she wasn't used to running on nervous energy. She'd been rude to Jess tonight on the porch, startling her father; she'd been snapping at Kelly. Probably the only reason she'd been decent to her mother was because she needed at least one ally. Where was she headed? How could so much bitterness and antagonism end up any way but badly?

Her voice was low and indistinct: "I'm sorry."

Had he heard right? Frowning, questioning his own ears, Jess glanced away from the road. "Pardon?"

"I said, I'm sorry. I hate this sort of thing. I can't go on this way."

She looked small, forlorn, frightened. Something tugged at Jess's heartstrings. "You've been worried. I understand, Casey."

"I've been behaving like a shrew."

"Don't be so hard on yourself. By the same token, honey, don't be so hard on me. Don't you believe that I wouldn't do anything to hurt Bobby?" Jess's expression brightened. "Casey, he's really something. Do you know what he did tonight? He shook my hand like a little man."

Heaving a sigh, Casey opened her eyes and raised her head from the seat back. "I know. I saw you arrive."

"You were watching?"

"From my bedroom window." Casey realized what the real problem had been tonight. She'd turned inside out with jealously over Bobby warming up to Jess. My God, was she really so petty? she wondered. She didn't much like the person she was becoming.

"All right if we drive down to the river again?" Jess asked. "I really don't know where else to go, Casey. Unless you wouldn't mind going to my place."

"Your place? No, the river's fine."

Jess gave a slight laugh. "I wouldn't suggest the river *or* my place if we were ready for a public appearance. But I don't think we are, do you?"

"This isn't a regular date," Casey agreed quietly. "Just go to the river. We'll talk a bit then go home."

"Right. That's what I was thinking, too."

When they were parked, Casey turned her face to the open window. The sun was low on the horizon, almost down, back-lighting the trees and brush that grew along the river's mean-dering path. It was a pretty spot, full of greens and yellows and browns; and the river was many colors—here gray, there greenish blue, with crests of sparkling, foamed silver wherever the moving water met and splashed against some obstruction to its flow.

The silence reached Casey's personal disquietude and meshed with it to produce a strange feeling of lonely upheaval. Here, in this placid, isolated place, even with Jess within reach, she all of a sudden felt as though she were completely alone in the world. Her sigh contained pathos and a little self-pity. She felt emotionally bruised, and wondered with a faraway vagueness if Jess had really thought her "easy," or had only lashed out because of her own shrewishness.

She had been that, she admitted with a ponderous sadness. She had been foolish, immature and easy. Regardless of Jess's careless what-the-hell attitude then, she could have kept things cool between them. She'd kept things cool with other men—rather, with the boys she'd been dating.

But Jess hadn't been a boy. He'd been a man—a worldly, self-assured, full-of-gusto male—and his handsome face and cocky manner had literally swept her off her feet. Right in this very spot, on a blanket, with the riverbank for a bed and the gurgling river water as music, he had taught her the joys of making love, shown her the strength and beauty of a man's body.

"What are you thinking about?" Jess asked softly.

Casey kept watching the river's slow passage. "Us," she murmured quietly.

"As we are today?"

"No. As we were six years ago." She heard Jess suck in a quick breath.

"Casey, try not to dwell on the past," he urged.

"I wasn't thinking of what came after that week. I was thinking about what happened during your stay."

"Oh."

She turned her eyes to him, and Jess saw how raw and ex-posed her feelings were. "How old were you?" she asked.

Jess swallowed. "Casey..."

"How old, Jess?"

He looked down. "I'm thirty-two now."

"You were twenty-six, then. You were very smooth, Jess, very...ardent."

He shook his head. "I was a jerk," he said gruffly.

"No. You weren't a jerk. You were the kind of man a young girl dreams about. Not that young girls should be dreaming about men like you, but then, teenage girls are notoriously romantic." Casey sighed again. "At least, I was."

"You were sweet—"

"I was a fool!" she snapped. Then, sorry she'd become angry again, she tried to release the tension from her face.

Jess eyed her thoughtfully. "You can't forgive yourself, can you? How can I hope you'll ever forgive me when you can't even forgive yourself? Casey, we made a mistake. Mine was worse because I was old enough to know better. But it was a mistake with a wonderful result: Bobby. Would you turn back time if you could and undo that week?"

Startled, Casey looked into Jess's expressive blue eyes. "I love him more than anything in the world," she whispered raggedly.

"If you didn't, you'd be a heck of a lot less than you are." Despite promises to keep his hands to himself, Jess slid across the seat. And when he put his arms around Casey and brought her head to his chest, she let him, just sighing softly. The loneliness she'd been enduring melted away in Jess's arms. She didn't want it to leave her because of Jess, but it did. His shirt was soft and heated by his body; his arms around her were a fortress of security.

He pressed his lips to her hair. "Stop punishing yourself, honey," he said softly. "I'm sorry I made that crack about you being easy. You were no easier than I was. I was as bowled over as you were. You were young and sweet and beautiful." Jess felt his body stirring and his blood heating from holding her. "You're still young and sweet and beautiful," he murmured.

He tipped her chin up and studied her face, and Casey stared back. There was a new tension in their locked gazes, and she knew where this was going, but she couldn't pull away. She wet her lips, and saw Jess watching. "I...can't get involved with you again," she said huskily.

"I want to kiss you."

"No." But she didn't move away, and Jess's face slowly descended. His mouth brushed hers. "Jess," she whispered in a weak stab at protesting. His lips grazed hers again. "Please," she begged, agonizing over the curling heat he was causing in her body.

His thumb caressed her cheek while his mouth teased hers with butterfly kisses. His eyes closed and opened, closed and opened again, giving her glimpses of the sensual nature of his feelings. His breath was minty, he was wearing that spicy scent again, and she absorbed the essence of Jess with every breath. Her head whirled with objections and old resolutions, and yet she sat still and let him go on teasing her.

But his nearness was bringing the past close enough to touch, too, and six-year-old sensations were beginning to cloud the present—not the hatred and vindictiveness she'd undergone after Jess left, Casey realized. What she was reliving were the feelings she had experienced in Jess Lonnigan's arms at seventeen. They shook her to the depths of her soul.

Jess was having no such crippling thoughts, however. His mouth was actively seeking hers. Casey turned her face, eluding his lips. "No, Jess," she pleaded, sounding strained.

"Honey..."

She made no reply. But when he continued to hold her, and she couldn't bear his insistent, quizzical look any longer, Casey reached for the door handle. Slipping from his arms, she got out of the truck. It was almost dark now, and the colors she had noted earlier had grown muted, flavored with the heavy grayness of late-evening light. Casey walked over to the river, aware of Jess behind her.

Her eyes were sad and questioning as she watched the water. "Why do you affect me like that?" she asked in such a quiet, unhappy voice that Jess frowned. "I don't want to want you," she whispered.

Jess took a step closer. "What can I say, honey?" he returned softly. "There's something between us, want it or not."

"I feel like I'm not in control of my own life anymore. One day, from out of the blue, here you are. You've changed everything, Jess. Why did you decide to come back here?" Casey turned with the question.,

Digging his hands into his pockets, Jess faced the river. "I don't know. There are a dozen other places I could have gone. I love Wyoming, and I remembered Blythe as a nice little town. But other than that, I just don't have a good answer, Casey. Maybe it was fate," he added musingly.

She gave him a sidelong glance. "Do you believe in fate?"

"I never gave it much thought before. I'm beginning to wonder, now. Something made this particular spot on the map stand out." He turned to her and put his hands on her shoulders. "Anyway, I'm here. I thought of looking you up, Casey. But not to make trouble for you."

She met his gaze evenly. "No, you thought we could pick up where we left off six years ago, didn't you?"

He thought of lying, for her sake, then trashed the notion. Whatever their relationship evolved into, it wasn't going to be based on lies. "Yes. That's exactly what I thought," he admitted with a trace of bravado.

Her eyes flickered. "Do you remember telling me you loved me?"

An invisible fist struck Jess in the gut. "No. Did I say that?"

An almost imperceptible nod of her head made Jess wince again. "And you believed me," he said with a profound sadness. His hands moved down to her upper arms. "Did you love me, Casey? Is that why you hated me so much after I left?"

At the feeling in his voice, Casey's knees got weak. She heard wonder, hope, curiosity in his question. And she remembered him ridiculing love, calling it a "foolish fantasy." Had he never been in love? She caught a sense of Jess's former life-style— towns blurring, women blurring, nothing ever real or solid to hang on to. *A different bed every few nights.* How many women had he shared those beds with?

She'd been only one of many. And he had been and still was the only man she had ever made love with. The inequity seemed overwhelming, stunning. And yet, for the first time, she was beginning to understand the man she had met six years ago. No family, the heady roar of the rodeo arena, a winner's adulation, rushing to the next town, the next fair, the next contest. My Lord, how would any man remember one seventeen-year-old girl in that confusing montage of everchanging scenes?

But could she confess that she'd imagined herself truly in love with him? No. A confession of that nature at this late date would accomplish nothing. Not when she was only one of the blurs in Jess's past. "I think my feelings at that time are better described as a rather serious crush," she finally replied, and saw a tiny flame die in Jess's eyes. He'd been hoping for more, Casey realized, probably because of his marriage proposal. Well, she might understand Jess a little better now, but she hadn't reached the point of saying yes to a loveless marriage.

She remained silent, leaving Jess to unanswered speculation. His hands flexed on her arms, and his gaze was relentless. Their conversation had been personal enough to have raised some provocative points. "Did you get married only to give Bobby a name, or did you care for the guy?" he asked.

Jess didn't know! Casey had actually forgotten that he didn't know about the farce of her pretended marriage. For a moment she battled with an urge to blurt it out, then common sense prevailed and she only replied, "I'd rather not talk about that, Jess."

"Casey, you talked about love last night. Did you love your husband?" he persisted.

"What difference does that make now?" she hedged.

His gaze roamed her face, looking beyond her features, probing her evasiveness. "Maybe none. I don't know. It suddenly seems important."

She was getting uncomfortable beneath his scrutiny. And he was too close again. She could feel him penetrating her senses; she was afraid of his power. Lifting her hands to his wrists, she tried to pull them away from her arms. "Don't push me, Jess," she warned unsteadily. "You said you wouldn't touch me and you keep doing it."

"Don't you question the feelings between us?"

The sky was dark now except for the faint, pearly reflection on the western horizon. They were shadowy figures on the bank of the river, visible to each other by shape and form, becoming less distinct, communicating through a contact Casey was finding increasingly disturbing. They had made love here, more than once, more than twice. Even in the dark Casey could pick out the spot where Jess had laid the blanket. Why did they keep coming back here? Even Jess's house would be more impersonal than this place.

Casey shivered, chilly from the night air, chillier still from the emotional drubbing she'd taken lately. "I'm going back to the truck," she announced. It was more than a hint, but Jess didn't take it. His fingers clasped and caressed simultaneously, warming her bare arms with the heat of his hands.

She knew what was in his mind; she knew what he was going to do. Later, when she remembered this moment, she asked herself why she hadn't broken away and run. But she didn't break and run. She let him pull her forward, and when his mouth claimed hers, she only moaned over her lack of control and kissed him back. On tiptoe, with her breasts squashed into his chest and his arms inching her closer, she opened her mouth and kissed him back.

It was a complex kiss from the outset, involving old memories and new desires. The firmness of his mouth was like an old friend, welcome, familiar. After six years it was *familiar*! Jess's way of holding her, one strong arm around her, positioned low on her back, lifting her up and to him was familiar, too, although Casey knew it wasn't something she'd spent time thinking about. His right hand twined into her hair, amassing a handful of curls, then releasing it to find another. He touched her cheek, her throat, with gentle but inquisitive fingertips, and he explored the heated moistness of her mouth with his tongue.

To Jess she was soft and warm and female. Her lips moved beneath his with emotion far surpassing what he'd hoped for. His body had responded quickly, and his mind went back in time in an attempt to associate the achingly desirable woman he was holding with the girl he'd seduced. He wasn't quite able to make the connection, but he only dwelled on the puzzle for a few heartbeats.

Casey was no longer chilly. Her temperature was soaring. She felt flushed, giddy. Breathing hard, Jess raised his head. She saw the reflected light of the rising moon in his eyes, in the wetness of his mouth. She couldn't deny what kind of kiss it had been; her breath, too, was coming in short spurts.

"Don't...don't do this because you want Bobby," she rasped hoarsely.

"I want you both, Bobby *and* you." He meant it. He could imagine nothing better than his own family, his own son, his own beautiful, sexy wife. And he had no doubt that Casey was a sexy woman. She'd been sexy six years ago—he at least remembered that very well—and if anything, she was even more so now. What more could a man ask for? Oh, yes, he'd meant his proposal of marriage with heart and soul.

Casey knew how aroused he'd become. The proof burned into her abdomen and ignited more intimate memories—Jess, naked on the blanket, without modesty, without the slightest embarrassment. He had a tiny little scar just over his left nipple, and another, high on his right thigh. She'd touched the scars, even kissed them. She'd done so much with this man . . . so much...all in the space of one week...all in the name of a love, a passion she hadn't been able to control.

She still couldn't. With Jess she was Silly Putty, with *silly* being the key word.

Casey placed her palms on his chest and pushed herself away. "I need time, Jess," she said as steadily as she could manage.

He held his hands up in a pleading gesture. His voice was ragged, gravelly. "How much time?"

"I don't know." She started back to the truck, but Jess caught her arm.

"Casey, we made a lot of headway tonight."

She stole a shaky breath. "Yes, but in what direction? What did we prove, other than how physical you are and how weak I am?"

Physical? Wasn't that what it was all about? Frowning, Jess followed on Casey's heels. He reached around her to open her door. "Maybe I'm dense, but what's wrong with physical?"

She paused to look at him. "Nothing, unless that's all there is."

"You're talking about love again."

"Yes, that's exactly what I'm talking about."

"Do you want me to tell you that I'm in love with you?"

Casey drew a shuddering breath. "My Lord, no. That's the last thing I want. I pray that no man ever says those words to me again unless he means them." She climbed up into the cab of the pickup. Jess stood by, one hand on the door.

"I think I'm finally getting the picture," he muttered, and gave the door a push to close it. When he got in the driver's side of the truck, he noticed that Casey had wrapped her sweater around her shoulders. "Would you like me to start the motor and run the heater?"

"I think we should just go," she demurred.

"In a few minutes. I want to explore something first. You're not going to marry me because we're not storybook in love, right? It just dawned on me when you made that remark about—"

"Jess." She sighed. "In the first place, getting married was and is entirely your idea. I never encouraged you in that direction."

"You said you'd think about it."

"It's only been a day," she reminded sharply.

Jess's eyes narrowed. "Yes. But I have a strong feeling your mind's already made up."

"Why is that such a surprise?" Casey questioned. "I told you last night how I feel about marriage."

His voice dropped several notches, becoming very serious. "Casey, I don't want just an affair with the mother of my son."

"Good Lord!" She sputtered out a stunned sound, something between a laugh and a scoff. "Where did you ever get *that* idea?"

Jess stirred uneasily. "Well, something's going to happen between us. There's too much chemistry to ignore it indefinitely."

Casey hid her eyes behind a weary palm in a this-is-too-much gesture. She had only herself to blame, she knew. Jess obviously listened more to actions than to words, and kissing him back and turning to mush in his arms apparently had made a much deeper impression on him than all her stabs at candor.

Dozens of interactions rushed through her brain, hers with Jess, Jess's with Bobby, her and Lucille's, Lucille and Ben's, even Ben and Jess's. The whole damned thing was getting mixed, co-mixed and intermixed, a tangle that threatened only deeper entanglement in the frightening future.

That she herself was at the heart of it, maybe even the cause of it with her ridiculous on-again, off-again feelings for Jess, only made Casey feel worse. An affair: that's what they'd had six years ago, a tasteless, thoughtless, *stupid* affair. And if she'd been old enough and experienced enough to sort it out, she would have recognized it for what it was. Instead, at seventeen, in her silly romanticism, she'd seen her feelings and Jess's lust as love.

At least now, even if nothing else positive ever came from Jess's return, she understood what had really happened during his first visit to Blythe. There hadn't been a speck of love between them—not *real* love. The man sitting beside her was still a stranger, albeit one who seemed in control of her baser urges. He was right about the chemistry between them, but that was all he was right about!

Dropping her hand, Casey prepared herself for a speech. She took a deep breath and found Jess in the dark with a relatively calm eye. "Your ultimate goal is Bobby, Jess. I have no problem with admitting I was terrified over the two of you even meeting. As little as we've talked, however, I feel that I understand you better now. Myself, too, I might add. I'm not afraid of what you might do about Bobby, at least. I think you have a lot of feeling for him already. But . . ."

"Like you said, he's easy to love," Jess put in.

"Yes, he is. That's not the point I'm trying to make, though. What's bothering me is you thinking in terms of 'us.' I don't want you counting on a future for the three of us. And I'm not saying that in anger, or with any thought of revenge, or with anything else the least bit vindictive. You and I are worlds apart. I can see now that even if you had stayed in Blythe six years ago it wouldn't have worked for us."

"How can you say that?" Jess intruded gruffly, and Casey heard a harsh note in his voice. "What do you mean, we're worlds apart?"

"Jess, you think the only relationship between a man and a woman is physical," Casey said with an odd gentleness. She had no desire to hurt Jess anymore, she realized. None at all. "I honestly believe that you don't have a romantic bone in your body. I'm not denigrating you for it, but I am saying it's not for me. I meant it when I told you I would never marry for any reason but love."

"Not even for Bobby, apparently," Jess replied sharply.

"Not even for Bobby," she echoed in choked agreement.

Jess took a breath that sounded painfully resigned. "Well, I guess you put me in my place, didn't you? In other words, Jess Lonnigan, forget everything except an occasional visit with your son."

"That's a rather cruel way to put it, but . . ."

"But it's all there is, right?" Now there was some of the old cockiness in Jess's voice. "Tell me something, honey. How do you know so much about this love you keep talking about? Have you experienced it? How many times? Was it far, far above the nasty old physical side of your nature? Who was the guy, your ex-husband? Did you two have such a lofty relationship, you never made love? And if it was so great, how in hell come you're not still married?"

Stunned, Casey heard the cockiness in Jess's voice turn to bitterness. The deluge of questions, coming one on top of the other left no room to jump in with any kind of answer, and barely gave her time to think. But they did accomplish one thing: they made her realize she was far from an authority on the subject of love.

But one didn't have to experience the emotion firsthand to know its strength and power. She'd grown up in a home with parents whose mutual love was a strong and abiding one. Her brothers both had happy marriages, Dee-Dee, too. No, she would never settle for less.

"Cynicism isn't going to change my mind," she declared.

"Yeah, and you're not going to answer my questions, either, are you? Just answer one for me, honey. Tell me how a woman with your sex drive keeps it under control while she's waiting for that great love to come along."

"My—! You're wrong about me, Jess. You're judging me again by the way I misbehaved six years ago," she stammered.

"I'm judging you on right now, sweetheart, on how you come alive in my arms, how your body curls into mine, how your mouth feels under mine. What do you want me to do? Pretend I didn't notice? Well, I did notice, and I know when the woman I'm holding wants exactly what I do."

Gone was her brief spurt of aplomb. Her voice was trembling again. "I admitted it, didn't I? Didn't I say only a short time ago that I didn't *want* to want you?"

"And it galls the hell out of you that you do, anyway. Well, let me tell you something, Casey. You might consider who you were at seventeen a silly, romantic fool. But you were one helluva lot more woman than you are now! At least then you weren't afraid to *live!*"

Angrily, with jerky, erratic motions, Jess started the truck and slammed it into gear. He drove away from the river with a rock-hard profile and a straight-ahead stare that, after one brief glance and a shiver, Casey refused to look at again. She had no idea just what Jess might do in a temper, and it was more than obvious he was boiling mad.

Well, she wasn't in the best of moods, either. He'd said some rotten things to her tonight, like that last crack. Afraid to live? Just because she didn't cater to his every whim? And what about that other insult, the one about *him* not wanting an affair with the mother of his child? Now, there was a laugh!

They drove up to the ranch in the same cold silence they'd left it with. Jess didn't get out and he didn't turn the engine off.

"Well, good night," Casey said after a moment, and reached for the door handle.

"I'll be by to see Bobby in a few days," Jess answered coldly.

"All right." Casey opened the door and slid to the ground. The minute the door was closed again, the pickup started moving, and when it was turned around it sped away, kicking up dirt.

Casey watched it go for a minute, then moved toward the house. It had been a difficult evening, she admitted wearily, and it had accomplished little beyond upsetting them both.

She knew she would think twice before going out with Jess again. They saw things too differently to ever do anything but fight, which she'd had quite enough of. He could see Bobby—simply because she suspected that Jess would make everyone miserable if she tried to stop him.

And she'd try to go on with her life as it had been before his return. She had her business to keep up and make future plans for, she had friends and family to spend time with, and if she wanted more, it wouldn't be hard to find a male friend. Wes Upton, for one. All she'd have to do was hint mildly, and Wes would jump at the chance to take her out.

She'd put Jess out of her thoughts once, and she could do it again. She *would* do it again.

Six

"Why, Lily! How nice. Come in." Lucille held the door for Lily Hastings and eyed the sizable box she carried. Lily owned and operated Blythe's one florist shop, and it was obvious she had driven out to the ranch to deliver some flowers.

"Hello, Lucille. Is Casey here? This is for her."

"She's out back with Bobby. Come in and have a cup of tea. I'll call her."

The two women went to the kitchen. Lily sat down at the kitchen table while Lucille called out the back door. "Casey? Could you come in for a minute, honey?"

"Sure, Mom." Casey had been playing catch with her son, and she gave the soft rubber ball one last toss. "Good catch!" She laughed. "I'll go see what Grandma wants, Bobby."

"Will you come back and play some more, Mom?"

"If I can, honey." Casey hurried into the house. "Hello, Lily," she exclaimed, surprised to see the small, pudgy woman in the kitchen. Casey's gaze fell on the florist's box on the table.

"It's for you," Lily announced, and gave the box a little push forward.

"For me?" Puzzled, Casey looked to her mother. "Who would be sending me flowers?"

Lily smiled knowingly, but she only said, "Open them, Casey. There's a card inside."

A sudden premonition hit Casey, but it was one she didn't quite trust. Surely Jess would never think of sending flowers to a woman.

She pulled the ribbon off the box and lifted the lid. Long-stemmed white roses greeted her startled eyes, and she breathed, "White roses. Oh, they're gorgeous!" Removing one from the box, she sniffed it and smiled.

"Read the card," Lily urged.

Casey picked up a small envelope. "It's sealed," she murmured.

"He wrote and sealed it himself," Lily announced with pride in her own integrity. "I never even got a look at it, but I know who it's from," she teased.

Breaking the seal on the envelope, Casey extracted the card. She quickly scanned the masculine handwriting.

Casey,
This romance thing is new to me, but I hope you'll consider this a start.

> Jess

It had been three days since that second night by the river, and Casey had just about decided Jess had given up on her. In one way, she was relieved; in another, strangely empty. Her ambivalence was showing again, Casey knew, but Jess had played too big a role in her past for her to just eliminate him now without some repercussions.

"They're from Jess," she told her mother in a strangely subdued voice.

"They're beautiful," Lucille remarked softly, then added briskly, "I'll get a vase."

Lily was chuckling. "Had to order these special, Casey. There's not much call in Blythe for white roses."

"No, I don't imagine there is," Casey agreed.

"That Jess is sure a handsome fella, Casey."

Casey smiled faintly. Lucille returned with a crystal vase, which Casey recognized as the best in the house. Smiling her thanks to her mother, she placed the rose she was still holding into the vase and reached for another.

When the flowers were arranged, Casey stepped back to admire them. "They must have cost a fortune," she murmured, more to herself than to either Lucille or Lily.

Lucille was pouring tea. "Would you like a cup, Casey?"

"No, thanks, Mom. Where should I put the vase?"

"Flowers that beautiful deserve a place of honor," Lucille declared. "Put them on the piano, honey."

"Good idea." Carefully balancing the lovely vase and roses, Casey smiled at Lily, then left the kitchen. After placing them just so on the piano in the living room, Casey sat down and pulled Jess's card from her pocket to read it again.

Was he going to court her? A funny little smile played on Casey's lips. Apparently, despite the black mood he'd been in when he dropped her off the other night, he'd given some thought to her arguments against a marriage of convenience. Even so, in spite of the vased evidence sitting on the piano, envisioning Jess as a romantic suitor was rather difficult. He was as physical as she'd pronounced him: earthy, rough around the edges, even crude at times. She could easily visualize him hopping in and out of bed with willing women, but romancing them?

Sighing, Casey sat back with her gaze on the almost pearlescent perfection of the roses. She had undergone quite a metamorphosis the past few days, she realized. She could think of Jess without hatred, without a knot in her stomach. Casey knew that understanding his old life-style had caused the change. Before Jess's return to Blythe, whenever he'd come to mind, she had seen him only in the context of their short-lived and heartbreaking relationship. Now she saw him in a broader sense. He'd been a man long before they met, and had lived a different kind of life than she could previously have imagined.

Her world had been confined to Blythe, the ranch and only a few forays beyond. Even after Bobby's birth she had relied on old habits and patterns. It had been more beneficial for her son to stay under Ben and Lucille Oliver's generous roof, and she'd willingly taken the easier route. Her small business provided the extras she would have hated asking her parents for, but would provide very slim support for herself and Bobby on their own. Staying on the family ranch had resulted in her living a rather insulated life.

Jess, apparently, had had no such buffers.

They were like night and day, black and white. Yet, because of an explosive passion between them six years ago, they had produced a child. There was an odd mystique about it, in retrospect. She might not have been in town that week; she might not have strolled down to the rodeo grounds with her friends that fateful first night. Jess might have bypassed Blythe. They might not ever have met. In which case, there would have been no Bobby.

A shudder of pure agony rocked Casey at the painful conclusion she had reached. No Bobby? Not even in her deepest depressions, once she'd held her son in her arms, had she ever wished he hadn't been born. Jess felt that way, too. *Would you go back in time, if you could, and undo that week?*

No! her inner spirit cried. Nothing could ever make her wish that Bobby wasn't a part of her life. He was the most important part of her life, and her love for him was like a living thing, an emotion that inhabited every cell of her body.

So, what about Jess's role in this? Would he do anything— even "romance" her—for the opportunity to openly claim his son?

It had surprised Casey that Jess hadn't come around for three days after he'd said he would—to see Bobby, of course—but the roses were now giving her some insight into Jess's absence. He must have been thinking, sorting things out. His apparent decision to "court" her made her feel strange, almost embarrassed, as though she had pushed him into something completely foreign to his personality. He'd obviously interpreted her stand against a loveless marriage as a bid for him to perform differently, when she hadn't meant that at all. It hadn't even occurred to her that Jess might attempt to change himself to fit what he'd labeled her "foolish fantasy."

He was obviously planning an all-out assault on her emotional defenses. What she *had* to do was keep her perspective. The roses were beautiful, but she didn't want to be courted simply to fulfill Jess's goal. She hadn't thought him devious, but now she was beginning to wonder. After all, as she'd told him, they didn't really know each other.

Female voices in the hallway broke up Casey's thoughts, and she got to her feet to thank Lily for the delivery. After goodbyes, Lucille closed the door, then gave her daughter a tentative smile. "Jess gave her a standing order, Casey. White roses each week for a month."

Getting another glimpse of Jess's determination created a frown on Casey's smooth forehead. Silently she pulled the card from her pocket and held it out. "Read it, Mom."

Lucille read the message quickly, then handed the card back and walked into the living room. Casey followed and stood by while her mother examined the bouquet again. "What do you think?" Casey asked uneasily.

Lucille smiled. "I think he intends to win your affection," she said calmly.

"It could be just a ploy to get Bobby," Casey warned, and met her mother's clear gaze with a troubled expression.

"One can fake feelings only so much, Casey. You'll know."

"Will I?" Casey replied uncertainly. She'd already been having a problem with the way Jess affected her physically. If he managed to do the same thing with her emotions, would she know anything?

Lucille patted her hand. "You'll know," she repeated—much too mysteriously, her daughter thought—and with another soft smile, left Casey alone with the roses.

Ben Oliver had confirmed the last weekend of July for the barn raising. In the meantime, Jess was to get the site prepared, and he'd been working on leveling the ground and constructing forms for the cement floor. As he wanted water in the barn, he also had to plan for water pipes and drains, a task that would have been a much bigger problem for an inexperienced builder without the aid and advice of another neighbor. Kelvin LeRoy understood plumbing and was generous with both his time and expertise.

Constantly amazed at the warmth and friendliness of his reception in the area, Jess had been working from sunup until dark every day to make sure everything would be ready for the actual raising of the barn. He had enjoyed the physical labor, and had found it therapeutic to the mental gyrations he'd been involved in since he'd last seen Casey. He'd been so deep-down stirred up and angry with her the other evening, he'd put in one helluva restless night and got up the following morning still angry.

Later, with a hot sun burning his bare back and shoulders while he shoveled and moved dirt from the building site, he'd thought it all out.

"So you think you want love," he'd muttered, and ferociously dumped a shovelful of dirt into the wheelbarrow. Then, another, and another. The physical exertion had felt good, had seemed to clear his head.

Finally, after dumping numerous overflowing wheelbarrow loads a safe distance from the construction area, Jess had mopped his sweaty forehead and admitted there wasn't any way on God's green earth that he was going to succeed in pushing Casey into marrying him, given her obstinate attitude on the matter.

It amazed him that she didn't see the issue as he did. What better reason could two people have for marriage than a great little kid like Bobby? It was so cut-and-dried for Jess. He had settled down with great plans for his horse ranch, and even if it took several years to really get it going, he had a nice sum in the bank—more than enough to support a family until the ranch began showing a profit. He couldn't figure out that obsession Casey had with finding a "great love"—not when she had the father of her son just begging for her hand.

By midafternoon he'd decided what he had to do: if Casey would only marry for love, love was what she'd get. He could be as romantic as the next guy, couldn't he?

Frowning, Jess had leaned on the shovel and thought about it. How did a guy in love act? Activities were limited around Blythe, but there were a few decent restaurants. At least the food was good. As for atmosphere, well, vinyl booths and neon lighting weren't very romantic in anyone's book. Scratch dinner out, Jess thought wryly.

Okay, what else was there? Flowers? Yes, there was a small florist shop on Main Street. Candy? Perfume? Jess had smiled smugly, positive he was getting the hang of it.

But, where would he take her? An occasional movie was fun—if the theater wasn't full of noisy kids, that is. What about a picnic? Or, yes, what about taking some horseback rides together? Riding off by themselves could present some interesting possibilities. They could go swimming, too, over at that nice little lake he recalled seeing about twenty miles to the south.

Besides, maybe it wasn't where they went that was as important as how he acted when they were together. He'd avoid arguments if he had to tape his mouth shut. He'd be polite and try not to cuss; and above all, he'd try not to pressure her.

That same afternoon he'd driven into Blythe to the florist shop, found out that the stock on hand was nice but ordinary, and made arrangements with the owner to order something special. After looking through a catalog, he'd chosen white roses, plunked down an outrageous sum of money and left instructions to make a delivery to the Oliver ranch each week for a month. He'd written a card giving Casey fair warning of his intentions, then waited the two days Mrs. Hastings said it would take for the flowers to be shipped in and delivered.

Now, today, he knew she would have received the flowers. And he had a plan in mind for the evening. At three o'clock he laid down his tools and went into the house to the telephone. Lucille Oliver answered his call, but Casey came on the line soon after. He heard her voice, that sexy little huskiness in it, and felt a tightening in his gut. Whether Casey liked it or not, she affected the hell out of him. "Hello, Jess."

"Hello, Casey. How've you been?"

"Fine. You?"

"I've been pretty busy." He proceeded to tell her what he'd been so busy with—the preparation of the barn site. "Anyway," he concluded, "everything will be ready when your dad and his friends show up."

"That's good. By the way, thank you for the flowers. They're very beautiful."

"I'm glad you like them. Are you free tonight?"

"Tonight? Why, Jess?"

"I'd like to see you."

"I've been expecting you to drop in to see Bobby."

Jess gave a dry little laugh. "I needed a little time to cool off. I was pretty hot under the collar the other night."

"Jess, I don't want to spend another evening fighting with you."

"I couldn't agree more. No more fighting, Casey. I promise."

"Well..."

"What I'd like to do is show you my place. I could pick you up around five and bring you over here. I've got a couple of nice steaks to barbecue. No funny stuff, Casey. Just dinner and a quiet evening together." He heard a sigh.

"Going to your house isn't wise, Jess."

"Casey, we're both adults. I'd suggest dinner in one of Blythe's cafés, but they're always packed. What I'd really like is an opportunity to talk, and we could do that a whole lot easier here than in a restaurant."

"I see." Casey was walking around with the phone to her ear, twisting the cord through her fingers. Since the flower delivery a few hours ago, she'd done almost nothing but study the situation. She had reached several conclusions. One, there was no keeping Jess out of his son's life, not unless she took Bobby and severed all connections with her home and family. Just moving away without a total break would accomplish nothing; Jess would follow her if he knew where she'd gone. Besides, running away would hurt Bobby. He was far too young to accept leaving his beloved grandparents, aunts, uncles and cousins without trauma. Even leaving the new puppies, who were beginning to open their eyes, wouldn't be understood by the little boy. He'd known only one home—the ranch—and uprooting him to the point of complete separation was too cruel to consider seriously.

Two, as a result of her first conclusion, Casey had realized she may as well cooperate with Jess on the matter of their son. She now believed that he wouldn't cause trouble, and she also believed he really thought marriage was the most sensible answer for the three of them. That was the point where she got bogged down each time she thought about it. She felt rather silly about inadvertently having pushed Jess into courting her, because he obviously thought he could win her affections with flowers and a more romantic approach.

People didn't fall in love that way, Casey strongly believed. They didn't set out to fall in love. It was something that happened or didn't happen, on its own. That Jess apparently felt differently about it only proved how little he knew, or had experienced, with the emotion. Not that she was any kind of authority on the subject, but at least she'd been exposed to solid, steady couples who *were* in love with each other.

Three, Casey recognized a strange void in herself. With the exhausting hatred she'd harbored for the Jess Lonnigan she'd met and made love with six years ago gone, there seemed to be a hole in her emotional makeup. She realized that she now had room for other relationships. For the first time in her adult life, she could see herself going out more, making more male friends, expanding her social activities. After Bobby's birth she

had dropped out and dedicated herself almost entirely to her
son. Now she felt freer, unburdened; and if Jess's return had
caused that—despite the anger and fear she'd initially suffered
over it—then perhaps she owed him the courtesy of friendship
at least.

Still, going to his house for an intimate dinner for two was
encouraging his romantic aspirations, wasn't it? Unless—

"How about me bringing Bobby along?" she suggested.

"Bobby? You'd do that?" Jess instantly got so excited he
completely forgot about the advantage he might gain while
wining and dining Casey alone. "Oh, honey, that would be
great, just great! What does he like to eat? Does he like steak?"

Casey laughed. "He'd prefer a hamburger, I'm sure."

"What else? I could go to Blythe and get—"

"Jess, a hamburger is plenty. He's not a big eater. Oh, if you
really want to impress him, he's a nut about chocolate pudding."

"Chocolate pudding. Well, I can probably figure out how to
fix it, huh?"

Casey laughed again. "It's easy. The directions are right on
the box. What time should we come over?"

"I could pick you up."

"No, that's not necessary, I'll drive us over."

"What time does he usually eat dinner?"

"Around five-thirty."

"Then that's when we'll eat. Casey, this is great of you. I'd
like to ask why, but I'm afraid of starting another argument."
Was it the flowers? Had they worked that fast? Jess wondered, puzzled about this romance thing. Maybe there *was*
something to it.

"We'll be there around five," Casey said, and put the phone
down with an astute smile. The enthusiasm in Jess's voice over
having dinner with his son far outweighed what she'd heard
when he'd posed the invitation just to her. She was very, very
right about Jess courting her only to get closer to Bobby. Which
she couldn't really fault, Casey admitted thoughtfully. But she
would have to make Jess understand that no amount of
"courting" was going to change her mind about marrying him.

Dinner went well—to a point. Jess and Bobby got along fa-
mously, with Jess definitely pleasing the child with bowls of

chocolate-pudding dessert. But Casey felt Jess's blue, blue eyes—so like their son's—on her as much as on Bobby.

Of course, she had taken special care getting ready for the evening. And she had even noticed, while putting on her makeup, that she seemed to have lost the harried look she had come to expect every time she looked in a mirror. Casey actually felt as if she'd been running a long, long mile and somehow had made it past a hurdle that had once kept eluding her. It was a strange feeling to sit at Jess's table and realize she was free of hatred and bitterness. She wondered if that was what Jess was seeing, or if he was merely responding to having a woman in his house.

Actually, Jess was doing both—and indulging in a bit of fantasy at the same time, too. Casey was wearing a gauzy pink dress, and she looked softer, more feminine, than he'd ever seen her appear before. It wasn't at all difficult to understand why he'd been so taken with her six years ago, not when he saw her like this.

She was wonderful with Bobby, he noted, loving but mindful of manners. Bobby ate like a little gentleman, and Jess was so proud to have him at the table he felt like bursting. Having Casey there involved some explosive feelings, too, although they were very adult, very sensual, explosive feelings. The fantasy in Jess's mind incorporated Casey and Bobby living there, with dinner together every night, a pleasant few hours together before bedtime, then bedtime.

Bedtime. They would tuck Bobby in, both he and Casey, kiss the little guy good-night, then go to their own bedroom. He would peel that pretty pink dress away...kiss that pulsebeat he could see at the base of her throat above the rounded neckline of the dress...and wear both of them out making love until the wee hours. Yeah, there was no doubt he still found Casey Oliver maddeningly attractive even if she maintained a cool, hands-off expression on her beautiful face.

When everyone had finished eating, Casey got up to clear the table and felt Jess's restraining hand on her arm. His voice was low and persuasive. "Leave them for now. Let's take Bobby for a walk while it's still light out."

For a moment Casey looked deep into Jess's eyes, and she realized how judicious her decision to bring Bobby along had been. Without their small son present, Jess would make a move, and with her heart skittering just from recognizing his mood and recalling how easily he could get to her, Casey knew that coming over here alone could very well have ended up in a way she was dead set against.

But Bobby *was* here, and Jess could give her all those steamy looks he wanted to. Nothing could come of them. Casey nodded her approval. "All right. Want to take a walk, Bobby?"

"Have you got any puppies, Jess?" the little boy questioned hopefully.

"Afraid not, pardner. Maybe I will have by your next visit, though. What's a ranch without puppies, right?"

Outside, Bobby ran ahead while Jess and Casey walked along at a slower pace. The sun was low but still warming the earth, and the evening quiet was lovely. As Casey looked around, she decided she liked Jess's place. The house was roomy and comfortable, there were six or seven big, old trees scattered around the backyard, and ahead of them, beyond the yard, she could see where Jess planned to build the barn and stable. "Your place is nice," she told him.

Jess gave her a wistful smile. "What's nice is this, Casey: the three of us together."

"It's been a pleasant evening," she agreed quietly. "Bobby seems to like you."

"And you?" He stopped walking, and Casey took another step, then turned to face him.

"I think we like each other well enough," she allowed.

Something flickered to Jess's eyes. "You don't hate me anymore, do you?"

"No, I don't. I think there's every chance of us becoming friends."

He shook his head. "That's not enough, Casey." He looked off at Bobby, who had climbed up on the corral fence to pat one of the horses inside the enclosure. "Even if Bobby wasn't in the picture, I'd want more than your friendship."

Casey's eyes narrowed. "I know what you'd want, Jess."

His gaze returned to her face and seemed to be assessing each feature. Casey looked away, but she still felt the impact of Jess's slow study. "Is that so terrible?" he asked softly. "Honey, I vowed I wouldn't put any pressure on you, but you're so damned beautiful. Maybe I'm too human, or, like you said, too physical. But when I look at you, I want you. I can't help it, Casey."

She cleared her throat with sudden nervousness. "I had hoped this wouldn't happen with Bobby here. Maybe it would be best if we called the evening to an end."

Sighing, Jess tore his eyes away from her. "I'm sorry. Let's go down to the corral so I can tell Bobby about the horses."

Casey stood by while Jess took Bobby into the corral and introduced him to his horses. "Can I ride 'em, Jess?" the little boy asked eagerly.

"Not tonight, pardner. But if you get your mom to bring you back during the day, you sure can."

"He has a pony at home," Casey called over the corral fence.

"But it's still fun to ride other horses, isn't it, pardner?" Jess returned.

"You bet!" Bobby agreed enthusiastically. "Mom, can we come back tomorrow?"

Casey sent Jess a silent warning. "Not tomorrow, honey. Maybe some other day, all right?"

Jess caught the message. "Well, maybe we *could* take a little ride tonight," he said at the disappointment in Bobby's big eyes. With that, Jess swung up onto the bare back of one of the horses. Then he put an arm down to Bobby. "Grab hold, pardner. I'll swing you up."

Casey watched with an odd constriction in her chest. The sight of her son and his father on the same horse was doing some funny things to her. They were so alike, Jess and Bobby— one big and handsome, the other small and handsome; the same black hair, the same blue eyes. Jess directed the mare with his knees and a hold on its mane, and horse and riders slowly circled the corral.

Bobby chattered and Jess replied, and Casey listened to the blend of their voices. With the sinking sun the air was growing chilly, and she hugged herself and watched the man and boy, noting after a while that her legs were shaking. She was getting too emotional over the camaraderie within the corral, she realized, trembling with more than just the late-evening air. Bobby was in seventh heaven with a man's total attention. He adored his uncles and grandfather, but Buck, Brady and Dee-Dee's husband, Ray, had their own children. As for Ben Oliver, he was a wonderful grandparent, but he was older and, although he was attentive to Bobby, his mind was often on the ranch or the daily news.

The heart of the matter was, no one loved or paid attention to a child as thoroughly or as selflessly as a parent. It was perfectly obvious that Jess was enjoying the ride every bit as much as Bobby was, and a niggling guilt began to eat at Casey. Was she being selfish because she didn't want to marry her son's father? Who, in all the men she knew and was likely to meet in the area, would ever care about Bobby as much as Jess already did?

Worried again and not very thrilled about it, Casey glanced at the setting sun and called, "I think we'd better go back to the house now. It's getting cool out."

They were laughing like old pals as Jess slid to the ground and lifted Bobby down. The pair ducked between the corral's pole fencing and the three of them started for the house. Casey swallowed a lump in her throat when she saw Bobby slip his hand into Jess's and try to match him step for step.

"Do you like cartoons, pardner?" Jess asked. "I rented a cartoon video today so you could watch it while your mom and I do a little talking."

Casey felt her pulse give a wild leap. "It's almost Bobby's bedtime, Jess. I'll help with the dishes, then we better be on our way."

"Aw, Mom, please?" Bobby cajoled.

"You can watch it until the kitchen is in order, honey. Then we really have to go home."

Back at the house, Jess took Bobby to the living room. Casey looked around the kitchen, then got to work cleaning up. She was still clearing the table when Jess returned.

"How about some coffee?" he suggested.

"None for me, thank you."

"Well, I'd like a cup. I'll put a pot on."

Casey began rinsing dirty dishes at the sink. Jess was moving between one counter and another, and he reached over her head to a cabinet for the coffee filters and murmured "Excuse me" when he brushed against her. When he did it a second time, Casey shot him a dark look.

"This kitchen is large enough for two people, Jess. I don't think it's necessary to keep bumping into me."

"I said I was sorry, didn't I?"

"You're doing it on purpose."

Jess switched on the coffeepot, then looked at the woman who was giving him such fits. She was small and very female in that pink dress, her auburn hair a cloud of curls around her face. She was determined to keep him at arm's length for only one damned reason: her own unwelcome reaction to physical contact with him. She could come up with fifty different excuses, reasons, justifications or explanations why there couldn't be anything personal between them, but they all boiled down to one thing: she was scared silly of him.

She knew, as well as he did, just how close to the surface lurked some very powerful feelings. Maybe they were entirely physical. Jess wasn't sure that he could dispute that. But Casey kept trying to ignore them, and that seemed childish to him.

His decision to give her space and time suddenly mocked him. How could he be anything but what he was? The flowers were fine. That was something he should do in any case. But the rest? Dancing around the obvious? What he wanted to do was to pull her into his arms and kiss her until she admitted the strong, compelling magnetism between them.

Instinct told him to do what felt right, and kissing Casey was suddenly as right as anything he'd ever encountered. He took the one long step that separated them, clasped the back of Casey's neck and tilted her head back. He caught only one glimpse of startled green eyes before his mouth settled firmly on hers.

Seven

Jess had the advantage. Casey's hands were under running water, a plate in one, a sponge in the other, her back to the kitchen; Jess had taken her completely by surprise. Her thoughts exploded in two different directions: Bobby's in the next room! and, Damn you, you promised you wouldn't do this!

Nevertheless, Jess *was* doing it. His mouth was firmly in command of hers while his hand under her hair kept her head still. Casey angrily refused to close her eyes or participate in the kiss in any way. Then her own libido began noticing Jess's scent. No man should smell that way—all spice and sex appeal, she thought wildly. His right arm boldly pressed into her breasts when he lifted his hand to her face.

Dripping water or not, sexy scent or not, she dropped the plate and sponge and grabbed at his arm, attempting to twist out of his hold. Instead of release, she got turned around and gathered up. His mouth never relaxed an iota either, and she still couldn't unleash any of the venomous phrases searing her brain.

His body and arms were unyieldingly taut, pinning her between the edge of the sink and him. Her brain devised savage revenge, to be heaped on this insufferable man when she was free again.

And then, in the midst of fury and the frustration of being the weaker sex, her own senses began to betray her. A choking, tight sensation in her chest, a pounding heart, a burning flame lapping at her insides—every trace of femaleness in her body began to respond.

I can't!

But she was. Desire hit her hard and fast. She wanted to lift her arms to his neck, to forget everything else and kiss him back, to fill her hands with his hair, to touch him and hold him and take him and have him. Six years and six million tears meant nothing in the heat of a kiss so sensual, so arousing. Tears glistened on the eyelashes that, only a few moments ago, she had been so determined to keep from covering her eyes.

Jess felt the change in her—the change he'd known would take place—and he relaxed his tight hold on her enough to explore the pink dress. His hands moved on her back, her waist, the curve of her hips, and she didn't pull away. Her breasts were plumped into his shirt, her lower body united with his. His lips relented to steal a quick, harsh breath, then took hers again. *And she didn't resist!*

One kiss demanded another. Casey's hands slid up his chest and around his neck. She was leaning into him, and her mouth was soft and open. His tongue moved into its velvety heat, and he emitted a quiet groan of intense pleasure. The hunger between them was growing, on the verge of an impossible intimacy, with Bobby in the next room. Yet they clung, their lips meeting again and again.

He was so hard and ready, he ached. But he kept torturing himself with more kisses, unable to refuse what she was offering now—soft lips, an ardent tongue, the pressure of her sweet body against his. In the background, from the living room, Bobby's youthful laughter mingled with typical cartoon honks, squeals and comical voices. While the innocent little boy giggled over the movie, his mother and father gasped and panted and groped in the kitchen.

There was something sensual even in that, Jess admitted behind the more urgent thoughts he was having about the woman he held. Their child, their flesh and blood, was proof of the passion they'd shared six years ago. And in that regard, nothing had changed.

Breathing hard, Jess raised his head and looked at Casey. "Marry me," he rasped. "Marry me and make us a family."

She couldn't speak for a moment. He'd sent flowers, he'd had them over for dinner, but he knew nothing of the real need in her heart, that part of her that longed for a normal relationship, with love as a strong foundation. Jess was impulsive and impatient, thinking he could have his son by kissing her senseless.

Well, not quite senseless. Even with her breasts rising and falling with overheated, rapid breaths, she was resenting Jess's presumption that an assault of wild kisses was going to dull her common sense. They stared into each other's eyes.

"I'm going home," she whispered raggedly.

Jess tasted the bitterness of defeat. "You're a coward, Casey." He dropped his hands and took a backward step.

"Don't start name-calling," she warned. "I don't want another fight, but I won't back down from one, either." She drew a deep, shaky breath. "Let me explain something to you. You've only recently discovered Bobby. I've loved and cared for him for nearly six years. Whatever I do with my life, it will never hurt my son."

Amazement entered Jess's eyes. "And you think marrying his father would hurt him?"

"I haven't finished. I won't do something to hurt Bobby, but neither will I hurt myself again. That's what I did with you six years ago, Jess. I didn't hurt you. I hurt *me*! It isn't selfish of me to want a good marriage. And I do know the difference between a good and bad marriage. Every member of my family has a good marriage, starting with my parents."

"Everyone but you, huh?" Jess drawled sardonically.

"What?" Startled, Casey caught herself. "Yes...yes, that's right. I...I don't want another mistake."

Folding his arms, Jess leaned his hips against the counter. "Tell me about your marriage. What went wrong?"

She dropped her eyes from his ruthless gaze, and as before when he'd asked about her "marriage," took refuge in "I don't want to talk about it." She moved back to the sink. "I'm going to finish the dishes and leave. When I came over here tonight, it was with the hope we might be friends. Apparently that's impossible."

"I told you friendship isn't enough."

She shot him a sharp glance. "It's all I have to give you."

"So take it or leave it? Is that what you're saying?"

Casey concentrated on a dirty plate, cleaning it under the stream of running water. "Don't court me, Jess. Cancel the flower order. Come and see Bobby when you want to, but leave me out of it," she said in a low voice.

He cursed under his breath. "This evening didn't turn out like I planned. You probably won't believe me now, but I didn't intend to make a pass. You affect me, Casey. I wish to hell you didn't but you do."

"No more than any other reasonably attractive woman, I'm sure."

He flushed. "There was a time when that was true. It's not true now." He moved closer again, his voice low. "Have you really forgotten what it was like for us?"

A rush of anger made Casey's voice caustic. "No, I haven't forgotten. But then I haven't slept with every available man across the U.S. either. Don't try to convince me now that that rodeo week six years ago made a lasting impression on you. You only remembered it *after* you returned to Blythe!"

"Aw, hell," Jess muttered, turning his back to her and raking his hair in frustration. She was right. The memories of Blythe and Casey Oliver had been only a vague pleasantness in a mind overloaded with similar memories.

The bottom line was that she wasn't going to be cajoled, persuaded or forced into anything. She was going to stay on the Oliver ranch—with Bobby—and he could like it or lump it.

Ignoring Casey's concern with the kitchen—at the moment he couldn't care less if the damned dishes ever got washed—Jess walked out and went to the living-room doorway. Leaning against the frame, he looked at Bobby. The child was sitting on the floor with his attention riveted on the television set. Completely oblivious to the tall man watching him from the door, Bobby laughed and bounced around periodically—a typically active, wonderful, adorable little boy.

Jess's mouth curled with bitterness. Why should his son grow up without knowing who his real father was? Why should he— Jess Lonnigan—live five miles away and pretend to be only a friend?

Jess had never felt so trapped before. His rootless life-style had given him hundreds of acquaintances, if few real friends; and casual acquaintances didn't rip a man's heart out and fling it back in his face. He'd played hard, but he'd worked hard, too, and he hadn't squandered his earnings, always knowing that someday he'd reach the point of wanting to settle down. He could equally thank and curse whatever fate had brought him back to Blythe. What a man didn't know didn't hurt him.

Jess's eyes closed for a moment, then jerked open. No, by God, he wasn't giving up!

Whirling about, he returned to the kitchen. Casey had just finished and was wiping down the countertops. "Thanks for doing the dishes."

She eyed him with a distant expression. "You're welcome." After drying her hands, Casey folded the towel and laid it on the counter. "We'll be going now."

"The movie's almost over. Let him finish watching it."

After a moment's thought, Casey relented. It wouldn't hurt Bobby to stay up a few minutes past his regular bedtime this once. "All right," she murmured, and bypassed Jess to go out the back door.

The night air was cool but felt good to her in her present state of feverishness. While she'd been alone, doing the dishes, she hadn't been able to think very far beyond Jess's kisses.

No, that wasn't quite true. Her thoughts had progressed far beyond kisses. She had too many memories of passionate, fulfilling lovemaking with Jess to keep her mind only on kisses. She knew what his body was like beneath his snug jeans and white shirt, and how his skin had glistened in the moonlight six years ago. She had memories as hot as an erotically explicit movie, although at the time, she'd only seen Jess's expertise as beautifully romantic. He'd had no qualms at teaching her what he liked and wanted, nor in discovering what pleasured her.

Did he remember any of that? Did he remember laying her down and kissing her thighs and . . .

Biting her lip, Casey hugged herself against a chill and leaned against a porch post. She heard the screen door open and close, and she lifted her eyes to the stars overhead, feeling Jess's presence behind her. He stood silently, and she felt that he was staring at her back.

Then he spoke, low, distinctly, urgently. "I want him, Casey."

Her heart skipped a beat, and all thoughts of passion fled her mind. What Jess aroused in her was a separate issue from Bobby. She didn't turn around. "You said you wouldn't make trouble."

"For him."

She turned slowly. "And for me? Do you think trouble for me wouldn't touch Bobby? What are you planning to do?"

His form was backlighted by the house behind, making him a tall, dark silhouette. "I don't know. Right now I have no plans, but I'm not going to stand by and do nothing."

Casey's mouth had grown dry. "You don't believe I'll leave, do you?"

"Leave if you want to. I'll find you. I know this country a helluva lot better than you do, and I'll find you." He paused, but began again before Casey could drum up a reply. "Let me tell you a few things about myself. I never had a home. My mother took off when I was about Bobby's age, and I never even knew which one from the parade of men before that was my father. I was passed around from one distant, reluctant relative to another. Then came the foster homes. Do you have any idea what that kind of life does to a kid?"

He'd spoken forcefully but without passion. There was no bid for sympathy in his voice. He'd presented the facts of his life as if he were talking about someone else. And he wasn't accusing when he added, "You couldn't begin to understand where I'm coming from. You have a great family—brothers, sisters, parents who are real parents. That's what I want for Bobby. You're a good mother. I know that. Watching you with Bobby, no one could doubt how close the two of you are. But a boy needs a father, too. And that boy inside *has* a father. Through my own stupidity I've already missed nearly five-and-a-half years of his life. I'm not going to miss any more of it."

A minute later Casey was glad she'd been too stunned for a comeback and that a stretch of silence had prevailed on Jess's back porch. "Mom?" Bobby was standing at the screen door. "The movie's all done, Mom."

Though her head was spinning, Casey pulled herself together. "All right, honey. Come out and say good-night to Jess while I get my purse." When Bobby came out, she went in. It took only a minute to retrieve the small purse she'd placed on a table earlier, so she was back at the screen door almost immediately.

Jess was on his knees and Bobby's boyish little arms were around his neck in a good-night hug. "We had a great evening, didn't we, pardner?" Jess was murmuring.

Bobby agreed with a nod of his head. Casey could see that her son wasn't questioning Jess's affection, and why would he? Hugs were commonplace and familiar to Bobby. Everyone in the Oliver clan hugged him frequently—even Kelly, who was at an age where affectionate displays were sometimes considered embarrassing. Bobby wasn't lacking in love, but watching him hugging Jess, and being hugged in return, touched Casey so deeply she felt tears in her eyes.

She blinked several times, then stepped outside. Jess rose slowly. "Well, thank you for dinner," she said briskly, and took her son's hand. "Good night," she called as she led Bobby to the car.

Just before he got in, Bobby yelled, "I'll be back, Jess."

As young as he was, Bobby's call had contained a note of masculine communication, a man-to-man sound. Dismayed, Casey hurried the little boy into the car.

After hearing Bobby's prayers and tucking him in, Casey locked herself in the bathroom and turned the bathtub's spigots on full blast. Ben Oliver almost always went to bed early, but Lucille and Kelly were still up. Casey didn't want to talk to anyone, though, and taking a bath would not only soothe her frazzled nerves, it would limit conversation about the evening with Jess to the few exchanges that had occurred when she and Bobby had first come in.

Lying back in the big old tub, Casey closed her eyes. She felt terribly burdened and worried, questioning her stand with Jess. Did she have the right to keep father and son separated? Were her own hopes and dreams of someday having a good marriage more important than giving Bobby the advantages of living with his own father? Jess already loved the boy, and it was all too apparent that Bobby could very easily love Jess.

Tears spilled out of Casey's eyes and slid down her cheeks. This was a serious, totally adult situation, and one that superseded what she wanted for herself. She had to think of Bobby and what was best for him. What Jess wanted, and what she wanted, was heartbreaking but immaterial. What was best for Bobby? Staying on the Oliver ranch—a home that guaranteed security for the little boy—and knowing Jess only as a friend? Or having his very own daddy?

Casey covered her eyes with her hand and wept. Jess had made threats tonight, but she doubted he'd follow through. That's not what was tearing her apart. He wouldn't do anything that would result in Bobby being hurt, she felt, which all but eliminated any kind of dissension, other than a private bitterness between her and Jess. But she couldn't stop thinking of Jess and Bobby together on the horse, and Bobby slipping his hand into Jess's while they walked. And the good-night hug, and the awful childhood Jess had had.

Wiping her eyes with the washcloth, Casey thought of asking her mother's advice. But with the next heartbeat she realized that only she could make a decision about marrying Jess. She'd leaned so heavily on Lucille in the past, cajoling her even into keeping the truth from Ben.

Wasn't it time she stood on her own two feet and stopped involving her mother in every move she made? At seventeen it was understandable; at twenty-three and with a near six-year-old son it was unforgivable.

It was hours before Casey found the blessed peace of sleep that night.

Ben Oliver had stopped by to check the progress Jess had made on the barn site. The two of them walked around and inspected the wooden forms Jess had built for the cement floor of the barn. "Looks real good to me, Jess," Ben commented.

"Everything will be ready for the last weekend of the month," Jess replied. "I sure do appreciate so many people giving up their weekend to build a barn for me."

Ben grinned. "You'll do the same for someone else, Jess. It all evens out."

Jess lifted his hat and settled it a little lower on his forehead. He had the strongest urge to confide in Casey's father, one he could hardly suppress. Ben Oliver was a very special man, and Jess could almost see himself telling him everything. *Bobby's my son, Ben. I was in Blythe six years ago.*

No, he couldn't confess seducing a seventeen-year-old girl and then walking away as if she'd been one of the free-and-easy women who hung around rodeo cowboys. Casey was Ben's daughter. He'd be hurt, wounded, by such a confession. In fact, Jess was discovering, every idea he came up with to get closer to Bobby would hurt someone. In the long run, the hurting wouldn't stop until it affected Bobby.

As painful as it was, Jess knew that his hands were tied. He'd put in a bad night, sleeping little, wrestling with irrevocability. Inadvertently, unknowingly, he'd already hurt his son enough. Casey, too. He'd leave them alone, or at least leave Casey alone. He'd have to see Bobby, and with friendship blossoming with the little boy's grandfather, no one would see anything strange in Jess Lonnigan dropping in every so often.

It wasn't until Ben was driving away, with Jess looking after him thoughtfully, that Lucille came to mind. Jess's heart started pumping faster. He'd completely overlooked Lucille. She knew the whole story. Would any good come out of talking to her? Casey had said her mother was understanding and easy to talk to. Lucille would be biased in Casey's favor, of course, but it might not hurt to approach her, maybe get her blessing as far as visiting Bobby went.

It was something to think about, at least.

When the rest of the week passed with no further word from Jess, Casey's nerves began to settle down. On Friday afternoon she made a delivery to Wes Upton, and at his urging sat down and accepted a cup of coffee. The attorney was a pleasant man with a mild, unobtrusive way of speaking and moving. He was calming, Casey realized. Just as Jess created a storm in her soul, Wes's personality calmed her.

They chatted about a number of topics—Wes's increasing practice, the possible potential of Casey's secretarial service if she rented office space in town, and several events around Blythe. Then, smiling pensively, Wes brought up his divorce and the fact that he'd been married for fourteen years. "The life of a bachelor isn't all it's cracked up to be, Casey."

She smiled, putting an understanding into the gesture she really didn't have. "No, I'm sure it's not. Do you have children, Wes?"

"Two boys. Brian is twelve and Tommy is nine. They live in Cheyenne with their mother."

"But you get to see them."

"Yes, of course. Not enough, though." Wes sighed then, giving Casey a glimpse of some profound unhappiness. "After the divorce I just wanted to get away from the whole mess.

I'm not sure now that it was the wisest move to make. I don't see the boys often enough, and I'm beginning to realize that I gave up a lot more than a lucrative law practice. It's not the money. I can see that in a year or so this will be a busy office. But my ex-wife wouldn't be caught dead camping out overnight. Boys need their father, Casey, or a darned good substitute. They need someone to be boys with, to camp and fish and hunt for frogs with, someone to cheer them on during a Little League game, or to take them horseback riding in the mountains."

Casey listened as if hypnotized. Bobby was only five and a half, still several years away from some of the activities Wes had mentioned. And she knew that her son would be welcome to go along anytime her brothers or brother-in-law took their own children on such outings. But would it be the same as having his very own father teaching him about camping and riding and fishing?

Maybe she was putting the cart before the horse, though. Would Jess even be that kind of interested father? Casey remembered very well all the time Ben had spent with her brothers. For that matter, Ben hadn't differentiated between his sons and daughters an iota. The girls were always invited on camping, hunting or fishing trips, the same as the boys. Only it was the boys who'd been giddy over such excursions, while Casey, Dee-Dee and now Kelly hadn't been all that thrilled with them.

It was another facet of the complex problem she was living with, Casey realized sadly. She felt bad for Wes, but Wes was more in Jess's position than hers. Like Wes's ex-wife with his sons, Casey had Bobby twenty-four hours a day. She was the recipient of his kisses and hugs and boyish humor. She was the one who shared those special few minutes at bedtime each evening, when all signs of little-boy toughness vanished and Bobby snuggled his favorite stuffed animal, a raggedy, disreputable tiger, under the covers with him. It was Casey who almost melted with tenderness and love during those beautiful moments, not Jess. Jess had never experienced them—not even when *he*'d been the little boy saying good-night.

Suddenly choked, Casey stood up. Her voice was huskier than normal. "I have to run, Wes. Thanks for the coffee."

Wes got up, too. "Casey, there's a dance tomorrow night at the Eagles' Lodge. Do you like to dance?"

She stopped and drew a shaky breath, pulling her emotional thoughts together. "Yes, I like to dance."

"Would you go with me?"

She could see that Wes wasn't very confident of an acceptance. He was such a nice man, and terribly lonely. In her present state of mind she was relating to his unhappiness a whole lot more than she might have a few weeks back. She hesitated, but only briefly. "Sure, why not?" she responded with a smile.

Wes heaved a relieved breath. "Great. What time should I pick you up?"

"I put Bobby to bed at eight-thirty."

"Nine, then?"

"Make it nine-thirty, all right?"

On the drive back to the ranch Casey thought about the date. She wasn't uncomfortable about spending an evening with Wes, but a niggling worry gnawed at her just the same. It had to do with Jess, and it annoyed her to realize she was concerned about how Jess might take her going out with another man. Not that it was any of his business. Jess Lonnigan had no claim on her whatsoever, on neither her time nor her affections. But she wondered if maybe he didn't think he did, which could possibly cause more problems than if she really were committed to him.

Jess was a part of the Blythe area and her life now, Casey admitted with a long sigh. Would he be in her thoughts forever, no matter what she did with her and Bobby's future?

Casey knew nearly everyone at the Eagles' Lodge and gladly introduced Wes to people he hadn't yet met. The attorney made a small joke during one dance. "I really didn't ask you out to make new contacts, Casey."

She laughed and glanced over Wes's broad shoulder. Wes wasn't a great dancer, but he was easy to follow and Casey had been enjoying herself. Seeing Jess standing at the wide doorway between the dance floor and bar instantly altered her mood, however. Her smile faded and she stumbled. "Sorry," she murmured absently, still watching Jess.

It was impossible not to notice his good looks and lean body. Jess had a way of wearing clothes that made them seem a part of him. His jeans and white shirt weren't a bit too tight, but the fabrics seemed to flow over his form.

His dark Stetson shadowed his eyes, but Casey knew where they were focused, all the same—directly at her and Wes.

"Another friend?"

A little embarrassed that Wes had caught her staring, Casey nodded. "Jess Lonnigan."

"Oh, really?" Wes turned his head to give Jess another look. "I heard he'd moved to the area. I'd like to meet him Casey. Would you mind one more introduction?" At the questioning look on her face, Wes added, "I understand he has some excellent quarter horses. My oldest boy, Brian, wants a quarter horse in the worst way, and his birthday is coming up."

"No, I wouldn't mind," Casey said quietly, wondering if Jess would have come to the dance if he hadn't somehow discovered she would be there. "We can go over right now, if you'd like."

With his hand on the small of Casey's back, Wes steered her through the couples on the dance floor and over to Jess, who watched them coming with an emotionless expression.

Casey looked great in a colorful floral-patterned sundress with narrow straps that showed off her smooth tanned shoulders, and a full skirt. She wore multicolored high-heeled sandals, and jewelry—bright pink earrings, and matching bangle bracelets on her left wrist. The man with her was big and stocky, a stranger to Jess.

"Hello, Casey."

"Jess. This gentleman would like to meet you. Wes Upton, Jess Lonnigan." The two men shook hands and made the usual polite comments about being glad to meet each other. "Wes is interested in your horses, Jess, so if you both will excuse me, I'll make myself scarce for a few minutes."

It wasn't until Casey was safely in the ladies' powder room that she acknowledged her feelings of the last few minutes. Maybe those feelings had been building from the moment she'd heard Jess's name at the rodeo grounds that day, but it made her almost ill to realize that whatever she'd felt for Jess Lonnigan six years ago, she felt now. She'd appeared calm during the brief introduction between the two men, but only through supreme effort. Now she felt the quaking of her interior spreading to her hands and her knees, and she wilted onto one of the chairs in the lounge area. How could she feel so much for a man who had caused her such unhappiness? And why now? Why tonight?

Casey put her head in her trembling hands, not at all happy with her discovery. Jess would marry her, but only to get his son. Oh, he'd make love to her; he'd already attempted that several times. But *love* her, as in falling in love? As in caring, for better or worse, for a lifetime? No. Hoping for anything resembling that kind of relationship was wasted effort. Jess was who he was—a rootless man—despite the ranch he'd settled on.

What was she going to do?

Filled with confusion, Casey sighed and got up. She knew she wasn't going to find an answer in this little room, possibly nowhere else, either. Maybe there was no solution to the dilemma she felt herself in—not one that would satisfy everybody concerned.

Casey was surprised to see Wes back at their table, sitting alone, when she walked out of the powder room. "Where's Jess?" she asked as she sat down.

"He said he had to leave," Wes replied. "I made an appointment to take a look at his stock tomorrow afternoon."

The evening progressed, but Casey functioned on two levels. Beneath her laughter and conversation were questions. Why had Jess dropped in at all, if not to see her? And why had he left again without so much as asking her to dance? She remembered them dancing in the high-school gym six years ago, and she could still feel the dizzying sensation of moving to music in his arms.

Maybe he *hadn't* known she was at Eagles' Lodge, and maybe he'd been upset to unexpectedly see her with Wes.

And then again, maybe he was only doing what she'd asked—leaving her out of his and Bobby's relationship. It was a surprisingly chilling thought.

When Wes stopped his car beside the Oliver ranch house shortly after midnight, Casey thanked him for a pleasant evening. He agreed it had been very enjoyable and asked to see her again socially. Casey looked straight ahead for a long moment, then faced the attorney.

"I won't be anything but honest with you, Wes. I'm...involved with someone." It was true. Until she made a final declaration about Jess, all her emotions were wrapped around him. The decision was still hers, Casey felt, even if

Jess's determination to get his son by marrying her was flagging.

"Your ex-husband?"

"My...?" Casey was dumbfounded.

Wes laughed uneasily. "It happens, Casey."

"No," she said softly. "He's not my...ex-husband."

"Well, whoever he is, he's a lucky guy. You're a nice woman, Casey."

"Thank you. You're a nice man, too. I probably shouldn't have accepted your invitation for tonight, but..."

"I'm glad you did. Are you and your...friend having problems? I'm not trying to pry, Casey, so if you don't want to answer that, just tell me to mind my own business."

Tears burned her eyes at the empathy she heard in Wes's voice, and Casey had all she could do to keep from shedding them. She had no intention of blurting out the details of her private life, but there was something about the attorney that invited confidence. "Very serious problems," she admitted in a low and husky voice.

"I'm sorry," responded Wes with a forlorn-sounding sigh. "If there's anything I can do, if you ever need someone to talk to, don't be reluctant to let me know, Casey."

She cleared her clogged throat. "Thanks, Wes. I'll say good-night now."

Wes walked her to the door. "Don't doubt the power of love," he said quietly. "If two people are truly in love, they can work most problems out." He looked away with an unhappy expression. "It's only when there isn't enough love that there's very little chance, Casey."

He was talking about himself, Casey realized sadly. But it fit her situation quite accurately. She knew Jess didn't love her and she certainly had no illusions about the wildly unsettling feelings she had for him. What she and Jess had was chemistry. Without Bobby in the picture, would she and Jess give each other even a moment of serious consideration?

Or was it possible that the flame that had ignited between them six years ago would be burning even brighter now, without her concern over Bobby's future restraining her impulses?

Eight

In the following week Casey saw Jess only twice, when he stopped in after supper on Tuesday and Thursday evenings, presumably for a few words with Ben. The two men sat on the front porch and discussed the construction plans for Jess's barn, with Bobby hovering close by.

Lucille and Casey knew the real reason Jess was dropping in, but Kelly was quite obviously perplexed. "I thought he was interested in you," she said to her older sister with all the finesse of a bull in a china shop. "Now you don't even show your face on the porch and he just sits and talks to Dad and Bobby. What's going on?"

"Kelly, it's none of your affair," Lucille chided.

"It's all right, Mom," Casey soothed. But it wasn't all right, and she'd been asking herself the same question. What *was* going on? Jess didn't ask for her or about her. He drove up, got out of his pickup and spent about a half hour on the porch with Ben and Bobby. After barely speaking to her at the dance, now he acted like she wasn't even on the ranch during his visits. Had he completely given up on any sort of a relationship with her? She'd told him to do just that, but, with a great deal of emotional dissemination, Casey began to realize it wasn't an acceptable solution to the situation.

Another disturbing aspect of the visits were Bobby's enthusiastic greetings. At the first sight of Jess's pickup, the little boy would run out to the edge of the driveway and wait for Jess to get out. Then he'd grin and say a deep-voiced "Hi, Jess" as if addressing a peer.

Casey's heart nearly stopped the first time she watched him do it from a living-room window. But when her son reacted the same way on Jess's next visit, she knew that something very real was developing between father and son. She watched them cross the lawn together, Bobby's small hand enfolded in Jess's, and with her heart in her throat, she saw that the little boy was even emulating Jess's walk.

On the second visit Lucille came up behind her. "I marvel that no one else seems to see the resemblance," she said in a very low voice.

Casey turned away from the window, with nervous tension on her face. Lucille's eyes searched her daughter's. "I haven't pressed you about talking to your father, but I think it's time, don't you?"

"Yes," Casey whispered meekly, ashamed of her procrastination. "I'll talk to him, Mom."

"When?"

Casey sucked in a startled breath. Lucille wasn't going to let her delay any longer. "I . . . I think I should talk to Jess first." The idea had come out of nowhere, but it seemed only sensible—and considerate—to let Jess know what had to be done. Friendship between him and Ben was growing, and this was a delicate matter. "Is that all right with you?" Casey asked anxiously.

Lucille nodded. "I think it's wise, yes. Talk to Jess first." She glanced at the door to the hall, which led to the front porch. "Tonight?"

"Not here, Mom!" Casey returned with a touch of panic.

Lucille sighed. "I know none of this is easy, Casey. But it simply cannot be put off any longer."

Casey brushed away a tear. "Dad's going to be hurt when I tell him how I lied."

"As I said before, don't underestimate your father's love for you."

"He...he might turn against Jess," Casey speculated with a strange twist of her heartstrings. It seemed odd to want to protect Jess in this, but she really didn't want a breach between the two men.

"Your father's a fair man. I'm sure he'll think before he does anything rash."

After Jess left, Casey went about her evening chores—seeing to Bobby's bath, reading him a story, tucking him into bed—with a divided mind. She was still a little girl where her father was concerned, she realized, and confessing her transgressions to him was a frightening prospect. It couldn't be put off any longer, though. When Lucille made up her mind that adamantly about something, there was no changing it. Casey knew that if she didn't tell her father, her mother would. And while she might still suffer pangs of immaturity with Ben, she was a grown woman and preferred that the story came from her. Besides, Lucille's role in the episode needed explanation, and Casey wanted to make sure her father understood that his beloved wife had only kept the secret because of Casey's impassioned pleas.

When all was quiet in Bobby's room, Casey took her purse and went downstairs. Lucille and Ben were in the living room, but Ben was in his stocking feet, his normal prelude to going to bed. "I'm going for a drive," Casey announced, and saw understanding in Lucille's eyes and surprise in Ben's. Casey never went out alone at that time of night, and her breaking a longtime habit was clearly making Ben uncomfortable.

As luck would have it, Kelly came bounding in. "Where you going, Casey?"

"Just for a drive."

"Great! I'll come along."

Casey's heart sank. "No, Kelly. Not tonight."

Ben frowned while Kelly's mouth dropped open. But before either could respond vocally, Lucille said firmly, "Run along, Casey. You don't have to have company if you don't want it. Kelly, stop looking like the last rose of summer. Your sister has a right to some privacy once in a while."

Casey quickly made an escape, tuning out both Kelly's and Ben's objections to her driving around alone after dark. She was going to see Jess, and it was with a serious enough mission that she was in no mood to worry about Kelly's pouts. Ben's concern was strictly parental, which was understandable when she still lived under his roof.

While she drove the five miles, Casey began to see her life differently than she had before Jess's untimely return to the area. Was it any wonder she still felt like a child in some respects? She'd never lived on her own, never fully supported herself, never assumed complete responsibility for herself, or her son. Why wouldn't Ben be worried about something as innocuous as her going somewhere alone after dark?

In all honesty, the time to get out of her parents' hair was long overdue. They shouldn't have to worry about a twenty-three-year-old daughter. They still had Kelly at home, which was enough after raising a big family.

All of which meant leaving the ranch.

Why hadn't she seen before how complacently she'd burdened her parents? Not that either Lucille or Ben would ever admit to such a thing. They'd never once so much as hinted that Casey and Bobby weren't welcome to spend the rest of their lives with them.

Well, she had some serious thinking to do. She would only move to Blythe, of course. Casey knew now that her threats to Jess had been only angry blusters. Leaving the ranch would be traumatic enough for Bobby without taking him very far away from all the people he loved. She could expand her business, or go to work full-time for Wes Upton. It would take some planning, but the thought of self-sufficiency was satisfying.

Jess's house was a good quarter mile off the highway, and right at the turn Casey could see that there were no lights on. Frowning, she proceeded toward it. It was nine, maybe a bit late for an unannounced call. Then, too, maybe Jess hadn't come home after he'd left the Olivers' front porch.

But no, his pickup was parked up ahead. Casey could see it beside the house. Was he in bed already?

She stopped behind the truck, without turning off the motor, and debated whether she should knock on Jess's door. A dog came around the house then, a big, shaggy, cream-colored dog with a wagging tail and a friendly "Woof!"

On closer inspection, Casey could see that the dog was pregnant, and she remembered Jess's comment to Bobby that a ranch wasn't much of a place without puppies. Her heart softened dramatically, and she turned the ignition off. This call was for Bobby and Ben, and maybe the first step in straightening out the convoluted mess she'd made of her own life. If she woke Jess, he would understand why after she'd told him the reason she'd come.

Casey opened the car door and stepped out. The big dog all but turned inside out welcoming her. "Some watchdog you are." Casey laughed softly, reaching down to pat the friendly animal.

"She's not a watchdog."

Casey looked toward the voice and found Jess standing with the front screen door partially open. Even in the dark she could see the delineation of skin and clothing, and it looked to her as if Jess had been to bed and only yanked on jeans when he'd heard the car. "I'm sorry to bother you this late. I didn't think you'd be in bed already," she said, putting a foot on the porch stairs.

"It's not that late. I wasn't sleeping, anyway. Come on in."

Casey slipped past him, avoiding contact. "When did you get the dog?"

"The other day." Jess snapped on a light, which revealed his bare torso and feet and a pair of jeans. "Her name's Sunny. A guy I met in town couldn't keep her because of the puppies due any day. Bobby will like her."

"Bobby will be delighted about the puppies," Casey agreed.

Jess gestured to a chair. "Sit down."

"Thank you." She wished Jess had more clothes on. His skin was as brown as toast, and her eyes kept going to the mat of hair on his chest. She cleared her throat and tried to appear calm, although her interior was quaking—because of her mission, because of Jess's half-naked good looks. Jess Lonnigan was as much of a flame today, tonight, as he'd been the first time she'd set eyes on him. There was a weakness in Casey Oliver Maddox, and this man, the father of her son, was at the heart of it.

Jess plopped into another chair and threw one long leg over its arm, stretching the fit of his jeans just a little too snugly for Casey's comfort. "What are you doing here?" he asked without a dram of tact.

"I need to talk to you about something."

"I was at your house earlier tonight," he bluntly pointed out.

"I know. But it's not something I wanted to discuss with an audience."

"Private subject?" he drawled with a suggestively raised eyebrow.

Casey colored. "It's not about us, Jess. Well...it is, but—"

"But not about marriage," he finished dryly. "For a moment I'd hoped you'd changed your mind. No such luck, huh?"

Casey sat back and looked at him. Why was she so against marriage with Jess? Almost every day something else happened to undermine her determination—thoughts of personal selfishness, recognition of what Bobby would gain from the union, the brand-new acknowledgement tonight that she couldn't continue living off her parents indefinitely. What on earth made her think that some great, profound, epic love awaited her? Jess was as close to love as she'd probably ever come. And he wanted to marry her, even if his reason was less than the romantic fantasy she carried in the back of her mind.

No! She couldn't marry a man who didn't love her. She just couldn't, no matter how many sensible other reasons she unearthed!

Giving her head a quick, sharp shake to clear it, Casey saw that Jess took it as a negative reply to his comments. She didn't alter his opinion. "I'm planning on telling Dad that you're Bobby's father," she announced, keeping her tone reasonably level and with very little inflection.

Jess's reaction was physical—a leap out of the chair. He walked around with a heavy, very serious-looking frown. Casey watched him pacing, then asked, "Do you object?"

He turned. "No. I think he should know. I almost told him myself the other day. Casey, I want to be there."

"When I tell him?" she asked, taken aback. She hadn't anticipated Jess's wanting to participate in the confession, and she immediately suspected it would make the ordeal more difficult. "I'm not sure that's a good idea," she said slowly. "Dad could be very upset."

Jess's mouth twisted grimly. "I wouldn't expect him to be anything else." His eyes, containing a hard light, landed on Casey. "Actually, I think he should know that I've offered to do the honorable thing."

She stiffened. "Don't you dare! No, I don't want you there. I only came to tell you about it because you and Dad are becoming friends." Besides, there was an aspect of the story that was none of Jess's business, her manufactured ex-husband. Ben had a right to hear the complete truth, but there was no reason for Jess or anyone else to know that Don Maddox was only a fabrication.

Lies were such a burden! This whole thing wouldn't have been necessary if she hadn't lied and forced her mother to lie. Yes, there might have been hell to pay when Jess showed up again, but it would have been an honest furor. Now Ben liked Jess, and Jess liked Ben; and who knew just what would happen between the two men when the deep, dark past came to light?

And none of them dared forget Bobby. The little guy was the focal point around which some very adult events were about to take place, and heaven help the one of them who hurt Bobby!

Folding his arms across his naked chest, Jess leaned against a section of wall with a determined expression. "Once Ben knows who Bobby's father really is, do you think I'm going to stay out of it? Forget that notion, if you have it. You bet I'm going to tell him I offered marriage when I found out I had a son. I might have made a bad mistake six years ago, but I'm willing to do just about anything to rectify it."

Casey gave him a cold look. "Even marry me. How noble and self-sacrificing. And of course, when Dad learns that I refused your proposal, I'll be the heavy, won't I?"

"Do you think that's how Ben will look at it?" Jess couldn't help the elation in his voice. If the Olivers lined up in his favor, wouldn't that influence Casey?

Well, strangely enough, he had some influence with Casey, too. So far she'd been fighting it, but Jess knew very well how strong the chemistry was between them. It suddenly occurred to him that they were completely alone—alone in his house. Casey looked beautiful, as she always did. Tonight she was wearing a red cotton skirt and a white blouse with a scoop neck and no sleeves. A lightweight white sweater was thrown over her shoulders, and the white blouse had minute red dots and red buttons almost as tiny.

Studying her, Jess relived last Saturday night when he'd walked into the Eagles' Lodge and seen Casey dancing. A wash of possessiveness, and especially a sting of jealousy, had nearly made him do something foolish—like walking out on the dance floor and hauling her out of that guy's arms. Jess had seen red, and only with supreme effort had he forced himself to stay at the doorway.

He'd been surprised to see Casey bringing the guy over, and his first impulse had been to ask her what the hell she was doing out with another man. When they'd been walking his way and he'd watched her skirt swaying with her movements and seen how incredibly sexy she looked in high heels, he'd actually wanted to punch the guy and drag Casey out of there. Again, common sense had prevailed, which, once Jess had talked to Wes Upton, he'd been darned glad of. Upton was a nice guy, and if he admired Casey, Jess could hardly blame him.

Since that night, Jess had asked himself a dozen times why seeing Casey with a date had affected him so adversely. He figured he had the best reason in the world for wanting her for his wife: Bobby. Along with that, Casey was an arousing, beautiful woman. Few men wouldn't get a few hankerings around her. But—and it was a damned big but—were the feelings he was noticing and trying to understand something more than a desire to experience her body again?

Something deep and masculine stirred in Jess. Right now Casey's pretty face contained the tension of worry and anger. But he knew he could soothe that away—very easily. She couldn't help responding to him, any more than he could help wanting her. That was the one area of their relationship where they were on the same wavelength, whether she wanted to admit it or not.

Moving almost lazily, Jess pushed away from the wall. Casey darted him a nervous glance but was still preoccupied with the horror of Jess announcing marital intentions to her father. Just how would Ben look at the situation if Jess butted in with that information? Casey knew that as kind and generous-minded as her father was, he was still a God-fearing, family-oriented man. He was also inclined toward that old saying, "If you dance to the music, you have to pay the piper."

Well, she'd danced—six years ago. And paying the piper, in Ben's eyes, could very well mean a marriage she wasn't ready for.

When Jess stopped right in front of her, Casey's gaze lifted to his face, and a sudden jolt shook her. She hadn't come here for a shot of Jess's physical persuasion, but the look on his face conveyed his intentions to be very different from hers. Casey's mouth went dry. "No, Jess," she warned.

He bent over, putting his hands on the arms of her chair. He was close enough to smell, and she caught a drift of mint, probably from toothpaste. His eyes contained a touch of laughter, giving him a boyish appearance. "You look good enough to eat," he told her in a voice that sounded both suggestive and admiring.

Casey's pulse had gone wild, but she tried to maintain a forbidding expression. "This isn't fair, Jess. I came here to tell you something that I consider very important. Please don't try to turn it into something else."

"I consider it very important, too. And I appreciate your coming by to let me know about it." The amusement left his eyes. "But we're all alone here tonight. Doesn't that do something to you?"

Apparently it did "something" to him. He was giving off sexually charged vibes, and she was picking them up, *soaking* them up, as if her flesh had suddenly turned porous and thirsty.

He raised a hand and touched her hair, following Casey's head back when she tried to avoid it. "So pretty," he whispered. "My son has the prettiest mama in the whole state."

"Jess..."

His eyes were darker and exuded a hot light, and he lazily wound a burnished curl around his forefinger. "Hair like silk, skin like satin, eyes like warm jade. But your mouth—ah, your mouth. There aren't words, Casey, none that I know of, to describe your mouth. It makes me feel, it makes me remember, it makes me want."

She drew a long, quivering breath. "I'm not... I won't..."

"You won't what?" He bent lower and brushed his lips along her hairline, tracing it down to her ear. "What won't you do, sweetheart?"

His voice was as much of a caress as his mouth. Casey's heart was pounding at a furious rate. She struggled against herself, against a liquefying weakness in her bones, against a curling heat in her stomach. She must remember how glib Jess had been six years ago, too, and not be overly impressed with flowery phrases.

But her senses were betraying her. She'd never wanted any other man. She'd never felt soft and liquid and so utterly female for any other man. This man, with his shock of shimmering, dark, unruly hair and sky-blue eyes, was the only man who had ever reached and stirred and tormented the woman in her.

Her hands were fluttering, afraid to light anywhere. The bronze sheen of supple skin over rippling, sinewy muscles, the dark mat of hair on his chest—she didn't dare touch him, not anywhere. He wasn't wearing a belt, and his jeans rode low on his hips, below his navel. He was half naked, and the half that was covered was straining against faded denim, reminding her of soft-summer nights beside a gurgling river.

"Leave me alone," she whispered raggedly.

His lips moved in her hair, heating her ear. "I can't leave you alone. I'm burning to death from wanting you."

"Any woman would do."

"No, any woman *wouldn't* do." Jess raised his head, tipped her chin and looked directly into her eyes. "I haven't so much as kidded around with another woman since I got here. I don't want any other woman. And even if I did, I wouldn't dishonor you or my son with some cheap affair."

Casey's eyes widened. "Since when have you become so scrupulously moral?"

He studied her. "Good question, isn't it?"

Casey's insides did a strange flip-flop. Even Jess looked surprised by what hung in the air, his own intimation that some kind of incomprehensible transition was taking place.

Well, she didn't understand it, either, and she was certainly too cautious to trust it. Just because Jess Lonnigan, rodeo star and first-class Casanova, had bought a ranch and settled down didn't mean he'd changed his philandering ways. By his own admission he'd played at life and love. The discovery of a son might have cooled his ardor temporarily, but leopards didn't change spots overnight.

Casey took his hand and brought it away from her chin. "I think I'd better be going."

That slow, heartrending smile of his appeared again. "Why?"

"I don't have to explain myself to you, Jess."

His hands cupped the arms of the chair again. "No, but maybe you want to. Maybe if you had the courage you'd say, 'Jess, if I stay I'm going to end up in your bed.' Maybe you'd like to say, 'I need you, Jess, I need you to kiss me and love me, like you did six years ago.'"

Casey turned her face away, eluding the compelling look in his eyes. "Don't be absurd."

He lowered his head until his lips were against the side of her throat. "Prove to me you don't want me," he murmured.

"I think that's exactly what I've been trying to do. You don't pay the slightest bit of attention to—"

"To lies?" Jess's hands moved from the chair to Casey's upper arms, and he straightened his long back then, pulling her up with him. His eyes bored into hers. "Stop being a coward, Casey. Stop pretending you don't feel what I do. Be your real self. Let yourself go."

Casey's knees were rubbery. *Let yourself go!* She closed her eyes and was immediately bombarded with emotions. *Be your real self!* Oh, Lord what was her *real* self? *Coward... coward... coward...*

Jess didn't hurry. His hands slowly moved around her and down her back. The white sweater slipped and he let it slide to the floor. He pressed his lips to her forehead, gradually drawing her closer. Her scent careened through his system like a speeding ball in a pinball-machine game, knocking against nerves, setting off bells and flashing lights. "Casey... baby..."

He caught her hands then and brought them up to his neck. His skin was warm and dry and vibrant with life. Casey felt his hands lock behind her, just below her waist, and she stared up into his blue, slightly hooded eyes. "Don't push me, Jess," she whispered.

"I can see in your eyes what you want."

"There's more at stake than..."

"You're too cautious these days."

"I have a son to think of."

"So do I, but making love isn't going to take anything away from Bobby."

Casey was desperately trying to cling to sanity. She knew she was at some sort of crossroad and that Jess had forced her there. It almost seemed like a battle for maturity; she was, after all, twenty-three and living a celibate life. By choice, of course. But it had always been so easy to do. Since that one week six years ago, she'd never been faced with the overwhelming desire for a man's body that Jess had provoked every time he touched her, until now. Yet, getting that involved with Jess seemed so traitorous to her situation.

And then Jess put into words some of the questions that had been hounding her. "Why do we have these feelings if they're so wrong, Casey? Why do we burn for each other? Why do I want you, and why do you want me?"

"Oh, Jess, I wish I knew," she lied, deeply shaken over her inner conflict.

His lips moved over her face. "There's nothing wrong with two people wanting each other. In fact, honey, there's something very right about it." His mouth rested on hers, and Casey sighed—deeply, emotionally—and parted her lips.

A sound resembling a growl came from deep in his throat and his mouth opened and possessed hers. His tongue slid between her lips and teeth, and his body molded around hers. Every dip and curve of Jess's form was hotly influencing. It was as if his chest were shaped to accept the configuration of her breasts, and there was no denying how perfectly their lower bodies melded. Even with the difference in their heights, they fit together as nature intended a man and a woman to fit.

Casey gave up on sensibility. She'd fought Jess since that day at the rodeo, and maybe more devastating to her, she'd fought herself. Perhaps she was completely wrong in everything she'd been feeling lately, or, at least, concerning the worries she'd had about Jess, himself. Maybe she *should* marry him. Maybe she should say goodbye to a dream and take what was available.

It was a subject that was easier to contemplate in Jess's arms than out of them.

She felt herself being lifted, swung up off the floor as though she weighed nothing, and she experienced only a small echo of remorse. Her heart was beating a wild cadence, and a strange joy that she was again going to experience Jess Lonnigan's magic filled her mind.

During the short walk down a hallway, Casey let her hands wander. His skin was smooth, hotter than before, and she turned her face into the hair on his chest and inhaled the male scent of him.

His bedroom was dark except for the pale, silvery moonlight. "Don't turn it on," she objected huskily when Jess stopped at the light switch by the door.

"Anything you say," he agreed softly. "This time," he added, and let her feet slide down to the floor. He straightened and reached for the tiny red buttons on her blouse.

Casey watched his face in the moonlight. It was shadowed and mysterious. She'd never made love as a woman, she realized. At seventeen she'd been eager but ignorant. Of course, by the time Jess left Blythe, she hadn't been at all ignorant. Yet, the sum total of her sexual experience was with this man, although he didn't know that. Jess still thought she'd been married, and he'd never asked about other men. For all he knew, she could be very experienced, very polished and sophisticated in bed.

The thought made her bolder—bold enough to caress and touch and run her fingertips over the planes of his bare torso. She could feel his heartbeat, a powerful, steady thumping under her fingers. His muscles were tight and firm, and he seemed quite controlled until she bent forward and licked at one tiny male nipple.

"Oh, baby," he groaned thickly, and twining his fingers in her hair, he tipped her head back and took her mouth in a hungry, devouring kiss. His tongue was insistent now, and within the dazzling effects of his increased desire, Casey felt his free hand working the rest of her buttons free.

With their mouths still united, Jess slid the blouse from her shoulders and arms. Casey was wearing a white teddy, and when he realized that, he undid the button on the waistband of her skirt and let it drop around her ankles.

Then he stood back a little to look at her. "You're so beautiful," he breathed hoarsely as he took in the long, tanned legs beneath the white satin of the sexy undergarment. Her nipples were visible bumps in the cups beneath two slender straps over her shoulders.

Jess opened his jeans—first the brass button at his waist, then the zipper on his fly. But he didn't push the pants down. Casey's startled gaze dropped to what she could see of maleness within the veed opening. Surprisingly enchanted with her curiosity, Jess slipped the teddy's straps down over her shoulders, and exposed the tops of lushly full breasts, then their pouty, dark nipples.

"Oh, Casey," he whispered raggedly, and bent his head to take one in his mouth.

"Jess," she moaned, and instinctively reached for that compelling vee in his jeans. He wasn't wearing underwear, which she'd already guessed, and his body was hot and rigid and velvety in her hands. She had touched him like this six years ago; he'd taught her, he'd shown her what to do. She'd been mesmerized by the intimacy then and, she realized, she was mesmerized by it now.

His tongue moved on her nipple, wetting it, while he gently sucked. She felt as if a live flame were loose within her, searing her breasts and leaping downward to a point of almost intolerable aching between her legs, only to crackle and shoot upward again.

Perspiring, Casey was having trouble breathing. A band had tightened around her chest. She wanted what she remembered from six years ago with an urgency that was becoming unbearable. After Jess had left Blythe and Casey had finally faced her predicament, she'd done a lot of reading. Several times, in novels, she'd encountered a female character who was considered frigid. It was one disadvantage she knew she would never have to deal with. She was far from frigid; not with the right man, she wasn't.

The right man! Casey's heart skipped a beat when the thought ran wild and encompassed the fact that Jess was the only man she'd ever really responded to.

The teddy was sliding down over her hips, and when it reached her ankles, Casey kicked it away. She pushed Jess's jeans down then, and he got rid of them just as easily as she'd disposed of her undergarment.

They fell to the bed and tangled into a sensual embrace, their mouths and hands searching. She felt Jess's hot breath on her ear. "It's been too long. I can't wait any longer," he whispered. "Are you on the Pill?"

"The Pill? No...no..."

Dazed, Casey watched him open the drawer of the nightstand and take out a small foil-wrapped packet, and when she understood what he was doing, she whispered, "Why didn't you do that six years ago?"

Jess shook his head. "We'll talk later."

She could see how agitated he was, how deeply aroused and excited he was. But so was she. Her breasts were rising and falling with harsh, labored breaths, and the fire in her loins was painfully insistent. He returned to her, laying himself within the cradle of her thighs, and sought her mouth for another soul-searching kiss that lasted until neither could breathe at all.

Casey's hands restlessly roamed his back. When her mouth was free she gasped for air and moaned. "Do it. Make love to me. Do it."

His penetration was swift and hot, and Casey whimpered with utter abandonment. Her hips rose, pressing him deeper. He was masterful, leading them both, and for the first time Casey really understood why, at seventeen, she'd mistaken this wild, mind-bending rush of feeling and emotion for love.

But she knew what it was now, and she could even label it. There wasn't anything wrong with recognizing one's sexual appetite, and as Jess had stated, there might even be something very right in it. She was years away from being a teenager, and sex was a very important part of adulthood.

The only thing slightly wrong with this was that she was awakening again for the same man who had hurt her so badly the first time around.

Casey didn't have to push the thought away; it quite easily dissolved on its own within the much stronger sensations of pleasure and desire controlling her mind and body.

It wasn't until it was over, until her skin and Jess's were both wet with sweat and her blood had stopped racing and her heart had settled down, that Casey realized she'd whispered words of love at the end. With Jess weighting her down, she tried to remember exactly what she'd said.

He raised his head and smoothed the damp curls back from her forehead. "That was perfect," he told her in a low, husky voice.

Her head bobbed once, a silent agreement. For pure physicality, nothing could ever be more perfect. But what about emotions? Hers were in a terrible snarl. How could she be in Jess Lonnigan's bed like this? She'd come to his house to discuss a serious topic, and that had been only her first mistake. How could things look so different in the space of a few minutes?

"Damn you," she whispered on a dry sob.

Jess stiffened. "Now you're mad at me?"

"Not just at you. I should have known better than to come here alone."

"Casey, whatever you do, please don't regret this. It was beautiful and right."

"It was as sordid as it was six years ago! Only I don't have the excuse of naiveté this time. Let me get up."

Jess tried to laugh, but it came out sharp and bitter. "I don't believe this." He moved away, freeing Casey, and watched as she got off the bed and searched in the near darkness for her clothes.

Nine

When they were both dressed and in the living room again, Jess tried to talk some sense into Casey. "You're wrong to take this attitude. We didn't do a damn thing we didn't have a right to do. Are you attached to anyone? Am I? We're consenting adults, and there's a lot of feeling between us, Casey."

He was right on that point. She had way too many feelings, which was part of the problem. But if genuine feelings were all there was to it, she might not be so upset. What hurt was that she knew all about Jess's feelings, and they were centered in one particular portion of his anatomy. She, stupid woman that she was, had succumbed again to Jess Lonnigan's fatal charm!

Casey retrieved her white sweater from the floor and gave it a shake. "I'll be speaking to Dad in the next day or so, whenever there's a good opportunity."

"Talk to me about this, Casey. Don't act like it didn't happen."

She swung angry eyes to him. "Oh, it happened, all right. But don't expect me to turn handsprings because I just proved again what a fool I am where you're concerned." Casey advanced a step, eyes burning. "I'm weak with you, Jess. I was weak six years ago and I'm still weak. It infuriates me, so don't *you* act all hurt and put-upon because I'm not thrilled about tonight.''

His eyes narrowed. ''Think what kind of marriage we could have.''

''One based on sex?''

''What would be so terrible about that? There isn't a married couple on earth who wouldn't be lucky to have what you and I have in bed. And don't forget Bobby. We'd be a family, and there's not a whole lot wrong with a family where the mother and dad can't keep their hands off each other. We could even have other kids. I'd like that, Casey. I'd like to fill this house with kids.''

Casey's memory had just gotten a nudge, and she wondered if she should ask Jess again why he hadn't used condoms six years ago.

''Casey, you'd be the most well-loved woman in the state.''

She almost made a very crude retort, because she was positive that Jess's affections had nothing to do with love. Instead, Casey drove both the question and retort from her mind and started for the door. ''I'll let you know how Dad takes it, if you want me to.''

Jess followed her. ''I'd still like to be there when you talk to Ben.''

''No.''

''Just like that, a flat-out no. You're not a very generous woman, Casey.''

''Just drop it, Jess. He's *my* father and you have no right to interfere.''

Casey was halfway through the doorway when Jess caught her arm. ''Maybe tonight gives me a few rights.''

She whirled on him. ''*Tonight gives you nothing!* Don't you dare try to make something out of what happened. I fully admit to being a fool, and I certainly don't need any pressure from you about it.''

Jess stared down at her with a hard expression. ''A half hour ago you were kissing me back and wanting more. I didn't force myself on you, Casey. You willingly opened your legs.'' She sucked in a startled breath, but he wasn't through. ''It's going to happen again, too. This kind of fire isn't extinguished with one glass of water, honey. I think you know that as well as I do.''

Casey tore her arm loose and lunged away. She knew Jess had come out of the house behind her, but she didn't look back. Her hands were trembling as she started her car, and then she glanced at the porch and saw him standing in a patch of light reflected from the living room. Casey drove away with tears running down her cheeks.

Casey put in a strange night. Oddly, as upsetting as it was, the evening with Jess also made her feel somewhat stronger. Her life was taking a new direction, one with a decidedly more adult perspective. While she showered and dressed the next morning, she visualized her future, both immediate and longer-range. She would talk to Ben first thing, then tell both parents about her decision to move to Blythe with Bobby. It was time she stood on her own two feet, and she couldn't do that under her parents' roof.

As for Jess, Casey's thoughts about him had gone around in circles. She could look on their lovemaking in two ways, she finally concluded: either Jess had just been, to put it crudely, horny and she'd been the only woman handy, or he'd deliberately tried sexual persuasion to get her to marry him—only because of Bobby, of course. No matter which, she'd be an even bigger fool than she already was to let it happen again, despite Jess's dire prediction.

Ben had already gone when Casey finally went downstairs. "Where's Dad working today?" she asked her mother who was the only person in the kitchen.

"He and the boys are moving some steers from one pasture to another. I doubt if you'll be able to talk to him until lunch, Casey."

"All right. I've got some typing to get out, so I guess I'll get that done. When Bobby comes down, have him come to the den."

Casey had fixed up one corner of the den for her work. It had a desk, a typewriter and a small cupboard for supplies. With a cup of coffee, she went to the desk and sat down. Lucille hadn't asked how the meeting with Jess had gone, and Casey was glad she hadn't had to talk about it. But she couldn't stop thinking about it.

Making love with Jess was like nothing else Casey had ever experienced. Of course, she had no other sexual encounters to compare it with, but how could anything be better? It was total immersion into sexuality, both hers and Jess's. He had the ability to draw her to a whole different level of emotion, one that was far distanced from the mundane aspects of life. In his arms she became beautiful, soft, a fantasy creature, and in retrospect, the memory was framed with sparkles of light and wind-chime tinkles.

Casey gave her head a shake. The reality of what she'd done was far from a star-speckled, musical dream. The reality was that Jess brought out her baser instincts, and what they felt for each other was only lust.

And he wanted to build a marriage on lust?

Disgusted with herself as well as Jess, Casey set her coffee mug down and opened a file folder. She had at least two hours of typing ahead of her, and then, later in the day, she would make her deliveries in Blythe. It would be a good opportunity to begin making inquiries about a rental house.

"I'll walk out with you, Dad," Casey announced when Ben had finished lunch and was preparing to go back to work.

"All right."

"Me, too, Mom?" Bobby enthused.

"No, honey. You stay with Grandma. I need to talk to Grandpa alone." Casey saw the pure, unmitigated nosiness on Kelly's face, but followed her father out the back-door without alleviating it.

They walked along in silence for a minute, then Ben gave his daughter a glance. "Something on your mind, Casey?"

"Yes."

Ben veered from a direct path to his pickup to a fence line and the shade of three massive oak trees. "Warm today."

Casey put her hands on the top rail of the white wood fence and looked at the horses that were contentedly grazing within the enclosure. "This is something I should have talked to you about years ago, Dad," she said quietly.

"Yes, I think you should have. It's about Bobby, isn't it?"

Casey's head jerked around. She searched Ben's eyes and saw that there never had been a secret! For a moment she was flustered. "You know?" she whispered.

"Most of it, yes."

"But, how..."

"Casey—" Ben sighed "—children have been asking their parents that question since time began. How do you know when Bobby does something you'd have preferred him not doing? You sense it, don't you? You know your own child so well that the slightest change in him alerts you."

"Dad . . ."

Ben smiled then. "Besides, your mother told me about it six years ago. You see, Casey, we don't keep secrets from each other."

Casey's mind was in a muddle. "But all this time Mom kept telling me I should tell . . ." Her expression cleared. "No, that's not true. She never said to *tell* you, she said I should talk to you." Casey's hand moved from the fence to Ben's arm. "I don't understand, Dad. I thought I had the secret, and all this time it was you."

Ben nodded. "Let's go back a ways, honey. When you were going through your trouble and confiding in your mother, you were very young and very hurt. Mom told me how you begged her to keep it from everyone in the family, including me."

"Especially you," Casey whispered brokenly. "I knew you'd be disappointed in me, and I couldn't bear it. Dad, it was wrong of me to ask Mom to lie, but I was so ashamed."

"Casey, everyone makes mistakes. Disappointed? Yes. I suppose I was, to a degree. But I was a lot more concerned with your and the baby's welfare than I was with my disappointment. At any rate, I decided to remain silent on the matter. You had enough heartache to deal with, and your mother was doing everything anyone could to get you through it. With circumstances being what they were at the time, I agreed that a manufactured husband was best.

"Honey, I knew that someday you'd talk to me about it." Ben slipped his arm around Casey's shoulders and hugged her. "When you grew up," he added quietly.

He hadn't mentioned Jess, and Casey's heart was doing flips in her chest. "There's more," she admitted weakly.

Ben cleared his throat and moved away. "You know, before Bobby was born and your mother and I talked about the baby's father, the man's name was mentioned only a few times. You were apparently convinced that there was no chance of locating him, and I gathered, from your mother, that you were in such a state, any attempt on my part to do so would only upset you more."

Casey was staring at her father in stunned silence. He'd known all along—everything.

"Besides, you were so young, and a forced marriage didn't seem like the best course to either your mother or me. That day at the rodeo grounds, when Jess's name was announced it rang a bell. But I didn't put two and two together until I saw your and your mother's reactions to it. Then, when I met Jess—and liked him, by the way—I decided again to stay out of it. The two of you are adults, Casey. It's for you two to work out—not me or your mother or anyone else."

Ben turned and faced his daughter. "Now, tell me what you feel about all of this."

"Oh, Dad," she whispered tearily. "I thought this was going to be so terrible. When I was younger I was deathly afraid of telling you, and then it became a humiliation I couldn't bear facing. I've been such a fool, in so many ways."

"Well," Ben mused philosophically, "foolishness is a human frailty. You don't have a monopoly on it, believe me. I doubt if there are too many people around who haven't done something in their lifetime that they don't regret."

Casey shook her head adamantly. "Not you, Dad. Or Mother. No one could ever convince me that either of you ever did anything even close to my mistakes."

Ben chuckled softly, as if remembering some long-ago indiscretion. Then he sobered. "I guess what's important is what you do from here on in, Casey. Jess and Bobby are developing quite a relationship, and I'd guess that dealing with that is your most pressing problem right now, wouldn't you?"

"They look so much alike. You've seen it, haven't you, Dad?"

"Yes, I suppose there's a resemblance. But Bobby looks a lot like your brother Brady, too."

Casey's eyes widened. "Do you really think so? Mom sees his likeness to Jess very clearly. Well, that's neither here nor there, is it? Dad, you really do like Jess?"

Ben nodded and replied firmly. "Yes, I do."

He wants to marry me! Casey tried, but she couldn't quite get the words out. Although, now that she thought about it, Ben probably knew about Jess's proposal, too. There really were no secrets between her parents, she was relieved to discover.

Still, if Ben knew about the proposal he also knew about her reluctance. And at this point she didn't want to even talk about it—not after last night. Instead she said, "I was afraid that once you found out, you might change your opinion of him. You seem to like most people, and the possibility of a breach between the two of you made me uncomfortable. He's just getting established here, and I know how much he values your friendship."

Ben gave her a long, in-depth scrutiny. "Do you still have special feelings for him, Casey? I know you must have had six years ago. You were an impulsive teenager, but you were never... Well, what's the word I want here?"

"Promiscuous? You're right, Dad. Jess is the only man I..." Casey stopped and looked away. She'd always been able to talk relatively freely with her mother, but there were some subjects that had never come up between her father and her. "I did have special feelings for Jess six years ago," she said softly, introspectively. "I imagined myself in love with him."

"Imagined? Why do you say 'imagined'? Weren't you capable of feeling love back then? Casey, don't denigrate what you felt. Subsequent events might have tarnished your feelings, or even destroyed them, but initially they were real. You have a right to remember that and to admit that Bobby's conception was a result of love."

Tears blurred Casey's vision. She *had* loved Jess. She had loved him so much she'd wanted to die when he left. And then the love had turned to hatred, to an obsessive, impossible wish for revenge. Now she didn't hate him, but she still wanted him physically; and what did one call that?

"Here, dry your eyes." Casey took the large red handkerchief Ben held out. "I'm glad it's finally out in the open, Casey."

"I am, too, Dad. What... what about the rest of the family? Do you think they should know?"

Ben frowned while he mulled it over. "I think that's something for you and Jess to decide. Apparently you've come to an agreement on him seeing Bobby, which I feel is wise."

Sniffling, Casey handed back the handkerchief. "Dad, there's something else I might as well say now, too. I've lived off you and Mom long enough. I don't completely understand it, but Jess coming back brought about an awful lot of change in me."

"You grew up, honey," Ben commented reassuringly.

Casey sighed. "Yes, I think I did. Anyway, I think it's time that I accepted responsibility for myself and my son. I'm planning to move to town. Wesley Upton has asked me to come to work for him full-time, and I can't see any reason why I can't handle that job and still keep up my business."

"Have you discussed this with your mother?"

"Not yet. But I will." Casey put her arms around her father's middle and hugged him. "Oh, Dad, why was I so worried about talking to you?"

"I don't know, honey. I never thought I was that tough to talk to, but maybe I was wrong. Listen, do you intend to tell Jess that I know the truth?"

Casey backed away. "I already told him I was going to talk to you."

"Yes, last night. Your mother told me about it after you left. How did Jess react?"

"He was glad. He said he almost told you himself one day. He wanted to be with me during this talk, but I preferred doing it alone."

"I would imagine Jess would like to openly claim his son?"

"Very much. I . . . I'm very undecided on that, Dad. What's best for Bobby? There would be so much talk if it got around. I don't know. It's a point I'm very confused about."

"Well, I'm sure you'll work it out."

Casey smiled faintly. "I'm going to do my best, Dad."

"That's all anyone can ask, honey."

"You're really not going to the barn raising?" Kelly asked in complete astonishment the Friday evening before the big event.

"No, I'm not," Casey replied.

"But, everyone's going! The whole family and most of our friends will be there. Mom, why isn't Casey going?"

"I'll tell you myself." Casey sighed. "I have a ten o'clock appointment tomorrow morning with Mrs. Loomis to look at that little rental house she owns on Third Street in Blythe. I'm moving to town, Kelly."

Kelly looked shell-shocked. "Moving to town! Why? What for?"

"Simply because it's time I took care of myself," Casey said quietly.

"Mom?" Kelly wailed.

Lucille walked over and hugged her youngest daughter. "It's your sister's decision, Kelly. We must respect it."

Casey and Lucille had had a long discussion on both the "secret" and the matter of Casey's proposed move. At first Lucille had been adamantly opposed to the idea, but she'd finally seen that Casey was right.

But Casey hadn't expected Kelly to be so unhappy about it. "It's only to Blythe, Kelly," she said gently. "You can spend time in town with me and I'll be back and forth a lot."

Kelly wiped at a tear. "I just don't see why you have to move. I'm not just being a kid about this, Casey. I honestly don't understand."

Casey looked at her baby sister and felt a deep tug of empathy for the teenager. "No, of course you don't. Take a ride with me and we'll talk about it. Mom, Bobby's sound asleep for the night."

"You two go right ahead. Bobby's just fine."

"Thank you. Coming, Kelly?"

"Yes . . . and thanks, Casey."

Casey took Bobby with her to look at Mrs. Loomis's house on Saturday morning, while the rest of the family departed for Jess's ranch and the barn raising. The little boy was full of questions. "Is this where we're gonna live now, Mom?" "Why?" "How come?" "Can I have a dog?" "Can I bring one of Pearlie's puppies with me?" "When are we gonna move, Mom?"

"Hush, son," she finally told him, then said to Mrs. Loomis, "You mentioned something about a deposit."

"I always get a cleaning deposit, Casey." The older woman hesitated, then smiled. "But I know your family so well, I'm sure I could waive the deposit in your case."

"That's very kind of you. I would never move out and leave the place dirty, Mrs. Loomis."

"I'm sure you wouldn't. Well, what do you think?"

The house was small, with two tiny bedrooms, a living room, a bathroom, a kitchen, which also did double duty as a dining room, and a storage room, which was plumbed and wired for a washer and dryer. What had caught Casey's eye about the little place was its large fenced yard. Also, Third Street was strictly residential and the traffic was minimal.

"Do you allow pets, Mrs. Loomis?"

"Oh, my, yes. I have two dogs and a cat, myself. Certainly this young fellow can have his puppy, Casey. Just watch that it doesn't chew holes in the carpet."

Casey had to smile to herself. The carpet was clean but had certainly seen better days. In all honesty, the house wasn't much. But it was a start at independence, and Casey could see herself and Bobby being quite comfortable in it after she fixed it up a little. Lucille had told her not to worry about furniture, as the Oliver ranch house had more than it needed and there were even some good pieces in the basement, only gathering dust.

After Casey had agreed to take the house, she put Bobby in the car and drove to downtown Blythe. The little boy chattered gaily during the short ride, and Casey wondered if he really understood what "moving" meant. He'd had no practical experience with it, because not even any of his aunts and uncles had moved within the realm of his memory.

Casey had promised her son a hamburger for lunch, and she parked in front of Summers' Café, which was across the street and down two doors from the hardware store. Getting out of the car, Bobby startled his mother by shouting, "Jess! Hey, Jess!"

"Bobby!"

Casey watched Jess lope across the street. She'd taken the coward's way out when she'd told Jess about the talk with Ben, using the telephone rather than chancing a face-to-face with him.

"Hello," she said, managing a semblance of calmness, which was nothing short of remarkable considering the way her insides had begun acting up.

"Hello, Casey." Jess knelt down and gave Bobby a hug. "How you doing, pardner?"

"We're gonna move, Jess."

Casey blanched when Jess gave her a cynically startled look. "Where to?" he asked, rising and letting Bobby slip his hand into his.

"To a house here in town." Casey answered. She could see that the topic infuriated Jess. "It's none of your business," she added tartly.

"The hell it isn't," he returned angrily, then glanced at Bobby and forcibly swallowed his temper. "I need to talk to you," he said to Casey.

"We have nothing to talk about." Casey took Bobby's free hand. "Come on, honey. Let's go get that hamburger."

Jess's lips were set in a grim line. "Tell me where and when, Casey, or I'll come to the ranch tonight and say everything I have to say in front of your whole family."

"What are you doing in town, anyway?" Casey hurled back.

"I came to pick up another keg of nails from the hardware store."

Bobby yanked on Jess's hand to get his attention. "I get to bring one of Pearlie's puppies to our new house, Jess."

Jess glared at Casey for a beat, then smiled down at his son. "That's great, pardner. Did your mom tell you about my new dog? Her name is Sunny and she had seven puppies last night."

"Seven?" Bobby's blue eyes were shining like new pennies. "Gee, I'd sure like to see them."

Jess looked directly into Casey's green eyes. "Have your mom bring you to my place this afternoon, pardner. You should be there, anyway, and so should she. No one should miss a barn raising. It's a very special event."

"Bobby's been to a barn raising before, and so have I," Casey replied coldly.

"Have I, Mom?" Bobby asked, his little face mystified.

"Last summer, son. Don't you remember that big picnic table with all that good food and running and playing with dozens of children? You talked about it for weeks afterwards."

"Oh, yeah, now I remember." Bobby's blue eyes turned to Jess. "Are you having a big picnic at your house, Jess? Are there lots of kids there?"

Casey was clinging to one of Bobby's hands, Jess to the other. Clearly the little boy was in the middle and neither Casey nor Jess wanted to let go. Two pairs of adult eyes locked and silently battled. Anger and determination and memories rode the paths of their gazes. "Bring him to the barn raising, Casey." Jess told her in a lethally quiet undertone. "I want him there."

"It's not your decision."

"I talked to your dad this morning."

"Drop it, Jess. I'm not going to discuss that now."

"I only said it to give you a preview of what's coming when we get a chance to really talk. Let's make it tonight, and since I've decided on the time, you get to name the place."

"You're the most exasperating..."

"Mom?" Bobby interjected. "Can we go to the picnic? Then I could see Jess's new puppies, too."

Casey glared a hole right between Jess's eyes. "I thought you wanted a hamburger," she reminded waspishly, then sighed and looked down at her son. His handsome little face was animated with eagerness, and what he was asking wasn't that terrible. "All right. We'll go to the barn raising," she finally agreed, but with obvious reluctance.

Bobby began hopping up and down. "Can I ride with Jess, huh, Mom? Can I, Jess? Can I ride with you?"

"If it's all right with your mother," Jess said quietly, giving his son a smile, then turning a hopeful look to Casey. "I'd take real good care of him, Casey."

A lump of solid tears clogged Casey's throat. She'd never been the sole recipient of her son's affections, although there'd never been a doubt that he loved her best of all the people who loved him. But the boy was turning to Jess in ways that would pinch any mother's heart. How did Bobby sense Jess's feelings for him so keenly? Casey knew he did. It was as her father had said: a parent recognized changes in her own child that no one else would ever notice.

There was camaraderie and boyish adulation in the look Bobby was bestowing on Jess, and Casey had to consciously swallow the sob that insisted on welling up. She cleared her throat and blinked at the hot tears threatening her last hope of maintaining her poise in this confrontation.

Jess frowned. "Casey..."

"No, it's all right. Bobby may ride with you. I'll follow in my car." Quickly she stooped over and hugged her son. "Don't forget to buckle your seat belt."

Then, with a brave smile, she turned and walked away, heading for her car. "Casey, I've got to pick up the nails before we leave," Jess called.

"Fine," she yelled over her shoulder, and climbed behind the wheel of her car, giving the door a hasty slam. The sight of Bobby and Jess carefully crossing the street, Bobby's hand in Jess's, the two of them talking together, brought fresh tears to her eyes.

While they were in the hardware store, Casey found a tissue and blew her nose. She was being silly, she told herself. She wasn't losing Bobby to Jess, and she *had* to adjust to the friendship between them. As Bobby grew older, Jess would probably request more and more of his son's time.

In a few minutes they came out of the store. Jess was carrying a keg of nails on his right shoulder and holding Bobby's hand with his left one. He dropped the keg in the back of his pickup, then got Bobby settled in the cab. Casey waited to start her car until Jess got into the truck, but she saw him say something to Bobby through the open window, then bound across the street again.

He came up beside her car and bent down to see her. "I just wanted to say thanks, Casey." His deep blue eyes contained a compassion she had never seen in them before.

"You're welcome. Make sure he buckles his seat belt. He forgets sometimes." Casey heard the raspy quality in her voice, evidence of the emotion she was still battling.

"I will. Casey..."

She bit her lip. "Please don't."

"I just want to say one more thing. Bobby's a happy, well-adjusted little boy because of you. I love you for that."

Casey sucked in a stunned breath, but before she could make a response, Jess was jogging back across the street.

Ten

The activity at Jess's ranch was just as Casey had anticipated. After a mammoth lunch the men returned to the barn construction, the women cleaned up and gossiped, and the children ran and played themselves into exhaustion. By the time darkness threatened, everyone was worn out, but the barn was up—walls, roof, windows and doors. So many men had shown up to help out, it had taken only one long day. The interior work was up to Jess, but the hard part was finished.

As families got into their vehicles to leave, Jess shook hands and expressed deeply felt thanks. Casey gathered up Bobby, preferring to leave while Jess was too occupied to notice. He looked as tired as the other men, but she suspected he would still want that talk he'd insisted on earlier, tired or not, and she would just as soon avoid it.

When she led Bobby to her car, however, Jess spotted her. "Casey! Just a minute."

"Get in, Bobby," she told her son. "I'll speak to Jess and then we'll leave." The little boy scrambled into the front seat and sat back without a word, and Casey smiled and shook her head. He'd had a wonderful afternoon and his eyelids were already drooping. He'd probably fall asleep during the short drive home.

Jess walked up. "I'd like you to wait until I say good-night to these good people."

"I can't, Jess. Bobby's completely done in." It was true, but it sounded like an excuse, even to Casey. "Some other time, all right?"

"When?"

Casey bristled a little. "What's this all about, anyway?"

Jess put his hands on his hips and looked away. Then his eyes refocused on her, a little more intently than before. "I talked to your dad this morning. You weren't completely candid in your discussion with him."

"I was as candid as I wanted to be. I certainly hope you didn't start something by talking about . . ." Casey glanced to the car. The windows were down and Bobby was probably listening. "I don't want to discuss this now."

Jess's expression didn't relent. "Then come back. Take Bobby home and come back." He saw another car pulling out. "I've got to thank those people, Casey. Either come back or I'm coming to you. Take your choice. We're going to talk here or at your folks' house." He bent over at the car window. "Good night, pardner. See you soon, okay?" Then he turned and walked away.

"You arrogant—" Casey whispered, stopping herself just short of a curse word. "It can wait until tomorrow," she shouted.

Jess kept walking, but he looked back. "No, it can't! One hour, Casey."

"One hour," she repeated under her breath. "Just who do you think you are?"

"Mom?"

Frustrated and angry, Casey climbed into her car. As she was driving away she saw her parents' car stop beside Jess. He bent over and shook hands with Ben, and it was obvious from his smile that everything was just great between the two men.

Heaving a disgusted sigh, Casey turned her attention to the road.

After Bobby was tucked in, Casey went downstairs. Lucille was in the kitchen putting away the leftover food she'd brought home. Every family had taken scads of food to the event, and while the hungry carpenters had definitely put a dent in it, it would have taken an army to eat everything. "Where's Dad, Mom?"

"Taking a shower, honey. Why?"

"Jess said they talked this morning and I'd like to know just what was said. Jess is insisting I go back to his house to discuss it, whatever *it* is. Do you know anything about it?"

"Yes, I do," Lucille said, and closed the refrigerator door. "Jess told your father that he'd asked you to marry him."

"I knew it!" Casey fumed. "Damn him! I told him to keep his big mouth shut about that."

"Casey, anger isn't going to help your situation. Your father already knew it, anyway, and he and I have discussed it. No one is going to pressure you into anything."

"No one but Jess," Casey retorted.

"Are you going back to his place?"

"He said if I didn't, he'd come here."

"Well, suit yourself about that. You can talk here as well as there."

That wasn't quite true, Casey acknowledged with an inward wince. There were things between her and Jess that she preferred to keep a secret from her family, such as her being dumb enough to go to bed with him again. "It's probably best if I go there," she decided aloud, and then asked, "Dad doesn't think I should marry Jess?"

Lucille had just rinsed her hands at the kitchen sink. She picked up a towel to dry them. "I didn't say that, Casey. Your father..."

"You're going to marry Jess?"

Kelly was standing in the doorway, and her eyes were as big as saucers. Casey groaned. The talk she'd had with her younger sister hadn't touched on Jess in the slightest. She had merely given Kelly the sound reasons she had for moving out on her own, which Kelly had seemed to finally understand. Or at least accept. But this had to be a surprise for the teenager, and with Kelly still so admiring of Jess Lonnigan, Casey didn't have the slightest notion how to explain what was going on.

She was about to appeal to her mother when she saw the weary expression on Lucille's face. Not only was Lucille exhausted from the long day, she had to be just plain tired of problems, Casey realized. That was one of the reasons she was moving to Blythe; she'd burdened her parents long enough.

"Kelly, it's like this. Jess has asked me to marry him, but I've told him no. My reasons are personal, although Mom and Dad know what they are. But I'm not going to discuss them with you or anyone else, and I'd appreciate your keeping this to yourself."

Kelly looked startled, but her sister's adult tone was more of a compliment than anything else. "Well, sure, Casey. It's your business. I understand."

Casey's features softened into a smile. "Thank you." She glanced at her mother. "Looks like I'm not the only one growing up around here."

Lucille hugged Kelly, then Casey. "You're both good girls, and I love you very much."

Casey used the drive to Jess's place to organize her thoughts. She was pretty confident of what was coming. Now that everything was more or less in the open with her folks, Jess was really going to press hard. The remark he'd made about loving her for being such a good mother to Bobby made Casey a little more tense every time it came to mind, and petty or not, she didn't like him playing the "wonderful father" role. Jess had only discovered his parenthood a short time ago, and she didn't want to hear his judgment, either good or bad, on the quality of her care of their son. The one point she intended to get across very clearly was, once she was settled in Blythe, Jess's visits would be highly regulated. She wasn't going to have him just dropping in and disrupting her and Bobby's schedule whenever the spirit moved him.

It was very dark when Casey arrived, and it didn't surprise her to see a light on in the new barn. Jess must have strung in an extension cord, she decided, because he couldn't possibly have completed the electrical work. Casey bypassed the house and stopped her car close to the newly erected structure.

She got out and saw Jess coming through one of the barn doors. His long, lean form was backlit, and that jab of intense awareness she was getting so accustomed to in his presence invaded her senses. But she didn't say hello; she wasn't there for polite conversation.

"Thanks for coming," Jess said, approaching her.

"You didn't give me much choice."

Jess jerked his head toward the barn. "Want to take a look inside?"

"I came because you demanded some sort of discussion, not to look at your barn."

"I know, but it's the prettiest barn any man's ever had, Casey." She had to smile, but Jess barely noticed. "I owe my neighbors more than I could ever repay," he continued softly, introspectively. "I was never in one spot long enough to make the kind of friends I have now. I've found a lot more here than I even knew existed—real friends, a son, you."

Casey's smile had slowly faded while Jess spoke. He was strongly and emotionally affected by the generosity of his neighbors, and his mood was reaching her. Yet she didn't want to be lumped with Jess's other newly recognized acquisitions. "Not me, Jess," she told him quietly.

His eyes lost their reflective cast and became laser sharp. "Tell me what to do and I'll do it. Tell me what you want and you'll have it. I want you for my wife. I want you in my bed at night. I want—"

Casey's anger suddenly blazed forth. "*You* want? What about what I want?"

"I just asked you what you want. Name it. If it's humanly possible, I'll give it to you."

Appalled, Casey took a backward step. "You're actually trying to *bargain* me into marriage! Do you think I'm looking for something material? Jess, I told you what I want out of marriage."

"Love," Jess said flatly.

"Yes. Love, dammit!"

He stepped closer. "Well, I love you."

Casey flushed three shades of hot red. "Like hell you do! Jess, just stop it. I like you a lot better when you're honest with me. I believe you want to marry me, and yes, I believe you want me in your bed. But, love? No. You didn't love me six years ago, and you don't love me now. You *love* Bobby. Jess, and I just happen to be his mother."

"That's not true! Casey, there was something between us six years ago, and there still is. Just because I was too damned thickheaded to know what it was didn't mean it wasn't there."

"The only thing between us was sex!" she snapped. "I've faced it. Why can't you?" Casey whirled and walked away, with Jess right behind her. "I asked you not to tell Dad about your proposal, and you did it anyway. Thanks a lot," she said sarcastically. She was at her car door, but Jess's hand on the handle stopped her from opening it.

"I felt he should know."

"Well, it didn't do you any good. For your information, he already knew, and Mom told me tonight that she and Dad aren't going to pressure me one way or the other. The decision is mine, Jess."

"Yeah, some great decisions *you* make," Jess jeered. "Moving Bobby to town—now there's a real winner. Just what will he be doing while you work every day in Upton's law office?"

"Oh, I see the grapevine is alive and thriving," Casey drawled. "Like it or not, Jess, I *am* moving to Blythe. And don't worry about Bobby. I have a very reliable sitter lined up. I think you know me well enough to know that I'd never neglect my son."

"*Our* son. I think you might be having a little trouble remembering that he's also *my* son."

"Don't kid yourself. It never leaves my mind for a second."

"You still wish I'd never come back to Wyoming, don't you?"

The accusation jarred Casey. In some ways Jess's return was a blessing. It had rid her of the immobility of hatred and given her life new direction. No, she wasn't wasting her time now wishing Jess hadn't come back.

The anger suddenly drained out of Casey's system, and she leaned against the side of the car with an unhappy sigh. "Oh, Jess, let's stop this. I'm so tired of fighting and bickering. All I want to do is get on with my life. I want to make a decent home for Bobby and myself."

Jess was staring at her with a stubborn expression. "I want you to move here, not to Blythe."

Casey drew a long, hopeless-sounding breath. "You never give up, do you?"

"Did you watch Bobby today? Did you see how excited he was to be with all those other kids? And the freedom he had? Is he going to have that in town?"

"No," Casey admitted uneasily. "No, he won't have the freedom he's used to, but . . ."

"Casey, you're doing this for you, not for Bobby. From where I stand, it looks like you're being damned selfish. You already had one chance at making that 'decent' home and it didn't work. Why don't you give me that same chance now?"

"What chance? Just what are you talking about? I've never lived anywhere but with my—" Flustered, as Jess's meaning struck her, Casey's words floundered. "Oh...I meant..."

But it was too late. All of the strange little omissions and mistakes Casey had made in the past weeks had rushed Jess in an explosive understanding. "You never were married, were you? That was another lie."

He sounded positively amazed, and his reaction infuriated Casey. "Don't you dare judge me," she raged. "While you were off enjoying your fun and games, I was seventeen and pregnant! Can you possibly understand what that's like for a young girl? That's why I thought my dad didn't know anything about it. I begged my mother to lie for me, to help me plan a marriage, a husband that didn't exist."

"Casey..." Jess's stomach was turning over. He couldn't have imagined Casey going through it alone. He'd thought, he'd *believed*, she'd fallen in love with a man willing to take her baby. He'd wondered why it hadn't lasted—hell, he'd even asked Casey why it hadn't—but he'd still believed she'd been married to a man named Maddox.

Casey heaved a dry sob. "Mom did tell Dad, but he's such a wise man, and he knew I would have been more upset than I was if I thought he knew the truth. I would have been, too. I felt safe thinking that no one knew but Mom—less ashamed. It took a while, even at that, but I eventually learned to hold my head up again. As a divorcee, my son wasn't considered a bastard, at least."

Jess sucked in a harsh breath. "He's not a..."

"It's not a pretty word, is it? Especially when it's applied to your own son."

For the first time Jess was getting a true sense of what Casey must have lived through, and he felt sick to his stomach with remorse and shame. Because of him, the Oliver family had gone through hell, with Casey bearing the brunt of it. It was a miracle that Ben would even speak to him, let alone give him his blessing as he'd done that morning.

These were good people. In fact everyone he'd met in Wyoming had been nice, and Ben Oliver was the best of the lot. And he, Jess Lonnigan, was the biggest jerk that had ever walked around on two legs. No wonder Casey didn't want to marry him. How could she ever forget what he'd put her through?

"I wish you had told me this before," he said in a low, anguished voice. "I didn't know, nor could I have guessed, what you went through. I visualized a man behind you, with you, caring about you, during those months. I'm not even going to say I'm sorry. There aren't words to express what I'm feeling. But I will say this, Casey: I'll leave you alone. I understand now why you could never marry me. As for Bobby, I'd still like to see him as much as possible, if you agree."

It was Casey's turn for amazement. "You mean you won't talk about marriage again?"

"Never. Everything that's happened between us makes sense now...the anger, the battles." Jess hesitated a moment. "Almost everything," he murmured, and Casey knew he was thinking about the night they'd made love in his bed. He sighed then. "Go on home, Casey. I've got a lot of thinking to do."

He walked off, and Casey felt almost glued to the spot. She watched him go around the back of his new barn, and then she heard a peculiar sound. Her thoughts tripped over one another. Surely Jess wasn't crying!

She moistened her dry lips, uncertain what to do. Jess's obvious sorrow wasn't something she'd wanted, not since she'd started understanding him. Before that, she would have relished this moment, she realized unhappily.

Moving slowly, Casey finally opened her car door and slid behind the wheel.

"You can take that sofa from the den, and there's a perfectly good dinette set in the basement." Lucille was making a written list while she talked. "Bobby's bed, of course, and dresser, and the bed in your room..."

Kelly suggested an end table from another bedroom, and lamps. The list was filling out nicely. "Oh, the mail's here, Mom. The truck just went by. I'll go out and get it."

"Thanks, honey. Casey, what about that bookcase in the upstairs hall? Is there room in your living room for it? And you've got to have a television set. We never use that small one in the kitchen. You can have that."

Casey was staring out the window. "Casey?"

"Oh, sorry. Yes, the small set in the kitchen will be fine, Mom. But just as soon as I can replace everything, I'll return all of your furniture."

"Nonsense. This house is overstuffed. It will be good to un-load it a little." Lucille smiled at her daughter. "Well, by to-morrow night you'll be in your own place."

"Yes." Casey sighed.

Lucille's smile evolved into a frown. "Casey, you don't have to do this, you know. You and Bobby are welcome to stay here forever."

"I know, Mom. No, it's best if I . . ."

Kelly burst in with the mail. "Casey, you got a letter from Jess!"

"From Jess?" Casey accepted the envelope. "Why on earth would he write a letter when he lives only five miles away?" She started to open it, then glanced at Kelly's avidly interested face. "I think I'll read this upstairs," she said, and got up from the table.

Kelly's disappointment was almost tangible, but Casey left the kitchen and hurried up to her room. She closed the door and sat in the bedroom's one upholstered chair.

The first thing she did was study Jess's handwriting on the envelope. She'd never seen it before, and his masculine scrawl somehow touched her heart. Since Sunday night Casey hadn't been able to get rid of the idea that Jess had gone behind the barn to weep in private. If he'd been that emotionally worked up, Casey knew he would seek privacy. He was exactly the sort of man who would think crying was effeminate and a sign of weakness.

To her, it denoted a sensitivity she found extremely moving. Jess's comments about the good friends he'd found in Wyo-ming were also meaningful. It seemed to Casey that Jess was doing some growing, too.

She tore the sealed flap loose and pulled out a folded piece of paper. Then her mouth dropped open, because when she opened the letter, a check fell into her lap. It was for three hundred dollars.

Quickly, then, Casey read the letter.

Casey,
Please don't tear up this check. He's my son and I want to

help with his support, I know your reason for hating me now, and you've been more than good about me seeing Bobby. It would mean the world to me to know that I was contributing to his care. Once you're settled in Blythe, I would appreciate a call so we can make arrangements for me to stop by. I meant what I said about not bothering you again, but I want to see Bobby. Please understand. I will send you a check every month.

Jess

Casey lowered the letter and stared across the room. She blinked at the tears in her eyes for a moment, then put her head in her hands and just let them flow. Emotions roiled and fed her unhappiness, and she wept until her eyes felt seared.

Then she sat back and admitted what she'd been fighting against for weeks now. She loved Jess. She would always love Jess. She hadn't merely been infatuated six years ago; she'd fallen deeply, irrevocably in love. No wonder no other man had ever moved her. No wonder she burned when Jess touched her.

She wiped her eyes. Was there the tiniest speck of honest affection developing in Jess Lonnigan for the mother of his son? They were becoming closer, even if it was caused by dissension. His arguments were changing. Hers, too, for that matter. Anger was becoming influenced by that infernal physical attraction neither of them seemed able to ignore. And he truly admired how well she'd raised Bobby. How, really, was she to read the signs?

Sighing, Casey refolded the letter and returned it and the check to the envelope. Then she got up and tucked it into her purse. She didn't know if she was going to keep the money and, in fact, didn't even want to think about it right now. She would make that decision later, when her mind wasn't so bogged down with frustration and, yes, self-pity. It wasn't fair that she'd been destined to love a man who didn't love her the same way—not fair at all.

The move was going smoothly. Buck, Brady and Ray were carrying the furniture Lucille had donated from the house to one of the ranch pickups, and Ben was overseeing its placement on the truck bed. Lucille was still digging out dishes, pans and cutlery for Casey's use. Kelly was filling a box with bed-ding, and Casey was packing up her clothing. Bobby had been given the task of putting his toys into two large cartons in his bedroom.

Casey folded another pair of slacks, then realized she wasn't hearing sounds from Bobby's room. She left her room and crossed the hall to Bobby's, intending to tell him to stop dawdling. "Son..."

She stopped. The little boy was sitting on the floor by one of the cartons, and crocodile tears were slithering down his face. Casey's heart turned over, and she quickly went to her son, dropping to the floor beside him. "Why are you crying?" she asked softly.

His big blue eyes, swimming in tears, lifted, and Casey saw what had happened. Bobby had finally understood what "moving" meant. Instinctively, Casey pulled him onto her lap and hugged him. "We must look at this as an adventure, honey," she said gently.

"But we won't be living with Grandpa and Grandma and Aunt Kelly anymore."

"That's true. But do your cousins live with Grandpa and Grandma? They come to visit, don't they? Well, that's what we'll do, too. Whenever you want to, we'll just get in our car and zip right back to the ranch. Think how glad Pearlie and the other dogs will be when we come driving up."

Bobby smiled. "Can I bring Rusty with me?"

Rusty was one of Pearlie's puppies. It had been a hard decision for the little boy to make when he loved each and every one of the litter, but Bobby had finally settled on a chubby little rust-colored pup.

"Of course you can. We wouldn't dream of leaving Rusty behind when we visit the ranch, would we? Now, let's both work on your toys. The men will be ready to load the boxes on the truck very soon."

Bobby slipped to the floor again and began scooping up toy cars and trucks, dropping them into the carton. "Mom?"

"Yes, honey."

"Does Jess know where our new house is?"

Casey's swift activity slowed. "He knows it's in Blythe, Bobby. I promised I would call him when we're settled."

"Maybe...maybe you should call him now. What if he wants to come and see me?"

Casey looked into her son's deep blue eyes. They were so like Jess's. Maybe she was the only one who really recognized the similarity, but when she looked at Bobby, she saw Jess. Her heart ached for this small boy, and for his father, too. How could she continue to keep them apart? They were becoming closer every day, regardless of anything she might do or feel about it.

Tears stung her eyes as she thought about the love developing between Jess and his son. Bobby sensed that he was special with Jess; he felt it and responded to it as a blossom reaches for the rays of the sun.

"I'll call him," she said huskily, and got to her feet, "Finish your toys, honey, and I'll go and call him right now. He'll know exactly how to find you in Blythe."

Jess didn't answer his phone, however, and Casey returned to Bobby's bedroom with an ardent promise to keep trying until she reached him.

That night was the first night Casey had spent away from her parents' home since she'd returned from "college" pregnant and supposedly divorced. Her bed was the same, but the tiny bedroom smelled and felt much different from her large room on the ranch. She'd left a small nightlight on in the hall in case Bobby should awaken and be frightened in the strange surroundings, and that little light gave Casey, too, a surprising comfort.

She wasn't afraid, but there were different noises to become accustomed to. The street was quiet, but still an occasional car passed by. Dogs barked, a cat screeched, someone banged a garbage-can lid, the little house creaked unfamiliarly.

There was so much newness to get used to. She would start working for Wes Upton on Monday, which gave her four days to get settled. It wouldn't take the entire four days, for she had scrubbed the house through and through before moving in. Her most important task, she felt, was to get Bobby oriented, and she planned to spend plenty of time with him. When he started school in September, he wouldn't be riding the school bus as he would have if they'd stayed on the ranch, and Casey wanted to walk the few blocks to the grade school several times with her son, making sure he understood the route and the danger of crossing streets carelessly.

She'd tried calling Jess several times throughout the day, but he'd never answered, and Casey had concluded that he was probably out working on his barn. Bobby had mentioned him again while he was getting into his pajamas, and Casey had again promised to keep trying until she got to inform Jess of their new address.

Now, while she lay in the feeble glow from the nightlight in the hallway, Casey felt a trickle of tears from the corners of her eyes. They were for her son, and she knew she couldn't go on battling forces that were growing stronger daily. Perhaps she had enough love for both her and Jess, she pondered emotionally. Maybe she was looking for the impossible, anyway. She wasn't apt to fall *out* of love with Jess, and even if she met a man who would really love her, how would she love him?

Casey let her mind take her into a future that included Jess as her husband. Her insides roiled at the image, but she tried hard to see him as a full-time father and mate. Jess had said, "Well, I love you," but she didn't feel it was true. She felt his desire and his determination, but not his love—although she very easily recognized that he loved Bobby.

Her thoughts turned to the more personal: to their lovemaking, to Jess's hard body, to his kisses. For purely physical love, she could ask for no more. Jess's sexual appetite was unquestionable. A touch, a look, a word, and he was ready to make love. He would be an ardent mate.

As for emotional love...?

Casey turned over in bed and quietly wept into her pillow. She was still romantic enough to want that special communion with the man she married. She'd seen her father and mother exchange thoughts without a word. She'd witnessed her brothers and sister and their respective spouses together, and while the air around them zinged with sexual exhilaration at times, there was also a quiet, secure aura about their communication. That's what she wanted with whomever she married. That's what she would give almost anything to have with Jess.

But maybe she should forget all that and settle for giving Bobby the best home possible. Casey flopped onto her back again and stared at the dimly lit ceiling. Perhaps she should let Jess know she was considering his proposal. She wouldn't rush into it, of course, but in a few weeks...?

One thing she knew for certain: she wasn't going to be mean about Jess's visits. He could see Bobby on his own schedule, not hers. She simply didn't have the heart for any more battles and ultimatums.

Casey fell asleep wrangling with it all.

"Jess! Jess!"

Casey went to the window and saw Bobby running to the front gate. Jess was climbing out of his pickup, which was parked right at the curb, with a broad smile. "Hi, there, pardner!" He came through the gate and swung Bobby up. The little boy wrapped his arms around Jess's neck and squeezed so tightly Jess yelped and laughed.

It was late Saturday afternoon and Jess's first visit. Rusty, Bobby's puppy, began yipping excitedly, and Casey smiled at the heartwarming scene. Then she went to the front door. "Hello, Jess."

He let Bobby slide to the ground, and his smile faded to somberness. "Hello, Casey."

Bobby was tugging on Jess's hand. "Come and see my swing, Jess. Grandpa put it in the big tree out back for me."

"Sure, pardner." Jess's eyes lingered on Casey for a moment, then he let Bobby lead him away. She watched them disappear around the corner of the house, then closed the door and went back to the dinner she was preparing.

The kitchen window was open and she could hear Bobby's excited chattering and Jess's replies. Bobby hauled Jess all around the yard, pointing out his play areas, the sandy patch of yard where he had a fleet of toy trucks and cars, the swing in the old oak tree, the plastic wading pool, where, he told Jess, "Mom lets me put water in it with the hose and I swim when I get too hot."

Casey's interest was more on what was going on outside than on the meat loaf she was putting together, and she stood close enough to the window to watch. Jess pulled something out of his shirt pocket and hunkered down beside his son, and Casey saw him press an object into the little boy's hands. She squinted to see what it was, but she couldn't make it out, although it obviously delighted Bobby.

"For me?"

"Yes, for you."

"Gee, thanks, Jess. I've gotta show Mom." Bobby ran to the kitchen door and burst through it. "Mom, look what Jess gave me."

Casey took the object and looked at it. It was a trophy belt-buckle, one that Jess had won in rodeo, intricately designed and engraved. "It's beautiful, Bobby. You'll have to take very good care of it."

"I will, Mom," he declared.

Jess stood at the door. "Come in, if you'd like to," Casey told him.

"Thanks." Stepping in, Jess smiled rather uneasily, "I thought Bobby might like the buckle. I hope you don't mind."

"No, I don't mind." When Casey had finally reached Jess by phone and given him their new address, she hadn't mentioned the check. It was still in her purse, and she was still undecided about accepting it. Oddly, if she hadn't admitted her feelings for Jess, she would have found it much easier to take his money. As it was, loving the man and knowing that she must keep it a private matter, she wasn't comfortable spending his money.

"Can you stay for supper, Jess?" Bobby asked eagerly.

Jess's eyes met Casey's, then slid away. "No, not tonight, pardner. Some other time, okay?"

Casey didn't encourage him to stay. She was finding her way, she felt, and soon she would talk to Jess on a different level. For tonight, it was best if he spent an hour or so with Bobby and then left.

Eleven

It was Jess's third visit—an after-dinner call—before Casey mentioned the check. Jess had stayed, at her invitation, to tuck Bobby in for the night, and he'd been grateful for the opportunity to share that special bedtime warmth with his son. As they left Bobby's room and walked into the living room, Casey said. "Would you like a beer or a soda? I need to talk to you about something."

Jess nodded. "Thanks. A beer would be great."

Casey went to the kitchen and returned with two bottles of beer. She handed one to Jess, then sat on the couch. Jess sank into a chair. "You've got the house fixed up nice, Casey."

"Thank you. It's small, but it's not bad little place."

"How's the job going?"

"Fine, really. I'm not fond of leaving Bobby all day, but we're both adjusting."

Jess's gaze held hers. "Are you?"

"Yes, Jess, we are," she replied evenly. Earlier, Casey had put Jess's check in her skirt pocket, and now she pulled it out. "This is what I want to talk to you about."

"You haven't cashed it."

"I've been undecided about keeping it."

"I'm sure you can use the money."

"That's not the point."

Jess took a long draft from his bottle, then gave her a hard look. "What is the point? I want to contribute to Bobby's care. Maybe it's not enough. Is that it?"

Casey's expression chilled. "I think you know me better than that. It's a very generous sum. It's the idea of taking your money, Jess."

"Is there something wrong with my money?"

He'd spoken cynically, and it struck Casey that since the night she'd thought she heard him crying, he seemed to have developed a rather hard shell. They were both going through a troubling period, she realized, which gentled her voice some. "Jess, there's nothing wrong with your money. But there could be something wrong with me taking it. You're playing the role of a friend, not a parent, and why should you—"

Casey didn't get to finish. Jess interrupted with a harsh "Playing a role? Yes, I guess that is what I'm doing." He drained his bottle and stood up. "Good night, Casey. Cash the check or tear it up. Do any damned thing you want with it."

With wide, startled eyes, Casey watched him go to the door. She rose then. "Jess, I'm sorry."

He turned, and never before had Casey seen him move so listlessly. His eyes looked older, tired, dull. "I'm sorry, too. I think this whole thing is getting me down. I don't like you and Bobby living here. I don't like you leaving him all day with a stranger. I don't like anything that's happening, but there's not a damned thing I can do about any of it."

"Dora Martin, the lady watching Bobby, is not a stranger. Come and meet her sometime. I've known her all my life. And please don't act like a working mother is some kind of misfit. Bobby is not neglected in any way."

Jess hadn't really touched Casey since the night they'd made love. But he moved to her and touched her now, and she didn't back away. His fingertips traced the curve of her cheek, and then her jaw, ending up on the side of her throat. "I know you don't neglect Bobby," he said quietly. "I just wish things were different."

So do I. Oh, so do I. Casey felt Jess in every cell of her body in a rush of radiating warmth that caused a lump in her throat and an ache in her stomach. She wondered if this was the time to tell him that she'd been doing a lot of thinking about his marriage proposal.

But he withdrew his hand suddenly and backed away. "Sorry."

She accepted the apology with a slight nod of her head.

"Good night. I'll drop by next Tuesday or Wednesday, if that's all right."

"Tuesday or Wednesday is fine."

After Jess left, Casey locked the door, turned out the living-room lights and sat on the couch in the dark. The only time she'd ever been unhappier was during the months she'd been pregnant. It looked to her now as if she'd handled Jess's return to Blythe as badly as anything she'd ever done.

To add to her misery, she was lonely. Was Jess going directly home? It was a Saturday night, after all, and there were places around the Blythe area where a single man could find anything he might be looking for. The thought of Jess with another woman was like a knife blade in Casey's heart, but she knew she had no right to object. He was a virile, healthy man, and he wasn't going to go without female companionship indefinitely, despite his remarks about not dishonoring her or Bobby by having some cheap affair.

Besides, there were plenty of decent women available, and not every affair would be cheap. And a lot of women in the area would jump through hoops to go out with Jess Lonnigan.

In the dark, sipping from the bottle of beer, Casey again visualized marriage to Jess. Maybe he would fall in love with her after they were married for a while, she mused. Was that possible? Or would she spend her life yearning for something he could never give her if she married him?

Sighing, Casey set the bottle on the end table and put her head back. Her job was going well. Wes Upton was a pleasant man to work for, which she'd anticipated. His law practice was gaining ground, but there were hours when Casey wasn't busy, and Wes had no objections whatsoever to her using the time to keep up her freelance secretarial service. She still typed Lloyd Abbott's manuscripts and did letters for several other clients. Her combined salary and fees wouldn't provide a princely income, but with sensible management, Casey knew she could support herself and Bobby.

Of course, there was the future to think of—Bobby's future. She would love to be in a position to assist her son financially, should he wish to attend college when the time came. Casey thought about it for a few moments, then took the check from her skirt pocket again. Yes. Now she knew exactly what to do with it. Three hundred dollars was an impressive amount for starting a savings account for Bobby's education.

Casey and Bobby spent Sunday at the Oliver ranch. The whole family was present, and the day passed normally, with noise, laughter and good food. The highlight for Bobby was an invitation from his Uncle Brady to go on a camping trip. It was Brady's son's birthday, and the youngster had requested an overnight camp-out as his gift. Bobby was thrilled to be invited along, and Casey agreed to have him ready to leave the following Tuesday afternoon.

At one point during the hectic day Casey found herself alone on the front porch with her father. They talked about her job and living in town, and then Ben asked, "How are you and Jess getting along?"

"Reasonably well. Do you see him very often, Dad?"

"Oh, now and again. I stopped by his place a few days ago, and he's just about got the interior of the barn completed. He's got plans for a twenty-stall stable, too, you know. He's a hard worker, Casey. His place is shaping up really well. His quarter horses are splendid animals, and buyers and other breeders are already coming to him. I firmly believe he's going to be successful with his operation."

Casey's expression was seriously reflective as her gaze absently rested on the children playing on the grass. "He comes by about twice a week to see Bobby."

"Only Bobby?" Ben inquired gently.

"I've been giving his marriage proposal a lot of thought," Casey said in a low voice. "Dad, Jess doesn't love me, but..." It was too painful to put into words.

"But you love him."

"I...I'm afraid I do," she whispered, then turned worried eyes on her father. "Please don't tell him."

Ben reached out and patted her hand. "I won't. So you're thinking of marrying him, even though you feel he doesn't love you?"

"I've weighed it from every angle, Dad. Bobby needs his father, more every day. Look how excited he got over the invitation to go camping with Brady. Jess adores his son, and what Bobby feels for him is becoming stronger by the day. As for me, I don't see myself falling in love with anyone else." She smiled weakly. "It's a big mess, Dad."

"Are you that sure of Jess's feelings? Or maybe I should say, lack of feelings?"

Casey hesitated. "Actually, I'm sure of very little. I can only go by what I feel from him. Jess would probably be...well, an affectionate husband, but I don't think it would be out of love." Casey's cheeks had gotten pink with that admission.

"Don't be embarrassed, Casey. There's nothing shameful about physical love between a man and women who are in love with each other."

She dropped her eyes. She and Jess didn't quite fit that mold, did they?

"I tried to call you, Jess, but there was no answer."

"I've been working on the barn." Jess was standing on the small front porch of Casey's house. He'd come to see Bobby, but Bobby had gone camping with his uncle and cousins. "I'll come back tomorrow night."

He was so excitingly handsome, standing at her door, and Casey's insides were acting up something terrible. His shirt was a white-on-white pattern, and fit his long, lean torso like a made-to-order glove. His jeans, dark blue and quite new-looking, hugged his narrow hips and muscular thighs. His skin was that lovely toasty color she found so fascinating, and his thick dark hair was neatly arranged, unusually controlled, just daring someone to muss it up with a flippant caress.

She didn't want him to leave.

"Would . . . would you like to come in?"

Jess's gaze shot to hers with the precision and impact of a well-aimed, steel-shafted arrow. There was no logical reason for the invitation, not with Bobby gone. He probed the depths of her green eyes for an explanation and saw a strange sort of confusion. "Yes, I'd like to come in," he said quietly, but his heart had begun pumping his blood faster.

Casey stood back from the door, holding her breath while he passed by her. Her emotions were turbulent, her mind a whirl-pool. She wasn't sure what she was doing, but she didn't want him to leave.

"Please sit down. I'll get us something to drink."

"Thanks." Jess perched uneasily on the edge of a chair, while Casey hurried to the kitchen. He heard the refrigerator door open and close, and then she was back with two ice-cold bottles of beer. She sat on the sofa, exactly as she had last Saturday night. Everything was like last Saturday night—where they each were sitting, the bottles in their hands—except for what was in the air. That was something new and incredibly exciting. Jess watched her while he tilted his bottle for a drink.

She stared back, then asked with studied nonchalance, "Are you dating anyone?"

Startled, Jess lowered his beer. "No, are you?" He was afraid to hope, but Casey had to be aware of the sexually charged atmosphere in the room.

"No."

"Are we having this conversation for a reason?"

Casey's heart was knocking against her rib cage. "I . . . I'm not sure. Do you object to it?"

Casey was wearing yellow shorts and a matching sleeveless, low-necked T-shirt. The day had been warm, and she must have changed clothes after work, Jess decided. Her feet were bare, but there was a pair of tan leather sandals in front of the couch. Her hair was tangled, as if it hadn't been brushed since morning, and her face was almost free of makeup. She hadn't planned this, Jess realized. Whatever was happening was spontaneous.

But . . . just what *was* happening?

"No, I don't object," Jess replied with less restraint in his voice. He'd been very careful with Casey ever since the night he'd learned that she'd never been married. He'd fully intended keeping his promise not to bother her again, and his visits to the house had been only to see Bobby. If he'd suffered at seeing Casey and knowing it was over between them, he'd kept it to himself. But this—her mood tonight—was an intriguing change of attitude. "I'll talk about anything you want to discuss."

"Well, I don't have a list of topics or anything," Casey said with sudden nervousness, which Jess didn't miss. "Actually, I was just making small talk, I guess," she added lamely.

Was he going to let her get away with that? Jess asked himself. It was a blatant lie. There was something on her mind. Or, on second thought, maybe it wasn't her mind she was having trouble with. Casey was a sensual woman. She'd been a sensual woman six years ago, although neither of them had had the sense to recognize her response for what it really was.

Old feelings swirled in Jess's brain. And memories of those nights by the river. He'd been a horse's patoot, maybe, but what man could have resisted the utter abandonment of this beautiful woman? Even then, she'd been completely female. It still amazed Jess that she'd been only seventeen.

Well, she hadn't been only seventeen the night she came to his house. And why was a woman with her drive and passion not dating someone? Why wasn't there a long line of men at her door?

He stretched his long legs out in front of him, adopting a deceptively lazy slouch. "All right. I'm game for a little small talk. In fact, I've got one question I wouldn't mind an answer to."

"Oh? What kind of question?"

"If it's too personal, just say so."

Casey's brief laugh sounded brittle, uncertain. "Of course."

"Fine. Other than the guy you're working for now, I haven't seen you with anyone. How come?"

Casey didn't answer right away. There were several different ways she could answer, and she needed to think about them. She was in a strange mood, she knew; a daring mood. It wasn't that she wanted to tease Jess or lead him on, but she hadn't wanted him to leave and then wonder where he'd gone. He knew almost everything there was to know about her now, and she suddenly realized she didn't want to kid him about her nonexistent love life.

Her gaze rose in a steady look. "Since Bobby was born, I've dated very little. An occasional movie, a dinner out, nothing even remotely serious."

Jess's system began a strange buzzing. He had to clear his throat to speak. "Are you saying what I think you're saying?"

Her eyes remained on him. "What do you think I'm saying?"

"That there hasn't been any other man."

Casey looked away for a beat, then returned her eyes to him. "There hasn't been. You're it, Jess."

"Why?" The word was sharp and piercing, then his voice dropped to a husky caress. "Why, Casey? Why hasn't there been someone else? You're an exciting woman. I can't be the only man who sees that, who feels it.''

Her eyes were a steady green glow, warm and clear within the dark lashes surrounding them. Her voice was sensually husky. "Do *you* feel it, Jess?"

Jess stared. She was issuing an invitation. She was sitting on that couch, kitten soft and radiant in that bright yellow outfit, with her long legs bare and tanned, her toenails painted a pretty coral, the peaks of her breasts all too evident under cotton knit, and issuing an invitation!

The buzzing in his system expanded into a dull roar in his ears. He took a long swig from his bottle, then set it down on the floor by his chair. He got up, slowly, unhurriedly, and watched her eyes follow his movements. She knew he was coming to her, and her reaction was a deep intake of air and a holding action, a waiting.

He crossed the room. It was only three steps on faded blue carpet, and he sat down beside her, not leaning back but sitting sideways, facing her. He took the bottle out of her hand and reached across her to deposit it on the end table. Then he took both her hands and brought them to his lips, watching her face all the while.

He saw the light of response ignite in her eyes, and heard the long release of the breath she'd been holding. "I feel it. I always feel it, Casey. You know I want you. I always want you."

She pulled her right hand loose from his grasp and reached up to touch his hair. "I want you, too."

His eyes searched hers. "Just for tonight?"

"Would you be angry if I said I didn't know?"

"Do you still think you're weak where I'm concerned?"

A silent renunciation took place behind Casey's eyes. *No, I'm not weak. I'm in love!* "You have something I've never found in another man," she said simply. "If responding to it is weakness, then I'm weak."

"My Lord," he mumbled, shaken to his soul. "Casey, I don't want to hurt you again."

"Will you?"

"Not intentionally. But I didn't set out to hurt you before, and look what happened." He'd promised never to mention marriage to her again, but the word was scorching his brain. If she wanted him so much, why not marry him? If she'd never found what they had with another man, why not seal their future with vows and wedding rings?

Casey had been staring at his mouth while he spoke. The power of the look was wringing Jess out. "Do you know what you're doing to me?" he whispered raggedly.

"I know what you're doing to me. Kiss me." She leaned forward, bringing her mouth to within a fraction of his. "Kiss, me, Jess. I'm burning for you."

Groaning, he wrapped his arms around her and kissed her fiercely, hungrily, His tongue was in her mouth for long, breathless moments, and his hand moved on her breasts. "Oh, Jess," she whispered breathily against his lips.

"Casey, Casey..." He pressed her down on the couch and their kisses got hotter and wilder. He pushed her T-shirt up, and then lavished all of the desire tormenting him on the beauty of her bared breasts.

"The bedroom," she whispered.

"Yes, the bedroom." His head spinning dazedly, Jess scrambled up. He took her hand and brought her to her feet, and together, arm in arm, stopping to kiss and taste each other every few steps, they made their way to Casey's bedroom. She closed the door, symbolically blocking out the world. This moment was hers—hers and Jess's.

In a minute they were naked. Casey moved to him and wound her arms around him, pressing her hot skin to his. Her mouth moved over his chest, his throat. "You're so beautiful," she whispered. "So utterly beautiful."

Her lips traveled downward, and then she was on her knees and kissing him intimately. Her aggressiveness drew Jess deeper into the smoldering caldron of their desire, and his pleasure at her boldness was so acute it brought a rumbling growl from his chest.

"I love you, Casey," he whispered hoarsely.

She didn't contradict him, remembering that he'd always been free and generous with such sentiments during lovemaking.

Jess took her arms and lifted her to her feet so he could kiss her lips. They moved to the bed, and he leaned over her while his fingertips adored and explored the curves of her body. His mouth followed close behind. His breath heated her breasts, her waist, her inner thighs and finally the very center of her desire.

This was not the first time Jess had made love to her like that. Six years ago Jess had turned her innocence to passion, and their lovemaking had been totally uninhibited. With Jess there were no taboos. She had fallen wildly, irreversibly in love with his reckless lovemaking, and the emotion was so strong now, she felt smothered by it.

She heard the whimpering deep in her throat, and remembered Jess's comment that day about wanting to make her whimper. He knew he could do it, and she knew it, too.

But she could also make him whimper. They had some mysterious sexual power over each other, and it had started six long years ago. Her only trouble with it was that she'd also fallen in love.

Casey's hands slid over his back and shoulders. She twisted her fingers in his hair. She traced the contours of his rugged features. And her desire rose and gathered and exploded into white-hot spasms of pure ecstasy.

Jess moved up and held her while her emotions cooled. Their bodies were no longer dry. The room was warm, though the window was open, and their skin glistened with a fine layer of perspiration.

When she was breathing more normally, Jess looked into her eyes. "We belong together," he whispered.

Her lashes fell, fanning out on the soft skin just below her eyes.

"Casey?"

"Don't talk, please." She knew he was right. They *did* belong together, and they were going to be together, too. But some small part of her still held out. One stubborn area of her brain still hoped and ardently wished he would fall in love with her. The words he uttered in the throes of passion meant little. She'd heard them six years ago, too.

Jess's promise to remain silent on the subject of marriage taunted him. And it was all too apparent that Casey still didn't want to hear about it, anyway. He sighed, lowered his mouth to hers and kissed her into a second response. When he raised his head, her eyes were dreamy and soft, containing that light of desire he knew he'd see.

He stretched an arm down to his pants on the floor and found his wallet. Again Casey watched the sensible process of birth control. "You've become more cautious," she said quietly.

He moved between her thighs and looked down at her. "Didn't I do that six years ago?"

"No, you didn't."

Jess shook his head. "I was a jerk, Casey. That's my only excuse, which is pretty damned unacceptable, I know."

She sighed. "You weren't a jerk. You probably thought I was on the Pill."

"I wish I could say that was true, but I honestly don't remember."

"I know."

He touched her face, caressing her lower lip with his thumb. "I feel you, Casey. In here." His hand detoured to his chest, then returned to her mouth.

"In your heart?"

"In whatever's in there. I want you so much—not for just tonight. Is that love?"

A small thrill darted within her, but just until she remembered that he was still as aroused as he'd been when they started. Only *she* had reached a more serene plateau, although Jess's body pressing into hers was again creating internal demands.

He held her face and kissed her lips, his mouth opening and taking hers, possessing hers. And then, while his tongue roamed and tasted and teased, he claimed her body.

Casey released a long, soulful breath and closed her eyes for the joyous ride. She knew what it was like with Jess, and it was what she had needed badly enough to invite him into her house tonight. Her hips lifted in unison with his thrusts, and he reached that point of searing heat within her that even her initial release, as beautiful as it had been, hadn't been able to quench.

It was the ultimate pleasure. No matter what else they did—the kisses, the caresses, the touching and fondling—no matter how exciting every other phase of their lovemaking was, this was the best. She was beginning to see herself readily settling for a completely physical relationship and giving her son his father. No doubt some very good marriages had been built on less, and perhaps her deep, abiding love for both Jess and Bobby would be enough to bond the three of them into a family.

Casey began to weep as sensation built and her emotions expanded. Jess was a masterful lover: strong, demanding, tireless. Casey's old bed rocked rhythmically with energies never before imposed upon it. Limbs intertwined and positions altered slightly, but the forces of nature never wavered. And gradually, excitingly, the explosion of completion drew nearer and nearer.

They climaxed only seconds apart, each crying out, each clinging to the other, taking gasping, needful kisses, whispering words and phrases of untamed, unthinking joy.

Then it was over. The bed was silent and still, the room was silent and still, the world was silent but spinning faster than normally. It took several minutes for Casey's racing pulse to relax. Her body was at peace—free from the feverish needs that had driven her to Jess's arms again. But it would happen again and again. Jess had said it aptly: one didn't extinguish this kind of blaze with one glass of water. In her case, Casey suspected the entire Pacific Ocean might not do the trick.

She stirred, moving her legs beneath the weight of his. Jess raised his head. His eyes were dark, his expression was sober. "We're not going to stay away from each other, are we?"

"Apparently not."

"An affair, then?"

The word *marriage* stuck in her throat. If he mentioned it now, asked her right now, she would say yes. But he had promised, and if it were to be discussed she would have to bring it up. She realized that she couldn't; the words simply would not come. Casey felt sick at the thought that if she couldn't talk about it at a time like this, when could she?

"Must we label it?" she whispered shakily.

"No, not if you don't want to." He pressed a gentle kiss to the corner of her mouth. "May I stay the night?"

Suddenly the world rushed into the room. She lived in town now; she had neighbors to think of, she had to get up early and go to work in the morning. "I don't think so."

He studied her. "When can I see you again?"

"You said you were coming back tomorrow night," she reminded.

"To see Bobby."

"Yes, to see Bobby."

"How will I see *you*?"

They both knew there was no chance of intimacy during Jess's visits to Bobby. And they had both stopped denying that intimacy was what they had to have from each other.

"Perhaps on Friday night. I could probably bring Bobby to the ranch for the night. I'll call my mother and find out for sure."

"Fine. I'll pick you up there."

"Yes, all right. Friday night. If Mom can't watch Bobby for some reason, I'll let you know."

There was so much unsaid between them. But Jess got up, disappeared into the bathroom for a few minutes, then came out and put his clothes on. Casey had donned a robe while he was gone, and she sat on the bed and brushed her hair while he dressed.

Their eyes kept meeting. They both knew their relationship was vastly different from what it had been, but neither felt they could comment on it.

"Walk me to the door?" Jess asked softly.

"All right." Casey put down the hairbrush and got to her feet. It had grown dark and Casey switched on the hall light. In the living room, at the front door, Jess put his arms around her. His kiss was warm and gentle and slightly inquisitive. Casey knew why. He was questioning her change of heart, or more accurately, her aggressive behavior tonight.

Her mouth lingered on his. "I love your taste," she whispered. His hand slid down her back to her hips.

"What else do you love?"

You! All of you! Every masculine inch of you! Your voice, your smile, your smell, your walk!

Deliberately she put on a seductively teasing smile. "What else do you think I love?"

He inched closer, pressing their bodies tightly together. "Casey, we're so right for each other, it boggles my mind."

"In bed."

"In bed, maybe out of bed, too."

Casey's breath caught. Maybe now...

"Well, I'll see you tomorrow night, but I'll be counting the hours until Friday night."

Her smile veiled the sadness in her heart. "I will, too. Good night, Jess."

Twelve

Friday saw the temperature soar. The law offices weren't air-conditioned, and Wes had placed several fans around for some relief from the unusually muggy heat. All morning Casey had battled a rather unique sort of anxiety, which was really a mixture of physical discomfort from the humidity and nervous anticipation of the evening ahead. Lucille and Ben were happy to have Bobby for the night and, Casey suspected, even happier because she was going out with Jess. It was increasingly apparent that her parents would be delighted if she and Jess were to marry.

Which was exactly the matter that had Casey on such pins and needles. She'd decided to talk to Jess about marriage that night. During his visit to Bobby on Wednesday evening, both she and Jess had been in obvious distress over maintaining a respectable distance from each other. Their mutual glances and a long, simmering good-night kiss had contained all sorts of sensual promises for Friday night.

At noon Casey drove home for lunch. She did that often, just to check on Bobby, although Dora Martin was a very capable sitter. They all had soup and sandwiches together, and Bobby prattled on about a variety of subjects. The camping trip was still a point of excitement, and the seven puppies on Jess's ranch another topic he never tired of discussing.

After kisses and hugs, Casey returned to work. The clock seemed to move slowly. While typing some letters for Wes, Casey thought of ways to begin the talk with Jess that evening. There was no reason to beat around the bush or play coy, she finally decided. She'd come right out and ask him if he still wanted to marry her.

The telephone rang a few times during the sluggish afternoon, and when it jangled at four, Casey reached for it as usual. "Law office," she answered, which was the greeting Wes had requested she use.

Dora Martin's voice was strangely abnormal. "Casey? I don't want you to become alarmed or upset. I'm sure he's not far, but Bobby's wandered out of the yard."

An icy hand clutched Casey's chest. "How long ago? When did you notice?"

"About a half hour ago. I've been walking around the neighborhood looking for him."

A lead weight seemed to have invaded Casey's midsection. "Dora, did you check the Monahans' place? They have three children that Bobby has played with a few times."

"Yes, and the Cartwrights', too, although their boy is older than Bobby."

Casey fought the panic closing in on her. Where would Bobby go? Why had he left the yard? She had laid down one irrevocable rule, drumming it into her son's head: *You must never, never leave the yard without asking permission, either mine or Mrs. Martin's.* She had repeated it until it was coming out of Bobby's ears. Or, so she'd believed.

"I'll be right there, Dora." In her haste, Casey slammed the phone down and took her handbag out of the drawer in one motion. She was on her feet and halfway to the door when she remembered where she was. Dashing back to Wes's open office door, she recited breathlessly, "I've got to leave, Wes. My sitter just called and said she can't find Bobby."

Without waiting to see or hear Wes's startled reaction, Casey ran from the office, down the hall, down the stairs and out to her car. Her driving was based strictly on habit, because her mind was already at home, running through the neighborhood, searching for places that her small son might have gone.

And then Casey remembered the puppy. Was Rusty at home? The fat, waddling little puppy was never more than a foot behind Bobby's energetic movements. Where Bobby went, so did Rusty. It seemed like a critical point to Casey. If the puppy was gone, too, then Bobby had merely taken a notion to go off somewhere. But if the puppy had been left behind . . .

Shuddering, Casey stopped herself from dwelling on the horrifying possibility of someone taking Bobby. The school! Yes, he might have gone to the grade school. He'd been enthralled with the school's ample playground, its swings and slides, its jungle gym. Periodically Casey had walked the route with Bobby, then let him enjoy the playground for a half hour or so, wanting to completely familiarize him with the three blocks he would be walking every day when school started.

Dora Martin was waiting at the front gate when Casey pulled up. "Is the puppy here?" Casey called as she got out of the car.

"No, the puppy's gone, too."

Casey heaved a relieved sigh. "All right. Tell me exactly what happened."

Dora couldn't quite meet Casey's eyes. "Bobby was playing in the backyard. I could hear him through the windows very well, and I sat down to read the paper. He came in once and got a drink of water and asked if he could have some cookies. I told him yes, and he went back outside. About an hour ago I realized that I hadn't heard him for a little while, so I went out back to check on him."

Casey could see that the older woman was devastated. No one could stare at a child for eight hours a day. Bobby could have wandered out of the yard just as easily with his mother present. "We'll find him, Dora. He couldn't have gone far in an hour. On the way home I thought of the school. That's the first place I'm going to look."

"I'll come with you."

"No, I'd rather have you check the neighborhood again."

"All right, Casey. I'll never forgive myself if some harm should come—"

"Don't even think it!" Casey jumped back into her car and started away. She drove slowly, peering in all directions, taking the same route that she'd taught Bobby to use to reach Blythe's elementary school. Any moment now she'd spot him, Casey told herself. Any second she'd see a small, black-haired boy in jeans and a blue T-shirt, with a fat little rust-colored puppy on his heels.

There were three children playing on the swings at the school's playground. Casey parked and walked over to them. "Hi, kids, I'm looking for my little boy. His name's Bobby and he has black hair. Have any of you seen him?"

The three shook their heads solemnly. Casey smiled tremulously. "Thanks. If you should see a little boy with a reddish-brown puppy, would you tell him that his mother is looking for him?"

The three nodded, and Casey gave the otherwise empty schoolyard a troubled, sweeping glance, then strode back to her car. She sat at the wheel a moment. Where next? Where would he go? What had been in his little-boy mind to take him through that gate and into a world he was just barely becoming familiar with?

He wasn't used to being cooped up, Casey thought with a rapidly sinking heart. On the ranch there had been only a few areas that had been off-limits—the breeding pens, the bulls' pastures—and Bobby had grown up knowing those particular sites were dangerous. Other than those, he'd had free run of the Oliver ranch. He probably didn't understand, despite warnings, why a simple excursion out of his own yard would panic his mother.

And his father!

Jess! She had to call Jess. Quickly Casey started the car and headed back home. Dora was on the street, and Casey stopped to pick her up. "He's not at the school."

"He had a quarter in his pocket, Casey. Would he have gone to the store to spend it?"

Casey remembered the quarter Bobby had found in the grass several days before, and how she'd told him he could keep it. Casey's spirits lifted a notch. "Why, yes, that's a possibility, Dora. We'll go and see."

But a check of the nearest store, and then several others within what Casey considered Bobby's walking distance, proved futile. Casey drove back to her house and parked at the curb. "I don't know where to look next," she said, her voice unsteady from mounting fear. "I've got to talk to... Dora, I'm going in and make some phone calls."

"Call the sheriff, Casey."

The two women's eyes met in a frightened exchange. Casey nodded numbly. "Yes. I should have thought of that myself."

Jess was in the shower, trying to hurry, when he heard the phone ringing. He'd spent the day working outside, and it was getting very close to the time that he was to pick up Casey at the Oliver ranch. Muttering an oath of irritation, he turned the spray off, grabbed a towel and dripped water all the way to the phone on the stand beside his bed. "Hello." It was said none too cordially.

"Jess, this is Casey."

His irritation vanished like a puff of smoke, but before he could say anything, Casey rushed on. "I've been trying to call you for several hours. Jess, I... we... no one... I can't find Bobby."

The words hit him like a ton of bricks, but it took a moment for any real comprehension. "What do you mean, you can't find Bobby? Where is he?"

Casey was so on edge, she let out a rude, disbelieving laugh. "If I knew where he was, I'd know where to find him, wouldn't I? Jess, half the town is looking for him. I've been calling you for..."

"You mean he's gone? How? I thought that sitter you have is a reliable woman. Wait a minute. Who was supposed to be watching him? Did it just happen, or—"

"Damn you! Don't you dare start looking for someone to blame. At this point I don't care who was supposed to be watching him, and besides, Dora Martin *was* watching him. He simply wandered off. It could have happened with me in the house."

"Not likely," Jess snorted. He was having trouble with the most consuming fury of his life. His son, his beautiful, perfect son was missing? How? Damn it to hell, *why*? "Where are you calling from?"

"Home. I'm at home."

"Stay there. I'll be there in ten minutes."

Casey put the phone down and burst into tears. She'd wept on and off since she'd talked to the sheriff's department. "We'll alert every car to be on the lookout, Mrs. Maddox," she'd been told. Which hadn't been a great deal of comfort. Rationally she understood that the world couldn't come to a halt because one small boy had disobediently sought excitement out of his own yard, but "rationally" didn't soothe her aching heart.

She'd called her mother then, and Lucille had immediately organized the family. Dora had gone up and down Third Street again, and within an hour dozens of people were combing the area. Casey heard over and over again, "We'll find him. How far could a little boy get in a few hours?"

How far? In what direction? For what purpose? Blythe was a small town, easily traversible by an adult on foot in a short period of time. But no one thought that the youngster had gone very far. The consensus was that Bobby was blissfully unaware of the furor he'd caused and was playing in some nearby neighbor's backyard. Casey prayed it was true.

House by house, street by street, the search began. Casey had run back and forth between her family, who were directing the efforts of the concerned volunteers, and her own house, trying again and again to reach Jess. She honestly hadn't expected him to get angry, and his reaction seemed like a final straw in the terrible day. It pointed up, much too clearly, that the two of them weren't even close to the kind of communication it took to make a happy marriage. On top of her almost insane fear for Bobby, the understanding that she'd been hoping for the impossible with Jess was too much to bear with any sort of stiff-upper-lip attitude.

Collapsing onto a kitchen chair, Casey put her head down on her arms on the table and wept with anger and frustration and fear. Where was Bobby? Where was her precious son?

Jess was driving fast, cursing one second, praying the next. His mouth was grim, his eyes full of pain. If something happened to Bobby, he wouldn't be able to deal with it. He'd never accept it, never.

Then his spirit rebelled at such morbid thoughts. Nothing had happened to his son. He'd find Bobby. The little fellow had only gone exploring. It was perfectly natural. Little boys were naturally curious creatures, easily forgetting rules and warnings.

He could remember his own boyhood. No, that wasn't a good example. No one had given a particular damn what he'd done. He could have stayed away from the house for days and no one would have cared. In fact, he'd done exactly that, sometimes sleeping in the streets.

Bobby was different.

No, it wasn't Bobby that was different, it was Casey. Casey was a wonderful, caring mother, unlike the woman Jess had called "Mom." Casey loved Bobby with the protective attention of a she-bear. Casey must be going through hell.

Jess mouthed a vile word, directed at himself. Casey had called, hoping for his support in this frightening situation, and had he given her any? No. He'd started looking for someone to blame!

Striking the steering wheel, Jess cursed his own stupidity. Would he ever learn? How much abuse would a woman take before she found the strength to put a man out of her life for good? Sure, they were great in bed, but a woman needed more than sex from a man. She needed support and confirmation and collaboration. She needed understanding and sustenance and . . .

She needed love. Casey needed love. She'd said it point-blank several times.

A choking sensation clogged Jess's throat, but along with it he felt as if he'd just been struck a blow. His vision cleared, his *inner* vision. How could he have been so blind? So dense? He loved Casey. *He loved Casey Oliver!*

Something joyous leaped through his system. But it was closely followed by a harsh dose of reality. At this point, nothing else really mattered but Bobby.

Jess rounded a curve in the road, traveling so fast that the tires on the pickup squealed in protest. And then, his eyes bugging out of his head in shock, he slammed the brakes on. The rear of the pickup fishtailed in a screeching stop, and Jess was out of the cab in a flash.

Bobby grinned. "Hi, Jess. Where ya going?"

The little boy's face was dirty and sunburned. He had a plastic bottle tied to his belt and he was carrying his puppy. "Rusty was getting awfully tired, Jess."

So much emotion rocked Jess that he couldn't speak at first. Then he knelt down in the dirt at the side of the road and put his hands on his son's shoulders. "Were you getting tired, too, pardner?"

"A little," Bobby admitted. "I was coming to see you, Jess. It's a long ways to your house, isn't it?"

"A long ways, Bobby." Jess glanced down at the plastic bottle. "I see you brought some water with you. That was smart."

"Uncle Brady told me that a good camper never goes anywhere without a water bottle."

"Well, your Uncle Brady is right. I was on my way to your house. How about you and Rusty coming with me?"

"Sure."

Jess knew his hands were trembling when he took the puppy from Bobby's arms. "Rusty seems all tuckered out."

"He walked an awful long ways, Jess. Then he just sat down. I called him and called him, but he wouldn't come. So I had to carry him."

Jess took his son's small hand in his. "Can't leave a friend behind, pardner." He helped Bobby up into the cab of the pickup, put Rusty on the seat beside him and climbed in himself. The boy and the fat little puppy, both with droopy eyelids, settled down. They were both "all tuckered out."

Jess drove the speed limit now. "So, you were coming to see me, huh?"

"It didn't seem so far before."

"That's because you rode, Bobby. Your mother's very worried about you."

Bobby's eyes got big. "Is she home from work?"

"It's getting pretty late, pardner. Didn't you notice the sun starting to go down?"

"Well, yeah, I was starting to get worried about that. But I thought I'd be getting to your place pretty soon. Is Mom mad at me?"

"I don't think she's mad, Bobby. But you should never go off like that without telling someone."

"I was going to, Jess, but..." The little boy looked shame-faced. "I guess I just forgot."

On the outskirts of Blythe, Jess slowed down, but he drove the shortest possible route to Casey's house. He spotted Ben on the street with some other people, and he tooted his horn and stopped. "Ben, he's all right. I've got him right here in the pickup with me," he yelled out the window.

"Oh, thank God." Ben, Lucille and a small crowd rushed over to the truck. After a brief explanation, Jess broke off the conversation with "I've got to get him home. Casey must be frantic."

"Yes, she is." Ben peered in at his grandson and received a weak smile. Clearly, Bobby was beginning to see the folly of his adventure. "I'll tell everyone and break this up, Jess. You go to Casey. And tell her we love her."

"I'll do that, Ben. I'll also tell her that *I* love her."

Ben smiled a slow smile of understanding, and when Jess drove away, he put his arm around his wife. "I think every-thing's going to be all right with our Casey, honey."

Casey heard a vehicle stopping out front, and she raised her head, suspecting that Jess had arrived. She didn't want to face his anger or accusations. She didn't want to hear that she'd been neglectful, that their son wouldn't be missing if she hadn't moved to town and put him in the hands of a sitter. She was having trouble enough with guilt-ridden indictments without hearing them from Jess.

And then she heard "Mom?"

"Bobby!"

Leaping out of the chair, Casey ran to the front door. "Bobby...oh, Bobby!" Lunging through the door, she caught her son up into her arms. She squeezed his small, solid little body and kissed his dirty face, laughing and crying all the while. Then she swatted his behind and hugged him again. "Where did you go? Where were you?"

"I went to see Jess. Mom, you're squashing me."

Casey let her squirming son slide down until his feet were on the porch floor. Then she looked at Jess. Rusty was in his arms, and for once the wiggly little puppy seemed content to be immobile. Casey avoided looking directly into Jess's eyes. "Where did you find him?"

"On the road, about three miles from town."

"Three miles?" Casey's mouth was dry, although it seemed that her eyes contained another bucket of tears just aching to be spilled. She blinked hard. "Let's go in. Oh! I've got to tell Dad and—"

"I already did. He said he'd let everyone know that Bobby's okay."

It was over. Casey's head was throbbing, her eyes were burning like two live coals from crying, but the nightmare was over. She would have to have a serious talk with her son, but not tonight. He was dirty, tired and had to be hungry. And her emotions hadn't settled down enough to discuss his misconduct with any degree of common sense. One instinct made her want to paddle his behind, while another urged her to pick him up and cradle him as she would an infant.

Maternalism took over. Inside the little house, Rusty padded to his box and curled up into a fat, rusty ball of exhausted puppy. Bobby was too dirty and sweaty to either eat or be put to bed. "I'll run a bath for you," Casey told her son. "Maybe Jess will help you with it while I make some dinner."

"I'll be glad to," Jess agreed quietly. Casey's red eyes and restless, fretful energy were clear evidence of the anguish she'd just lived through. He wanted to soothe her, to take her in his arms and stroke her hair and tell her he loved her, that he'd finally realized how much she meant to him. He wanted to beg her forgiveness, plead for an understanding that he was afraid to really hope for. When she had desperately needed him, he'd given her negativity, disapprobation. He felt sick to his stomach with shame and self-reproach.

Bobby was too tired to eat much. Shiny clean, wearing his pajamas, he was falling asleep at the table. Casey got up. "Come on, honey. Let's get you tucked in."

Jess stayed seated. He hadn't eaten much, either. He sipped from his glass of iced tea while Casey put Bobby to bed. She hadn't invited him to the evening ritual, and he felt he shouldn't intrude. Not tonight.

Casey returned very quickly. "He's already sleeping," she said as she began to clear the table.

Jess watched her closely. She was calmer than when he and Bobby had first arrived, but there was still an underlying tension in her movements. "Three miles is quite a hike for a little guy."

Casey carried a stack of dishes to the sink. Then her shoulders squared and she turned. "Jess, I don't want to go on with our..."

There was determination in her green eyes, but also a strange cast of sadness. "Our affair?" he finished softly. "I couldn't agree more." He stood up. "Something happened to me today. I don't know what to call it, Casey, but a bolt of lightning couldn't have struck any harder. I was driving fast, trying to get here. I was furious, raging at fate or whatever it was that was threatening Bobby."

He moved a step closer. "Then I remembered your call and how I'd reacted." He took another step.

One of Casey's hands came up in a restraining gesture. "Don't, Jess. I don't want you to touch me. This conversation is not going to lead to the bedroom."

His voice dropped. "And if I touch you, it will?"

Casey's chin came up. "It's not enough anymore. All you and I have is sex. There's more to life and relationships, Jess. There's respect and communication, there's..."

"Love?"

The word intruded, almost rudely. Casey hadn't expected it, and it stalled her train of thought. She stared into blue eyes that looked startlingly, rebelliously alive.

"I love you, Casey. That's what I've been trying to tell you. It hit me all of a sudden, from out of nowhere. It was just before I saw Bobby."

Powerful emotions attacked Casey, weakening her, liquefying her bones. She turned to face the sink, and she held on with both hands while her eyes squeezed tightly shut. Her mind wouldn't quite take Jess's words in, and they hovered on the edge of her consciousness. All of the doubts that today's horror had brought so vividly to light again buffeted her. It could be a trick, a ploy. He'd been scared senseless, just as she'd been. He might do anything to get Bobby under his protection.

She felt his hand on her back. "Casey? Look at me."

Her eyes opened listlessly. "Go away, Jess. Please just go away and leave me alone."

"You don't believe me."

"Did you expect I would?"

Her voice was dull, lifeless. He hadn't anticipated out-and-out denial. His feelings were so real now, so defined. But how could he convince *her* of that?

"Go away," she whispered.

"No, I'm not going to go away. I love you, and I'm going to find a way to prove it to you."

She turned then, and a spark of anger showed in her eyes. "How?"

"Why would I lie about it?"

"To get Bobby."

"Bobby." Jess's gaze flicked toward the hallway, which led to the bedrooms, and he realized that even if there were no Bobby, God forbid, he would love Casey. This mess was all his doing. He'd all but ruined Casey's life six years ago, and then, when he'd returned and found out he had a son, he'd used any and all means to cajole Casey into marriage. No wonder she wouldn't, or couldn't, believe him now.

His eyes misted. "Is it really that hopeless? Casey, I'm baring my soul to you. I love you with everything I am. Lord help me, I don't know why it took so long to realize it. Or maybe it just happened. I don't know. I don't have any glib answers."

Casey took a shaky breath. There was moisture in Jess's eyes and a stunningly different expression on his face. Her senses warred. She'd wavered back and forth so many times on Jess, and she was afraid to believe him. But she wanted to, she desperately wanted to. She knew she had to guard against her own feelings influencing her. If she were to trust Jess, she must do it because of him, not because she was still putty in his hands.

"We'll talk," she said huskily. "Give me a few minutes alone." Slipping past him, Casey went down the hall to the bathroom. Her hands were trembling while she washed her face and brushed her hair. She took the time to put on just a little makeup, as her face was pale and drawn.

Then she went across the hall to Bobby's room. The little boy was sleeping so soundly, Casey could hear him breathing. He'd walked more than three miles, he and his puppy, trying to pay

Jess a visit. Why? What mysterious force of nature had made Bobby disobey explicit orders and set out on a fifteen-mile walk?

Of course Bobby didn't understand distances very well. In a car one made the trip in a very few minutes.

He loved Jess, didn't he? This small boy loved his father, without even knowing that Jess *was* his father. It was probably a response to what he felt from Jess; no man had ever given him the undivided, unconditional affection that Jess did. Ben and Bobby's uncles were wonderful to the little boy, but Bobby felt the extraspecial emotions he aroused in Jess; he sensed Jess's love for him.

Casey choked on the thought. It was what she had to have from Jess to believe him—that *sense* of love.

She bent over and kissed her son's smooth, warm cheek. The least she owed him—and herself, too—was to make the effort of a completely honest discussion with Jess.

Thirteen

When she walked into the living room, Jess got to his feet. He probed Casey's facial expression, searching for a clue to what she might be thinking after having had some time alone. There was little to be seen in her face, although she did look calmer. "Are you all right?"

"Sit down, Jess." He'd been at one end of the couch, and while he resumed his seat, Casey chose a chair. "I think it's time that you and I stopped even the slightest bit of game playing. I'm going to be totally honest, and I would appreciate the same from you."

"Agreed," Jess said quietly, willing to do whatever she might suggest.

"I had made up my mind to talk to you about marriage tonight." At Jess's startled expression, Casey held up a hand. "Let me finish. From the time you first brought up marriage, I've gone back and forth on it. I fought a dozen emotional battles because of Bobby. He took to you right away, and I went through jealousy, resentment and guilt because of it. I really didn't know that the two of you would become close so quickly, and I didn't like it."

"That's understandable," Jess put in.

"Yes," Casey agreed. "It was understandable. What wasn't quite so easily grasped were my own feelings for you. Under all the hatred and anger and resentment lay something I didn't want to face. I fought it with every ounce of my strength, Jess. I had to ask myself why, when I had such positive proof of the kind of man you are—or were—was I so weak with you? Why, when you touched me, did I forget all the pain and humiliation I went through because of you?"

When her pause stretched on, Jess asked softly, "And did you find an answer to those questions?"

"Yes." Casey lifted her chin. "I fell in love with you at seventeen, Jess, and after you came back, I fell in love with you again. Maybe it never stopped. Maybe, even while I was hating you, I loved you. I don't know. Like you said about yourself a few minutes ago, I don't have all the answers."

Jess wanted to rush across the room and gather her into his arms. But Casey's expression deterred the impulse. She spoke again. "I knew that you didn't love me. No, please don't deny it. You didn't. But we had . . . other things."

"Sex," Jess interjected in a voice that was beginning to relay the anguish Casey's honesty was creating.

"Yes, sex. I wanted more, Jess. I wanted what my parents have, what my brothers and sister have. I wanted harmony, and closeness. I wanted that special communication that only occurs between people who are really in love with each other. But then I decided to settle for less. I thought all kinds of crazy things. Maybe you'd fall in love with me after we were married, for one."

"Casey. . ."

"Anyway, I was going to talk to you about it tonight. Then Bobby disappeared. I called you two and three times every hour. I was afraid to leave town and drive out to your place, so I kept calling. I was sure you were working outside and couldn't hear the phone, but I knew you'd want to know. I was scared to death, and the thought of you coming and sharing the agony with me was comforting. I kept calling."

Jess's skin had paled to a sickly gray. Casey went on. "You were cruel on the phone, and I knew then that we had no chance of having a stable marriage. I felt it would be a travesty, with no possible conclusion but unhappiness for all three of us.''

Jess slumped back on the sofa, looking at her, staring at her. When she remained silent, he asked, ''Is that all? Are you through?''

''Yes.''

''All right. Your honesty hurts like hell, Casey. I was already so full of self-disgust I didn't think there was room for any more. But there was. I've been the worst kind of jerk there is, and I'm not going to try and soft-pedal anything I've done.'' Rising, Jess restlessly paced the small room.

''When I decided on Blythe, you came to mind. I remembered you as a sexy dish. Yes, I know that's an insult now, but that was what was in my mind. I thought of looking you up, and when I saw you at the rodeo grounds, I was thrilled. You were beautiful—even more beautiful than I remembered. Your hatred baffled me.

''I found out later that day that you'd been married and had a son. But I was glad again, because I also found out you were divorced. I was sure you couldn't possibly hate me—you had no reason to hate me—and I planned to see you again.''

He turned and looked at her. ''Casey, even before I knew Bobby was my son I wanted you. But I won't lie. My feelings were strictly below the belt. You're an arousing, exciting woman, and I wanted to...'' Jess stopped talking and raked his fingers through his hair, then started pacing again.

''Then I figured it all out. Bobby was my son. If you only knew what that did to me. My son.''

Casey heard the emotional cracking of his voice, and she couldn't help a rising empathy. Whatever doubts were tormenting her, she had none where Jess and Bobby were concerned. That bond was firmly set, as surely as if Jess had always been a part of his son's life.

She spoke with more gentleness. ''I did know what that did to you. It was the reason why I began to understand you. Then you talked about your childhood, your life, and I realized how different your background was from anything I'd ever known. You were a different kind of man than I'd ever known. It was probably what made you so attractive six years ago. You had a reckless, go-to-hell, cocky attitude, a swagger in your walk. And, oh, you were sexy.''

Jess had stopped pacing, his eyes on Casey. They exchanged a long look. "Casey, I love you. I love you so damned much. You just said you love me, too. Let yourself believe me, honey. Please.'' Closing the gap between them, Jess knelt beside her. His face expressed an impassioned plea. "Look at me. Look at my eyes. Can't you see how much I love you? Casey, it wasn't there before, but it's there now. You've got to be able to see it.''

She did look. She studied and probed the depths of his eyes. She was afraid to trust the adoring light she saw, and yet she was moved by it. Her resistance slipped, but a tiny flame of fear still burned. "I won't settle for second best, Jess. I can't. I know that now.''

"You won't have second best. You'll have a man who loves you. No one will ever love you more.''

She sighed softly. "Oh, Jess, I want to believe you.''

She was still wearing the blue dress she'd put on for work that morning. It was rumpled and wrinkled, but she'd forgotten it in the events of the day. Stunned a bit, she realized that Jess's right hand was sliding beneath her skirt, heating the bare skin of her thighs. "That's not going to clarify matters,'' she protested over a suddenly too rapid heartbeat.

"Maybe it will,'' Jess whispered, burying his face in the curve of her throat. "Love me, Casey. Let me love you. Let me show you how much I love you.''

"Jess, you never play completely fair,'' she whispered as his hand nested around the mound of her femininity.

"I'm playing for keeps this time.'' He pressed his lips to the pulse in her throat. "Your heart's beating a mile a minute. So's mine.'' Under her skirt he found the top of her panties and pushed his hand down into them.

"Bobby!'' she gasped, reaching for the one excuse that might stop this delicious onslaught.

"Bobby's sleeping. And if he should happen to wake up and see his mother and father in each other's arms, it wouldn't be the end of the world. He's got to know, Casey. He's got to be told.''

"I know," she moaned. Jess's fingertips were sliding back and forth over her most sensitive spot. "Oh, Jess. What am I going to do with you? You're an incorrigible man."

"You know several things to do with me, honey," he whispered thickly. "I've thought of this ever since Tuesday night. I thought you'd be in my bed, but yours will do just as well."

He was doing it again, making her forget everything else in the heat of his sexuality. That's why she hadn't wanted him to touch her in the kitchen. She knew she couldn't resist his magic. She never had been able to. In despair, Casey began to weep. Tears flooded down her cheeks, and she just let go and sobbed.

Jess froze for a moment, then raised his head. His hand was still under her skirt, and he withdrew it slowly. Strangely, he knew what the problem was. It was almost as if he were reading Casey's mind. He cleared his throat and took her hands in his.

'Casey, look at me."

Sniffling, she brought a watery, resentful gaze to his face. "What for?"

"I love you more than I ever thought it was possible to love someone. I didn't know feelings like this existed. You and Bobby have taught me more about love than anyone else and all of my entire past life has. Will you marry me, Casey? Will you do me the honor of becoming my wife?"

A proposal. A beautifully said, impassioned marriage proposal. Was that what she'd been waiting for? "How...how did you know that's what I was thinking about?" she whispered.

"I sensed it."

He'd said the right thing. He'd unknowingly pushed exactly the right buttons. "Oh, Jess." She slowly slid her hands up his chest and around his neck. "Maybe you do love me."

His eyes were suddenly swimming with tears. "I do, Casey. I love you more than life. I've been the world's biggest idiot. It's so crazy, because I understand why you're afraid of me and yet I can't let it go at that. We're meant to be together. We've always been destined to be together, only I was such a fool. Maybe someday you'll be able to forgive me, but I don't know if I ever will."

Closing her teary eyes, Casey put her forehead against Jess's. She believed him, she realized in a whirling tide of emotions.

She believed him. He loved her. She felt it in every fiber of her being, in her very soul. A sense of peace overlaid the desire to weep and laugh and just let go. Her voice was husky with feeling. "I love you. I love you so much I could die from it."

They held each other, and then Jess laughed. It sounded shaky and more filled with emotion than mirth. "Well, don't die, honey. Not when we're just now getting together." He got to his feet, pulled Casey up from the chair, picked her up, carried her to the couch and settled her on his lap. And then they held each other again—silently, tenderly.

Casey finally stirred, feeling reborn, complete. They exchanged sweet kisses interspersed with words of love, until their feelings were no longer soft pastels but brilliant streaks of aroused reds and greens and blues. Jess whispered against her lips with a note of teasing, "We can talk some more or we can make love. Which do you vote for?"

She nibbled his lips with a happy laugh. "Both."

He enclosed her in a fierce embrace and conveyed his love, which was expanding more with each passing second, in a long, hungry kiss. His voice was hoarse when they finally both needed air. "I love you, lady."

"I love *you* cowboy."

"Can I play under your skirt now?"

She laughed gaily, freely. "You're a wicked thing, aren't you?"

His hand snaked under her dress. "Is this so wicked?"

She sighed and relaxed her thighs. "That's wonderful," she murmured, and after a minute, "Oh, Jess, you make me want you so much," she said needfully.

"You make me want you just by being in the same room. You make me want you when I'm miles away and your beautiful face comes to mind. I honestly don't know how we're going to live in the same house and get anything done, do you?"

Casey gave a weak, fluttery little laugh. He was teasing, but there was a lot of truth in it. Their relationship had begun, so long ago, because of their powerful sexual attraction, and if anything, it was even stronger today. She put her mouth to his ear. "I want your body, cowboy," she whispered seductively.

A lazy, slow smile curved his sexy lips. "Honey, you've got it. Forever and ever. This ramblin' man is ready to settle down for good."

"For good," Casey whispered dreamily. "Those are beautiful words, Jess."

"Beautiful words for a beautiful lady. Oh, Casey," he murmured, suddenly staggered by the need to possess her. The past hours had been emotionally strenuous—for her, for him. Jess wanted to bind their love, to prove it with action, and he began with a kiss containing all the heat in his feverish body.

Happiness mingled with Casey's desire as she returned Jess's passion. The sensation of oneness she was feeling with Jess was what she had dreamed of all her adult life. She had somehow always known that real love would feel like this.

She wanted to show him with her body how much she loved him. Her face was flushed, her lips wet and provocatively swollen, when she tilted her head back and began unbuttoning his shirt. Their gazes met and held until the shirt was open, and then she pressed her mouth to his bared chest. "I will want you just as much in ten years, twenty," she told him.

"Yes," he agreed huskily. "This is for keeps, Casey."

She undid the buckle of his belt. "We won't always see eye to eye on everything."

"Undoubtedly."

She slowly slid the tab of his zipper down. "But we'll talk those times out."

"Definitely."

Casey looked down at the impressive display of aroused masculinity she had uncovered, then raised her eyes to Jess's again. "You're a very beautiful man," she whispered. She watched the drift of smoky emotions on his face as she caressed him intimately. Leaning forward, she pressed her lips to his, slipping her tongue into his mouth.

Groaning, Jess clamped his arms around her, holding her to him with mounting desperation. "Maybe we'd better get out of the living room," he murmured shakily. "I'm on the verge of getting very carried away."

Casey got off of his lap and took his hand. Her legs weren't quite steady, and she teetered slightly as Jess got up. He noticed. "Are you all right?" The day had been traumatic, and Casey would have every right to feel shaky.

She wrapped her arms around his waist and laid her cheek on his bare chest. "I'm fine. You affect me so strongly, Jess."

He held her tightly. "We affect each other. We always did, we always will." Moving away, he bent over, placed an arm behind her thighs and lifted her off the floor.

Casey closed her eyes for the short journey to the bedroom. Once inside, Jess let her feet slide to the floor. "Turn on the lights," he instructed as he closed and locked the door. "I want to see you."

She nodded. She wanted to see him, too—every wonderful inch of Jess Lonnigan. They undressed quickly. Casey threw back the covers of the bed, but before she could lie down, Jess came up behind her. He pressed his nakedness against her back, and his hands began moving over her breasts, her stomach, downward to the triangle of auburn hair at her thighs. His lips warmed the side of her throat.

Heat and desire spiraled through Casey. She felt him lift her left foot to the bed, and the erotic position opened her to his searching fingers. The dizzying sensation of unleashed passion ricocheted through her mind and body, taking her to a new plateau of awareness when she felt the hard shaft of his manhood seeking entry.

"Oh, Jess," she moaned hoarsely when they were tightly joined.

"Do you like it this way?" he whispered.

His fingers were a torment of pulsing rhythm, driving her wild. "I won't last," she rasped.

"Don't try, honey. Go with the flow." Slowly, deliciously, he began to move within her. "I want to give you pleasure," he breathed in her ear.

"To make me whimper," she gasped, referring to the day he'd told her he wanted to undress her and make her whimper.

He remembered that day, too, and his responsive chuckle was low and gravelly. "Yes, to make you whimper."

She could barely speak. "You do that . . . very easily. Oh, Jess . . . Jess . . ." The room turned upside down as the rapturous spasms began, and when she was weeping softly and weakly leaning all her weight back against him, he held her until she had calmed.

Then he left her body and turned her around. His gaze moved over her features. "I love you, lady."

She touched his face. "I love you, Jess. So much."

He brushed at a tear on her cheek. "Jade-green eyes that spill pure diamonds," he whispered.

She smiled. "The result of those whimpers you like so well. I expect you will see a lot of them."

He steered her to the bed. "No matter how many times, it will never be enough." With Casey on her back, Jess leaned over her. He touched a nipple, tracing the rosy areola, then fingering the center bud to rigidity. "We're going to be together every day, every night, from now on. It's a fantastic thought, isn't it?"

"Very." She sighed as his mouth opened around the nipple he'd been teasing. "Very fantastic," she repeated huskily.

Sometime in the night Casey awoke. She lay quietly, then realized that Jess wasn't sleeping, either. "You're awake, too?" she whispered.

"Hi." He turned onto his side and pulled her closer. "I've been lying here thinking about Bobby. Are we really going to tell him who I am?"

"I think we have to, don't you?"

"I'd sure like to, but he's just a little kid. Will he understand?"

"Jess, he has to know. Everyone has to know. Lord," Casey groaned, "the gossips will have a field day."

"Exactly. Honey, we know, you and me. And your folks. Why does anyone else have to get in on it? I'll bet that attorney you work for could draw up adoption papers."

Casey bolted upright. "You'd do that?"

"When Bobby's old enough we can tell him the truth. But what's the point of everyone talking it to death? It's no one else's business, Casey, and Bobby doesn't need to grow up with that kind of gossip about his birth. Yes, I'd file for his adoption, if you agree it's best."

Casey nestled back into his arms. "It's best, but I never would have dreamed of asking you to do that. Jess, you're a surprisingly wonderful man."

He grinned. "Yes, by cracky, I am, aren't I?"

"By cracky?" Casey exploded with laughter. "You're also conceited, by cracky," she quipped when she could speak again. "But you have a right to be." She sighed dramatically. "You're only the sexiest guy who ever walked around on two legs."

Jess laughed. "I love you, lady."

Casey yawned and snuggled closer. "I love *you* cowboy." She was almost asleep when she murmured. "Casey Lonnigan. It has a nice ring, Jess."

He smiled and closed his eyes. The future looked bright and beautiful. Casey, Bobby and Jess Lonnigan. Yes, it did have a nice ring. A very nice ring.

* * * * *

SILHOUETTE® Desire™

COMING NEXT MONTH

#607 GLORY, GLORY—Linda Lael Miller
Years ago, Glory Parsons had been forced to flee her hometown—and Jesse
Bainbridge. Now she's returned with shocking news about his adopted niece.
Could Jesse ever forgive Glory's special secret?

#608 LOOKING FOR TROUBLE—Nancy Martin
Police officer Sheila Malone knew Max Bollinger spelled *trouble*. She thought
the sexy aristocrat was innocent of murder, but proving it would've been easier
if he hadn't also stolen her heart!

#609 THE BRIDAL PRICE—Barbara Boswell
Marry without love? Never! But cool, sophisticated Carling Templeton did just
that to protect her father...never expecting arrogant rancher Kane McClellan
to be the man of her dreams.

#610 UPON A MIDNIGHT CLEAR—Laura Leone
Bah humbug! That's how Fiona Larkin felt at Christmastime. But when
mischief at her pet motel called for the help of security consultant Eli Becker,
Fiona discovered a season of love.

#611 THE PENDRAGON VIRUS—Cait London
When *Ms.* Dallas Pendragon bet macho bachelor Sam Loring that he'd fail
trying to act as a working mother for a month, he expected to win—more than
the wager....

#612 HANDSOME DEVIL—Joan Hohl
Selena McInnes was undaunted and unimpressed by strong men, until she met
December's *Man of the Month*, handsome devil Luke Branson, in this
passionate sequel to *The Gentleman Insists*.

AVAILABLE NOW:

The tradition continues this month as Silhouette
presents its fifth annual
Christmas collection

SILHOUETTE

Christmas

STORIES
1990

The romance of Christmas sparkles in four
enchanting stories written by some of your
favorite Silhouette authors:

Ann Major * SANTA'S SPECIAL MIRACLE
Rita Rainville * LIGHTS OUT!
Lindsay McKenna * ALWAYS AND FOREVER
Kathleen Creighton * THE MYSTERIOUS GIFT

Spend the holidays with Silhouette and discover
the special magic of falling in love in this
heartwarming Christmas collection.

ARE YOU A ROMANCE READER WITH OPINIONS?

Openings are currently available for participation in the 1990-1991 Romance Reader Panel. We are looking for new participants from all regions of the country and from all age ranges.

If selected, you will be polled once a month by mail to comment on new books you have recently purchased, and may occasionally be asked for more in-depth comments. Individual responses will remain confidential and all postage will be prepaid.

Regular purchasers of one favorite series, as well as those who sample a variety of lines each month, are needed, so fill out and return this application today for more detailed information.

1. Please indicate the romance series you purchase from regularly at retail outlets.

Harlequin	Silhouette	
1. ☐ Romance	6. ☐ Romance	10. ☐ Bantam Loveswept
2. ☐ Presents	7. ☐ Special Edition	11. ☐ Other _____
3. ☐ American Romance	8. ☐ Intimate Moments	
4. ☐ Temptation	9. ☐ Desire	
5. ☐ Superromance		

2. Number of romance paperbacks you purchase new in an average month:

12.1 ☐ 1 to 4   .2 ☐ 5 to 10   .3 ☐ 11 to 15   .4 ☐ 16+

3. Do you currently buy romance series through direct mail?   13.1 ☐ yes   .2 ☐ no

If yes, please indicate series: _____
(14,15)   (16,17)

4. Date of birth: _____ / _____ / _____
(Month) (Day) (Year)
18,19   20,21   22,23

5. Please print:
Name: _____
Address: _____
City: _____ State: _____ Zip: _____
Telephone No. (optional): (___) _____

MAIL TO: Attention: Romance Reader Panel
Consumer Opinion Center
P.O. Box 1395
Buffalo, NY 14240-9961

Office Use Only   DDK

Take 4 bestselling love stories FREE

Plus get a FREE surprise gift!

PASSPORT TO ROMANCE
SWEEPSTAKES RULES

1. **HOW TO ENTER:** To enter, you must be the age of majority and complete the official entry form, or print your name, address, telephone number and age on a plain piece of paper and mail to: Passport to Romance, P.O. Box 9056, Buffalo, NY 14269-9056. No mechanically reproduced entries accepted.

2. All entries must be received by the CONTEST CLOSING DATE, DECEMBER 31, 1990 TO BE ELIGIBLE.

3. **THE PRIZES:** There will be ten (10) Grand Prizes awarded, each consisting of a choice of a trip for two people from the following list:
   i) London, England (approximate retail value $5,050 U.S.)
   ii) England, Wales and Scotland (approximate retail value $6,400 U.S.)
   iii) Carribean Cruise (approximate retail value $7,300 U.S.)
   iv) Hawaii (approximate retail value $9,550 U.S.)
   v) Greek Island Cruise in the Mediterranean (approximate retail value $12,250 U.S.)
   vi) France (approximate retail value $7,300 U.S.)

4. Any winner may choose to receive any trip or a cash alternative prize of $5,000.00 U.S. in lieu of the trip.

5. **GENERAL RULES:** Odds of winning depend on number of entries received.

6. A random draw will be made by Nielsen Promotion Services, an independent judging organization, on January 29, 1991, in Buffalo, NY, at 11:30 a.m. from all eligible entries received on or before the Contest Closing Date.

7. Any Canadian entrants who are selected must correctly answer a time-limited, mathematical skill-testing question in order to win.

8. Full contest rules may be obtained by sending a stamped, self-addressed envelope to: "Passport to Romance Rules Request", P.O. Box 9998, Saint John, New Brunswick, Canada E2L 4N4.

9. Quebec residents may submit any litigation respecting the conduct and awarding of a prize in this contest to the Régie des loteries et courses du Québec.

10. Payment of taxes other than air and hotel taxes is the sole responsibility of the winner.

11. Void where prohibited by law.

COUPON BOOKLET OFFER TERMS

To receive your Free travel-savings coupon booklets, complete the mail-in Offer Certificate on the preceeding page, including the necessary number of proofs-of-purchase, and mail to: Passport to Romance, P.O. Box 9057, Buffalo, NY 14269-9057. The coupon booklets include savings on travel-related products such as car rentals, hotels, cruises, flowers and restaurants. Some restrictions apply. The offer is available in the United States and Canada. Requests must be postmarked by January 25, 1991. Only proofs-of-purchase from specially marked "Passport to Romance" Harlequin® or Silhouette® books will be accepted. The offer certificate must accompany your request and may not be reproduced in any manner. Offer void where prohibited or restricted by law. LIMIT FOUR COUPON BOOKLETS PER NAME, FAMILY, GROUP, ORGANIZATION OR ADDRESS. Please allow up to 8 weeks after receipt of order for shipment. Enter quickly as quantities are limited. Unfulfilled mail-in offer requests will receive free Harlequin® or Silhouette® books (not previously available in retail stores), in quantities equal to the number of proofs-of-purchase required for Levels One to Four, as applicable.

OFFICIAL SWEEPSTAKES
ENTRY FORM

Complete and return this Entry Form immediately—the more Entry Forms you submit, the better
your chances of winning!
- Entry Forms must be received by **December 31, 1990**
- A random draw will take place on **January 29, 1991**
- Trip must be taken by **December 31, 1991**

3-SD-3-SW

YES, I want to win a PASSPORT TO ROMANCE vacation for two! I understand the prize includes
round-trip air fare, accommodation and a daily spending allowance.

Name_____

Address_____

City_____ State_____ Zip_____

Telephone Number_____ Age_____

Return entries to: **PASSPORT TO ROMANCE**, P.O. Box 9056, Buffalo, NY 14269-9056

© 1990 Harlequin Enterprises Limited

COUPON BOOKLET/OFFER CERTIFICATE

Item	LEVEL ONE Booklet 1	LEVEL TWO Booklet 1 & 2	LEVEL THREE Booklet 1, 2 & 3	LEVEL FOUR Booklet 1, 2, 3 & 4
Booklet 1 = $100+	$100+	$100+	$100+	$100+
Booklet 2 = $200+		$200+	$200+	$200+
Booklet 3 = $300+			$300+	$300+
Booklet 4 = $400+	____	____	____	$400+
Approximate Total Value of Savings	$100+	$300+	$600+	$1,000+
# of Proofs of Purchase Required	4	6	12	18
Check One	____	____	____	____

Name_____

Address_____

City_____ State_____ Zip_____

Return Offer Certificates to: **PASSPORT TO ROMANCE**, P.O. Box 9057, Buffalo, NY 14269-9057

Requests must be postmarked by **January 25, 1991**

--------------------------------✂--------------

ONE PROOF OF PURCHASE

3-SD-3

To collect your free coupon booklet you must include the necessary number of proofs-of-purchase
with a properly completed Offer Certificate

© 1990 Harlequin Enterprises Limited

See previous page for details